**ue wanted to bite him, to taste his blood and learn if it was as rich and xciting as the man.**

But there was a certain danger in that. Summer had no idea what Nicolo was.

What would she impart in Nicolo's mind if she drank his blood? If he were merely human would she drive him mad?

Couldn't risk it. He needed her. And she wanted him to trust her.

"Don't let this happen," Summer muttered.

But they were only words. Her heart had already made a leap. And while that scared her, she was always one to follow adventures. Even the kind Summer had never pursued before, like the adventures of the heart.

# THE VAMPIRE'S PROTECTOR

## MICHELE HAUF

First Published in Great Britain 2016
By Mills & Boon, an imprint of HarperCollins*Publishers*
1 London Bridge Street, London, SE1 9GF

ISBN: 978-0-263-92174-8

89-0616

Our policy is to use papers that are natural, renewable and recyclable products and made from wood grown in sustainable forests. The logging and manufacturing processes conform to the legal environmental regulations of the country of origin.

Printed and bound in Spain
by CPI, Barcelona

**Michele Hauf** has been writing romance, action-adventure and fantasy stories for more than twenty years. France, musketeers, vampires and faeries usually populate her stories. And if Michele followed the adage "write what you know," all her stories would have snow in them. Fortunately, she steps beyond her comfort zone and writes about countries and creatures she has never seen. Find her on Facebook, Twitter and at www.michelehauf.com.

To all the orchestra geeks. You rock!

# Chapter 1

Summer Santiago followed the scent of dust and dirt down the hallway of a nineteenth-century brownstone nestled in the middle of the tiny Italian village of Cella Monte. The place had been shuttered up and locked for decades. She'd been told so by the village *sindaco*—the mayor—who had given her a key after she'd explained she wanted to conduct some historical research. She'd flashed her credentials indicating she was an archaeologist who worked for Rutgers University.

Of course, she had neglected to mention that the research project did not exist. And that she was not an archaeologist. The credentials were a clever forgery. So she'd also touched his neck, with the excuse she was shooing away a bug. But in those seconds of skin-on-skin contact she had used her vampiric persuasion to convince the mayor to cooperate with her and hand over the key.

Persuasion, or the ability to enthrall a mortal, came in handy for her job. As a Retriever for Acquisitions, a division of the greater Council that oversaw the paranormal nations, she tracked down and obtained objects of magical or volatile nature and handed them over to the Archives for storage.

This mission rated a mere two on Summer's scale. One being easy-peasy, ten heart-thumping challenging. Find and seize a violin that had once belonged to the famed composer and musician Nicolo Paganini. The violin was supposed to possess magical power. Possibly even a curse placed upon it by the devil Himself. The electronic dossier Summer had received for the retrieval had been sketchy at best. What little she knew was that rumors hailing from the nineteenth century told if Paganini were to have played the instrument all hell would have been unleashed.

Apparently, that had never happened, because the world was still relatively the same as it had been in the nineteenth century. It did not abound with creatures from Hell—or Beneath, as Summer and other paranormals referred to that dark and demonic realm. Not to say that demons and other nasties didn't inhabit the Mortal Realm; they did. But they had insinuated themselves amongst the varied mortal population.

A man who valued all instruments, Paganini had designated in his will this particular violin be destroyed following his death. Good call. But for some reason it had instead been hidden away.

The home where the violin had been last seen, according to the Acquisition's dossier, had been sitting untouched for over seventy years.

Summer turned the knob on an inner door and

opened it wide to a gaping blackness. A chill as cold as winter crept over her skin. A shiver lifted the hairs on her arm. With a thought, she adjusted her body temperature and took a few steps downward into the darkness. Vampires were crafty like that. Able to regulate their body temperature with but a thought. Came in handy during the winter. She hated the cold. If ever a job in a tropical clime were offered in the winter she'd jump at it.

But she did love a good creepy adventure.

As she descended the stairs, the wood steps creaked in protest until her purple Chuck Taylors landed on a dirt floor. Darkness sweatered her, and while her sight was excellent, in the absence of light even vampires needed a bit of help. She tugged out her iPhone from her jeans pocket and turned on the flashlight. The beam fell across the imprints her shoes had left in the thick dust on the stairs behind her.

She was accustomed to decrepit old buildings. She'd grown up with a brother who had liked to explore the darkest, dankest, creepiest of places. And since Johnny had always offered to babysit her when their parents needed the help, Summer had explored right alongside him. Now she was drawn to the unknown and mysterious. And it wasn't just buildings, but also experiences and people.

Vampires were not inherently evil. It was difficult enough to deal with the fact she'd been born different from all the other vampires—someone who imparted madness into her donors' psyches every time she pierced them with her fangs. But she was coping. Mostly.

Summer floated her fingers across the gold-and-

emerald flocked damask wallpaper as she strode down
the dirt-floored hallway. The walls were sheetrocked
for some distance. Then the paper ended, as the smooth
walls segued into dirt. Or rather—she pressed a palm
to the cold, dry surface—limestone.

Were she descending into the catacombs beneath
Paris, not much would be different. Just another adventure spook-out with her brother. Except they avoided
the touristy Catacombs in the 14th arrondissement and
only ventured into the forbidden tunnels frequented by
cataphiles.

With a smile in anticipation for whatever delicious
surprises awaited in the dark, she wandered forward
and downward as the floor slanted. The narrow aisle
suddenly turned right and opened into a room stuffed to
the ceiling with boxes and crates. She flashed the light
beam across an old wicker dressmaker's dummy. Head-
less, it was also, sadly, naked. What looked like two
chairs from the Louis XV time period, upholstered with
pale pink damask, were stacked in one corner with no
regard for their value. Every spot on the walls was covered with paintings depicting portraits of men, women
and even a few dogs.

"Interesting." But she wasn't into art. Or dogs. Especially the werewolf kind. Okay, so she made an excep-
tion for her grandfather, Rhys Hawkes, who was half
vampire, half werewolf. As well, her uncle Trystan was
full werewolf.

The flashlight beam swayed from side to side in the
room before her. She was looking for clothing on racks.
Nothing. Summer sighed. She always got her hopes
up when exploring old storage rooms such as this one.
Wasn't like she'd expected this mission to actually pro-

vide the bonus of vintage clothing. She favored a pretty man's frock coat or jackboots. The dresses and flouncy stuff never interested her. Leather pants or jeans and a T-shirt—as she wore today—were her usual choices.

Tucking the phone into her pants front pocket so the flashlight end beamed out, Summer strode about the tiny open space corralled in the center by all the gathered treasures.

A hobby horse sat to her left. The red leather seat was worn and cracked from frequent use. She tapped the dusty rope mane, thinking how children from the past would be stupefied by today's young, who would likely run right past the wooden horse and straight for any electronic gadgets. Plant themselves in a chair and look up only when their mothers called for lunch.

She loved her electronics, but was very choosey about who she friended on social media. She did have a Facebook page, but it was strictly for family and very few friends. She didn't pin pictures on electronic boards, nor did she Tweet about what she had for lunch. Because really? No one needed to know she'd had A positive for lunch yesterday.

And she was feeling a bit peckish. She'd have to make a stop for a snack before she hit the road home for Paris.

Focusing her search, she lifted the cover from a cigar box and peered inside. No silver coins but plenty of rusted straight pins. She put the cover back and spun to sit on a gray velvet divan. A cloud of dust frothed about her, and she quickly stood, having forgotten the perils of such ancient conditions. Waving her hands to clear the dust, she choked and coughed.

Good thing her allergies were only to demons.

Next to her butt print on the divan sat a jewelry box. She pulled it onto the cleared velvet, knowing it wouldn't contain a violin, but being a slave to curiosity, and flipped up the heavy cover. Inside lay a few diamond necklaces and rings. She wasn't much for the sparkly stuff, preferring the simple hematite band she wore on her thumb. A gift from her dad, Vaillant, who preferred flashy silver jewelry himself.

"Bet these are worth a new Audi," she said of the jewels.

Alas, she didn't need another car. And she was not a thief, and nothing inside this home belonged to her. The items she was sent to retrieve on missions were taken, though. By gift or by force. Whatever means necessary. For reasons humans could never comprehend. The items the Retrievers tracked were deemed dangerous and best hidden away from chance human discovery.

Summer would leave everything in this room as she found it and report the contents to the mayor later. If relatives could be found, the items would be returned to them, and if not, perhaps the village would hold an auction. Or perhaps they'd simply abide the dying wish to keep the place sealed off. Had it been because of the contents of this room? Or because of one particular item? Had the owner been aware of the violin's volatility?

"We'll never know," she muttered, and her gaze scanned for something of interest.

Across the room, between an upended jacquard sofa and a stack of large paintings, there looked like a door. Summer tugged out the phone and as she squeezed between stacks of old crates, the light beam fell over an iron ring on a small door that might suit a hobbit.

"The secret passageway," she said with glee.

Testing the iron ring with a tug, she saw that the iron frame about the door jiggled. After placing the phone in her mouth to direct the light on to what she was doing, she then grabbed the ring with both hands and pressed one foot against the wall beside the door. With some effort, she was able to ease the entire door out of the frame.

Vampires were like that, too. Pretty damn strong when they needed to be.

Though there was too much stuff stacked around to pull the door out and set it aside, she was able to move it to the left and shove it away from the opening, only to realize the inside was more like a small storage closet that went back only about three feet.

Kneeling and creeping forward, she pushed aside a lightweight metal box that might contain documents. Sliding aside a wooden crate stuffed with porcelain-faced dolls, she spied a familiar object tucked beneath an ell of dusty blue fabric.

"A violin case."

Her heartbeats pounded. Whenever she found her assigned object she had to suppress a squeal of glee. Too girlie. And really, she took more pleasure in a mental pat on the back for a job well done.

The director of Acquisitions, Ethan Pierce, had assigned her this mission because he knew she was a musician. She could play virtually any instrument placed in her hands, but she didn't practice or keep up with any particular one. Playing music was such a solitary, static thing. An abandoned hobby of hers. She preferred to be out adventuring and getting her hands dirty. Or, give her a car to take apart and she landed on cloud nine, tools in hand, grease smeared across her cheeks.

Yet she had been a good choice for this mission because she'd take the caution necessary when handling the object, the director had stated.

As well, she could appreciate any style of music, not in the least, classical. What kind of geeky fantasy would it be to actually hold Nicolo Paganini's violin?

Summer slid a palm over the top of the case. It wasn't hard plastic like most violin cases nowadays, so she carefully lifted the thin, leather case until she could grasp the handle, which was placed center top, and carried it out into the main room, where she could study it. She set the case on a wooden crate and found that only one leather buckle with brass fixings was still intact. And rust crusted over that one. She could easily force it open, but she didn't want to damage the leather case or break the strap, so she wiggled carefully at the mechanism until finally the strap slipped from the buckle.

"Nice." Summer pumped her fist in elation. "This is freaking cool."

It would be insane not to take a look inside. To keep it closed and simply carry it home to Paris and hand over to the Archives? So long, so good to have known you—for a day?

No. She had to look at it. First, to ensure there actually was a violin inside. Second, to touch the instrument the famed violinist had once owned.

Nicolo Paganini had been a remarkable man, lauded by the masses. Summer would go so far as to label him a rock star for the nineteenth century. Gifted beyond belief. Or had he been cursed? The rumors told that Paganini had sold his soul to the devil to play the violin with such spectacular skill. His contemporaries had accused him of being the devil's familiar, or even a witch's son.

Modern-day science told a more truthful story. Paganini had been afflicted with a condition called Marfan's Syndrome, which hadn't elongated his fingers (as rumors had whispered) but rather had made his connective tissues so flexible as to allow his fingers to span three octaves across the four violin strings and thus create amazingly complicated compositions. Yet to his contemporaries he had seemed to possess superhuman ability.

But if the mission dossier was correct, this violin had not been played. So the deal with the devil could have never been made. Maybe?

Summer would never know the real story without raising the violinist from the dead and asking him herself. And that certainly would never happen. So she'd verify the instrument was intact, hand it over to the Archives and then on to the next job.

The case top lifted with an ominous creak. Inside lay a violin. A black violin. Its condition startled her. The ebony finish gleamed as if it had just been polished with linseed oil and a soft cloth. And the strings!

"They're tight," she said with curiosity and a wrinkle of her brow.

She touched each of them in turn—without actually plucking them to produce a tone—E, A, D, G. The string tension was about right from what she remembered the few times she'd played violin when she'd been younger. So tight, it was as if someone had just finished playing it.

"That's...impossible."

This Cella Monte home had been sealed for seventy

years. The mayor had told her all things inside had remained untouched. Evident from the dusty clutter she'd seen while making her way down to this room. Yet, a violin left to sit so long would certainly show its age. The wood body would dry and likely crack. The fingerboard might even separate from the neck. And the strings would loosen for sure, requiring careful tuning. After so many decades, surely new strings would be needed.

She lifted the instrument, finding it only slightly heavier than the electric version Domingos LaRoque used when he played for Bitter/Sweet. That vampire played in her brother's band, which combined electric guitars with cello and violin for some truly kick-ass gothic heavy metal. Summer had once owned a classic wood acoustic violin. It was probably stored away in her parents' mansion, but she hadn't thought about it since she'd set it aside as a teenager.

The bow sat nestled next to the violin, so she took that out and studied the bow hairs. They were pristine and off-white and smelled of rosin, but they weren't thickly coated with the substance. Someone had cared for this lovely prize. Or maybe it had never been played, for the bow hairs were not discolored near either end from repeated use.

Was it really Paganini's violin? Or simply a family instrument passed down through the ages, of which stories had been concocted about its legacy. And as the generations passed along the tale it had been forgotten which parts of the verbal history about this black violin had been embellished.

Because really? The legend told that on his deathbed

Paganini requested this violin be destroyed. It had been tasked to his son to ensure it was done.

Why had it not? And what made Acquisitions believe *this* particular instrument was the real thing? What was it about this violin that made it a danger to others? Did it possess magic? Had it been magic that had given Paganini his unprecedented skill?

Summer believed in magic. Witchcraft. That was real. Tangible. Explainable. But fantastical bob-bib-be-bo that swirled about a thing with Disney sparkles? Not so much.

She had to remind herself that oftentimes the items she sought appeared innocuous and common.

A stroke of her finger across the violin body glided over the slick, lacquered surface. Did she dare? If she pulled the bow across the strings would the instrument crumble and fall to pieces? Violins actually seemed to improve with age. There were centuries-old Stradivarii that sold for millions at auction. Was this a Strad?

Aiming the flashlight on her cell phone, she checked inside the body of the violin. There wasn't a paper designating the maker and year, though some writing did show on the curved inner rib. She couldn't make out what it said. If she had one of those flexible gooseneck tools with a light on the end she could thread it inside the instrument and learn more about it. But even if she could read it, it would likely be in Italian. She spoke and read only French and English.

She checked the case and found nestled in a square of soft fabric a round lump of amber rosin that should rightfully be as hard as glass. Instead it smelled sweet and had the slightest give to it. She ran the bow across it quickly, and the hairs took on the sticky rosin, which was designed to give the hairs good grip.

Something at her ear whispered softly, like a teasing springtime breeze coaxing her to walk outside, enjoy the absence of snow. She really hated the snow. Flowers and the warmth of the sun (albeit felt through sunscreen and protective clothing) made her giddy. She couldn't get the image out of her brain. And the idea that playing the violin would sound like spring coaxed her forward.

She plucked the E string and...it sounded in tune. More weirdness. A quick pluck of the A, D and G strings found the same.

"Holy crap," she muttered.

Giddy excitement coaxed her to place the base of the violin against her shoulder and hug it with her chin. Grasping the neck with her left fingers, she—

"No."

She quickly set the violin back in the case.

"You are not that stupid, Summer. If playing the violin was some means to calling up Beneath or the devil or some dark curse, then I'm not going to risk it."

Besides, she prided herself on following the rules, or at least, not rocking the boat when it came to her missions. She did her best and did not raise questions. She liked maintaining that militant control while on the job. Because in life? Not so much control. Especially when she bit people for sustenance. She did something to them. They were never the same. And that lack of control required balance in all other aspects of her life.

Holding a hand over the violin, ready to touch it, she flinched when the breezy whisper felt more like a shove into the springtime than a suggestion. Almost as if something *wanted* her to touch it.

That was creepy. And not in the good way.

"Nope. Not going to play it."

She inspected the end of the bow, wondering if she should loosen the hairs a few twists because it wasn't good for it to be kept tightened when not in use. Yet she'd found it in this condition. Obviously, this was some sort of magical violin.

Placing the bow in the case, her wrist suddenly twisted and the bow glided across all four violin strings in rapid succession.

"Oh shit. I did *not* do that."

She dropped the bow, but it landed on the strings, and again, drew out a series of notes.

"No, no, no. It's not me. I didn't do it!"

She looked around. A weird feeling that someone was watching and would finger her as the culprit crept up her neck. A strange silvery whisper tickled her ear, and she shook her head and slapped at her long blond hair near her ear.

The tones from that weird, accidental bowing of the strings had sounded incredible. As if the violin had been waiting ages, endlessly, ceaselessly, for someone to come and release that sound.

"But not me. Oh no." She took a step away from the open violin case. Staring hard at the bow, she waited for it to move of its own volition. It didn't flinch.

Dashing to the case, she slapped the lid down and rebuckled the latch. Then, tucking the case under her arm, she raced down the dark hallway, fleeing toward the cool morning daylight.

For once, she'd creeped herself out. And the last thing she needed was to be accused of playing a violin that would put her in league with the devil Himself.

# Chapter 2

*La Villetta cemetery; Parma, Italy*

"Hexensohn!"

At the sound of the guttural accusation, the man sat up—and banged his forehead on the stone directly above him. He pressed a hand to the flat surface. Solid and cold. He pushed. It didn't move.

He opened his eyes to…no light. Darkness muffled. And cold, so cold. Sucking in a breath, he couldn't feel his heartbeats.

But he didn't panic. The realization that he was trapped inside a container was only a minor distraction. What disturbed him was that he was aware of his thoughts. And that he was thinking. Again. After…

His death.

Sitting up in a panicked lunge, this time his forehead did not connect with stone, but rather, he felt a sludgy resistance as he rose upward and moved through the stone. His body ascended with little effort until his hands and shoulders felt the warmth of sunlight on them. Slapping a hand onto a hard surface, he levered his body up and out until he sat upon a stone monument.

"What in all...?" His shoulder bumped a stone pedestal, and he leaned against it. Not relaxed, by any means, but more getting his bearings. He sat up off the ground a few feet, one leg dangling over the edifice. Columns surrounded the area, and around that, a black wrought iron fence. Had he just risen from a sarcophagus?

Hmm... Looked like a fancy monument to someone long dead. Could it be his own? He had died. The knowledge was instinctive and ingrained. A certain fact. And he recalled that last, painful, gasping breath so clearly. Had it only been just yesterday?

A deep breath took in his surroundings. The air smelled of mildew and jasmine flowers. Birds twittered nearby. And the weird rushing sound of something unfamiliar not far off. Gasping out a breath, he pressed fingertips to his chest and realized his lungs were taking in air. He breathed? But how? He— Wasn't he dead?

Something had sung to him. Called him. Summoned him with that vile curse *hexensohn*. It meant witch's son, and he'd hated it once and already hated it again. Yet accompanying the curse he had felt the music. The pure and rapidly bowed tones from an instrument that had once facilitated his very livelihood.

Glancing about, he took in the close-spaced tombstones and nearby mausoleums. He sat in a cemetery, upon a large tombstone. And that startled him so that he slid off the stone sarcophagus, stood, wobbling as he stepped a few paces, and then turned to study the bust placed upon the pedestal where he had just risen. He narrowed his eyes. The face and hair on the bust looked familiar. Though it wasn't life-size, perhaps a bit bigger. Had he ever appeared so…regal?

"Not me. Can't be," he muttered. "I'm dead. This is a dream. Some means of Hell torture. It has to be. No one comes back from…"

His eyes took in the area. The entire monument he stood within was about ten feet square with eight columns, two supporting each corner of a massive canopy. Wandering to the edge and stepping down onto the narrow strip of loose stones circling the structure, he turned and looked high over the front of the canopy.

And he read the name chiseled into the stone above. "'Nicolo Paganini.'"

He grasped his throat, marveling at the sound that had come from him. Because… "I could not speak for so long."

Years before his death he'd lost the ability to speak. It had been miserable, and he'd to rely on his son, Achille, to press an ear to his mouth so he could hear the barely imperceptible sounds he'd made and then interpret to others.

"Achille?" Where was he? How many days had it been since his death? Had his son buried him? How had he come to rise from the grave?

What was happening?

The brimstone bargain? No. He had not fulfilled his portion of that wicked bargain. And yet…the sound of a violin had woken him from his eternal slumber.

He tapped his lower lip in thought and then was surprised at the feel of his skin and—he opened his mouth.

He had teeth! All of them, in fact. They had all fallen out in the years before his death.

Looking at his hands, he marveled that the age spots that had once marked his flesh were not there. He pushed fingers up through his hair. It was long and tangled, but it felt soft, not dry from years of sickness. His face, too. The skin was smooth and taut. Had he grown young in his death? Impossible.

Again, the steady heartbeats prompted him to touch his chest. And then he beat a sound fist against his body. When had he ever had such firm, well-developed muscles as he now felt beneath the clothing?

What foul magic was this?

Was he alive? Was this his body or that of some creature? What diabolic magic had been enacted to conjure him from his very grave?

"It can't be."

He thought of the devil Himself. That wicked, foul beast. The ruler of Hell, or rather, as the creature had called it, Beneath.

"That bastard wouldn't. He had made the offer to me so many times. Every time I refused."

Many a night Himself had set the black violin before Nicolo's old and decaying body and told him he had been born with supernatural power. Why must he continue to deny his birthright?

Nicolo had always denied that wicked magic. Many times over the decades he had performed, he had steadfastly refused the bargain Himself offered. Because he'd not wanted his son, Achille, to see him as a monster. For he knew that by drawing the bow hairs across the violin strings, he would become evil. A creature like the devil Himself.

Supernatural power or not, he could have never lived with such a selfish choice. Instead he'd used the talent that he'd honed since a young child. And even with death withering his skin and bones, he'd not the urge to accept Himself's final bargain on his deathbed.

"Pick it up," the Dark Lord had said of the black violin that gleamed with promise. "Play one song and you shall have it all. Your legacy."

Never, Nicolo thought.

And yet, is that what had happened now? No, he'd not played the violin. He'd instructed Achille to ensure it was destroyed after his death. So how was he now standing before his final resting place?

Very much alive.

It was a rather fine-looking tomb, if he did say so. Quite a large pediment and a glorious monument to the maestro.

The maestro himself. A man now seemingly unhampered by age and time—even death—and feeling rather as if he was in his twenties again.

How much time had passed? Closing his eyes, Nicolo concentrated on the sounds, moving beyond the birds and weird rushing nearby to that minute rhythm. It wasn't coming from a window or even a distant concert hall. It was coming from *within* him. From his very soul.

Did he have a soul now? Should not death have released his soul?

A profound thought.

A few simple notes had woken him. Not even a tune or melody. Bow across strings. Almost accidental, really. Yet those notes had sung to him. Calling him. Luring him. Gesturing with a coaxing finger for him to follow.

Achille must not have destroyed the black violin. Had someone found the instrument? Were they playing it right now? It had literally pulled him up from death. He knew that as he knew his heart beat now.

Nicolo turned about, lost in the odd sensation of being lured and yet feeling as if he'd just been reborn. His eyes fell to a nearby tombstone that detailed Marie Grace's final rest taking place in 1920.

"1920? But that's…"

He had died in 1840 after living fifty-eight years. A splendid life. A troubled life. A boisterous and desperate life. But he regretted none of it. For he had lived for his pleasure and had fathered a smart and kind son.

Had so much time passed then? Eighty years? The woman's tombstone looked old. A corner was chipped, and soot and moss covered half the surface. It could be even later than 1920. Yet the idea of stepping into the world so far into the future was impossible to fathom.

Nicolo stepped forward and gripped the wrought iron fence encircling his tomb. Where must he go? *How* would he go? And with what means would he survive? And what would he do now that he'd risen from death? Would the violin continue to sing and lure him down the dark and evil path he had literally been born to follow?

The music grew more insistent, and his newly beating heart answered those desperate questions for him. There was only one thing he could do to ensure that bedamned bargain did not claim him. He must find the violin that had called him up from death. And destroy it.

Sitting in the silver Audi with the windows rolled down, Summer glided her fingers over the leather violin case nestled on the passenger seat. Since discovering the instrument an hour earlier she'd been hearing the silvery whisper intermittently. It wasn't a voice, more just a sound, a distant note on a violin. So far away that she had to lean forward and tilt her head to hear it, but she wanted to hear it. To answer it.

And that was strange. She likened it to her vampiric persuasion. Had she fallen under some weird thrall when uncovering the violin? If it really had come from the devil Himself any number of malevolent spells or hexes could be attached to the instrument.

The thought gave her a shudder. It took a lot to scare her. Devil's magic was number one on that very short list. Demons ranked number two.

Her reflection in the rearview mirror showed a tired blonde with dirt smeared across her cheek and dust still cluttered in her hair. She'd driven straight from Paris to Italy and hadn't slept since two days earlier. She required a few hours shut-eye each night. That's what she was considering now as the car idled roadside at the edge of Parma.

She rubbed at the dirt on her chin, but didn't bother when it smeared. She was used to being dirty. In her spare time she liked to work on cars, and getting greasy was part of the fun. Makeup and hair spray? Ugh. Leave the war paint for the girlie girls. Much to her ultrafeminine mother's annoyance, Summer was a tomboy to the bone.

Probably another reason why the Retriever job fit her like a glove. She didn't mind the tough work, long hours, travel or the dirt. And she really didn't mind the creep factor.

Except when said creep factor was accompanied by a violin that played itself. But had it really? Or maybe the unconscious fear of evil she had was putting that freaky scenario in her brain. It could have been that she'd dropped the bow, the bow hairs had slid across the violin strings, and, *voilà*. A few random notes had sounded. Shouldn't raise the dead or Beneath.

She hoped.

"Paganini's violin," she whispered with awe. "Nice snatch."

Now to get it to Paris. Without falling asleep. A sip of blood should do the trick to keep her awake, so she'd keep her eyes peeled for a potential donor. Someone nondescript, young, not terribly attractive, but not a vagrant. She preferred mousey and bookish, actually. Though, considering what she did to them, she should probably go after criminals. But then, she argued that changing a criminal would only make him a worse danger to others. A normal person? With hope, they could handle the results of her bite.

There was nothing she could do about it, and she did have to take blood. Bags of blood from a blood bank wouldn't cut it. A vampire had to drink blood with a heartbeat to survive.

Initially, she hadn't realized what her bite did to humans. Her father, Vaillant, had been the first to notice. He'd gone along with her those first times when she'd come into her fangs at puberty and had taught her to stalk the shadows and take a donor without killing. Yet, her father had noticed that her donors were different after Summer's bite. Some struggled with voices about them that they grasped for as if at insects. Others shouted out to nothing but the madness inside them. It seemed a condition that lasted for hours.

Over the years, her family had figured that Summer's

bite was somehow changing her donors. A little or a lot, depending on how large a drink she took from them. A long drink? The donor very possibly went mad. It had frightened her to know she had such an ugly power. And confused her. Why only her? Other vampires did not impart madness with their bites. Nor did her bite seem to affect the paranormal breeds. But she could hardly keep her blood drinking only to paranormals. Humans were so much more abundant.

Fortunately, she had a strong family support system and had learned to control her hunger as much as she could. Which meant taking only a small sip and then hoping the donor would be okay. Just a touch of madness.

It was no way for a vampire to exist. But it was her life.

What she wouldn't give to be a normal vampire who could take a nice long quaff from a pulsing vein and then walk away, whistling a show tune.

Her job did make avoiding that emotional struggle a little easier. No time for empathy for others or personal-relationship woes. She kept busy. Focused on the prize. And never got involved with distractions such as families who may own the sought-after magical item, or humans who wished to challenge her for the prize, she, as a Retriever, had been assigned to obtain.

Life was basically good. And it would be much better when she dumped this weird, whispering violin.

"I'm going to bring you in to the Archives to be cataloged, tagged and stored. Never to be played," she said and followed with a sigh. "That's so wrong. This violin is exquisite."

Whatever horrible powers it might possess could be counteracted with a witch's spell, yes?

No. She wouldn't go there. Dark and dangerous things were best kept under lock and key. And wards. And spells. And any other magical device that could be slapped on to the thing. Better safe than sorry.

She picked up her phone and scrolled to the director's number, when it suddenly rang. From the director.

"Yes," Summer answered. "I've found the black violin. Got it in the case and sitting next to me right now."

"Excellent. So you'll be flying it to Paris today?"

"Uh, you know I drive." Because, adventurous as she was, soaring up to thirty-thousand-feet altitude in an airplane? Not going to happen. She was a creature of the earth and intended to remain as close to it as possible. It wasn't that she was afraid of flying, she was merely sensible. "I'm sure I can have it there by tomorrow evening. Monday morning at the latest. I might find a place to pull over and rest because I've been driving all night."

"That's fine. As long as it's secure, there is no rush. Go ahead and bring it directly to the Archives for cataloging."

"Uh... Director Pierce?"

"Yes, Santiago?"

"What is the thing with this violin? I mean, it seems innocuous. It's just another violin, albeit remarkably well preserved. The strings were even tight—"

"You didn't play it, did you?"

"What?"

"Don't play that violin, Santiago. All of Beneath will, quite literally, break loose if anyone should play that violin."

"Uh..." Gulp. *All* of Beneath? That covered quite a

lot of area. And included its ruler and nemesis, Himself. But *really*?

"Summer." The director rarely used her first name, so that set her back in her seat. "Tell me you did not play the violin."

"I did not play the violin."

"I'm sensing there's a *but*?"

She sighed heavily, and with a glance to the violin case, nodded. "But I did drop the bow, and it slid across the strings. It wasn't as if it was purposefully played. It made more of a noise than anything."

"Fuck."

She had never in her service to Acquisitions heard Ethan Pierce swear. And now Summer noticed her hands shook. What the heck? She hadn't done anything cataclysmically wrong. She was still alive. A vile nest of demons had not been released from the depths of the storage room where she'd found the violin. The sky was still blue. The earth still circled the sun. The birds were chirping. The…well, really. Everything was cool.

"Summer, Paganini had specifically stated that violin be destroyed. He did so because before his death the devil Himself made him an offer."

"I know the history."

"Yes, the history you can read in books and on the internet. But the real history—the one Archives records in the *Book of All Spells*—details that if Paganini had played one song on the instrument he would have been granted all the power the devil possessed."

"Yes, but, Director Pierce, Paganini is dead. And like I said, it was just a note or two. Some noise. I did not play the violin. I'm pretty sure the uh…" No one spoke the devil's name too much. Say it three times? You've invited him for lunch. "…the Big Guy hasn't risen either. Everything is cool."

"Is it?"

"You know I'm an ace at the smooth, clean mission. Why are you so worried?"

"It may be a precautionary worry. And I certainly hope it is. But what if playing a note or two disturbed the dead Nicolo Paganini? It's a probability I have to consider due to the nature of the strange magics with which we often encounter."

Summer let out a burst of laughter. And then she silenced. Director Pierce had not offered equal levity with return laughter. "Really? No. That's— Why the musician? It was just a note or two."

"Where was the violinist buried?" She heard clicking on his end, indicating he must be doing a search on the computer. "Parma. Not far from Cella Monte."

"Yes, I'm just outside Parma now. I pulled over to…" She wouldn't admit she'd been considering a nap.

"Then you can ensure your little mishap didn't stir up trouble. You must go to the grave site to check that the musician's grave is undisturbed."

"Seriously?"

"Santiago, it is essential. You have either dallied very closely with a wicked bargain, or have, in fact, released a malicious force into the world."

He had a way of making it sound so devastating that Summer shrank even deeper into the car seat. But then she sat up straight and hit the steering wheel with a fist. "I have done no such thing. Have you ever known me to mess up a mission, Director Pierce?"

"No, and I don't want to jump to conclusions with this one. But that violin has been forged by Himself.

I will hazard no foul-ups regarding any such object. The important thing right now is that you must go to the cemetery. Yes?"

She nodded. "What about the violin?"

"Keep it safe. And unplayed."

"I can do that."

"I know you can, Santiago. You have served Acquisitions well over the years. I'm sure this little mishap was nothing more than that. An accident."

"It was. I swear to it. You know I would never lie."

"I do know that about you. Call me as soon as you've confirmed the Paganini grave at the Parma cemetery remains intact."

"I'm off to do a little grave digging." Yikes. "Sorry, Director Pierce."

"Every Retriever faces a life-altering challenge at one point or another in their career. This may be yours."

Life altering? He was really laying it on thick. "I'm always up for a challenge. Goodbye."

She slunk back into the seat and closed her eyes. "Good one, Santiago. You may have just unleashed untold evil into the world."

It always sounded more ominous in the movies. Of course, the movies had a soundtrack that made everything ominous.

"Good thing there's no soundtrack today," she muttered.

Had an accidental slip of the bow across the strings disturbed the famed violin maestro in his grave?

Only one way to find out.

"Guess there's no rest for this wicked violin thief." She swallowed, wishing she'd found a donor to slake her thirst earlier. "This is going to be a long day."

# Chapter 3

The Villetta cemetery in Parma sat close to the edge of town, nestled near residential areas. On one side of the cemetery stretched gorgeous vast green fields and trees. Summer drove along the road edging a field, feeling as though it were a little oasis within the bustle of the busy world.

It was nearing noon, a lazy time of day that found most inside eating or relaxing before a meal. She wore her sunglasses, and she tinted all the windows in her cars for protection. A vampire could certainly venture out in the daytime, even in the sunlight. But they did burn much easier and faster than most, and direct sunlight could leave nasty sores and burns. So she never went anywhere in the summertime without a sweatshirt jacket and sunglasses. Sunscreen helped a bit, as well.

Though homeschooled by her parents, she'd been

allowed to study those subjects that had most appealed to her and had basically designed her own education. Music and mechanics had topped her study list. So what she knew about Nicolo Paganini was that he had been buried in the cemetery only after much struggle to actually allow his body a proper burial. History books told that he'd refused the last rites on his deathbed, so the priest had denied him burial in consecrated ground. His son, Achille, had fought and struggled for years and had finally, after decades and agreeing to donate the remaining bulk of his father's estate to the Catholic Church, won his father a resting place in Parma.

One could read the details of that weird burial struggle and assume Paganini had refused the last rites because he had been dabbling in the occult and perhaps had even made a deal with the devil, but it was also known that, at the time of refusal, he hadn't thought he was going to die.

But it didn't make sense to Summer. If he'd refused to play the violin then he couldn't have been the devil's associate, as so many had accused him.

Then again, what did she know? The musician had a sordid and interesting history. Accused of deviltry merely because he had been a prodigy on the violin? Stupid. But not for the time period, she supposed. And if he really had made a deal with the devil that would easily explain his phenomenal talent.

Summer knew people made deals with Himself every single day. And they were real and signed in blood and paid with breath and bone. She'd had a run-in with Himself once. She tried very hard not to ever let that happen again. And she had a built-in warning system thanks to her allergy to demons.

Checking the GPS map on her phone, which she'd attached to a plastic holder on the dashboard, she verified the cemetery wasn't far off. She'd not once been in Italy before today, but appreciated the quiet afternoon drive. With luck, the cemetery would be as peaceful. And if she had to actually do some grave digging she would be granted privacy.

If she arrived at the graveyard to find that indeed the grave had been disturbed and the body was gone, she'd...

Summer blew out a breath. "I have no earthly idea what I'll do."

Her Retriever training had not covered tracking a newly unearthed dead man and returning him to the grave. Though, now she thought about it, all she had to do was rebury him. Right? It made sense. But what about a violin raising hell did make sense? And was it all of Beneath, or was it a metaphorical hell in the form of the man being some kind of demon or hellish being?

"You're thinking about this too much," she muttered as she drove by a man wandering along the road's edge.

The single-lane tarred road was paralleled with grass growing high in the ditches. In need of a mow, but she liked the overgrown nature. A quaint countryside drive. So seeing a man wandering by in a black suit, looking rather dazed, gave her pause. She slowed the vehicle and peered in the rearview mirror. He stared after her, yet continued walking. Dressed in a long black coat, black pants and white shirt, and with long black hair. Was the coat actually a tux? The tails of it went to the back of his knees. His eyes looked like black voids from the distance. He was slim, but not unattractive. Maybe a little dirt on his face and hands?

In that somber suit he looked out of place against the cerulean sky and emerald field. On the other hand, maybe he was coming from a funeral that had just been held at the cemetery?

Or he could be...

"No. Freaking. Way."

Summer's heartbeats dropped to her gut, and she slammed the Audi to a halt. Grabbing the cell phone from the dash, she clicked online, thankful that she got Wi-Fi out here. Searching for Paganini brought up a page full of images. Tall, slender and darkly handsome for a nineteenth-century guy. Some caricatures made him look comical with a bent spine and spider-long fingers as he viciously attacked the violin. No actual photographs, though. She supposed photography had been invented a little later.

She shook her head as she gazed at the man walking away in the rearview mirror. "Can't be. He looks... healthier, if not...normal."

Shouldn't a guy risen from the dead look...dead?

Tapping the steering wheel with her thumb, she then rubbed the hematite ring along the leather wheel. She was seeing things she didn't want to believe. The director had spooked her with his warning about disturbing the dead. "He's just a local. Wandering home from a funeral. Yeah."

She shifted into Drive, but didn't take her foot off the brake pedal.

The cemetery loomed ahead, within shouting distance. Could he really have climbed out of a grave and now be wandering the countryside? The man had been buried—she quickly did the math—around one hundred and seventy-five years ago. Wouldn't her car freak him out? And the modern paved roads and—hell, everything?

"This is insane. He's not a dead guy. He just happens to look like Paganini." She was in Italy. All the guys were darkly handsome, right?

But she had to be sure. She wasn't going to let this mission get any more messed up than it already was.

Shifting into Reverse, she backed the car down the road. When she paralleled the man, he paused and cautiously stepped back from the car as if it were a vicious bull staring him down. After a few moments of consideration, he leaned forward and peered through the window at her.

She rolled down the window. Grabbing her cell phone and clicking on one of the pictures, she then held it out, to compare images side by side.

"Ah shit. It's him."

Nicolo marveled as the dark glass window in the moving carriage slid downward to allow the driver to speak to him. A female driving a carriage without horses? Such a wonder the world had come to. He could not even be frightened at the strange prospect of allowing a woman such leeway as to drive about unescorted.

She held a small device out toward him and asked, "Is this you?"

What? Him? He leaned forward and saw there was a small painting on the device. Or rather it looked like a sketch. Of him. He'd seen that sketch. Sir Edwin Henry Landseer had done it during a concert when Nicolo had performed at the Royal Opera House in London.

"Yes, me," he said in French because she had used that language. He spoke Italian and French.

"You are Nicolo Paganini?"

"But of course." He leaned closer to her, but wasn't sure about touching the carriage. It gleamed silver. Not a bit of wood to its construction. "How do you know this? What magics do you practice to identify me as such? And what witchery is contained in that box you show me?"

"It's called the internet and this is a cell phone," she said with a wave of the object before pulling it back inside.

He understood neither of those words.

She opened the carriage door and got out. The woman was petite and…dressed most strangely. Yet, Nicolo had seen a few women since wandering out from the cemetery. All wore trousers such as a man and close-fitting shirts with sleeves short enough to reveal more than enough arm, and on some, the necklines were so low as to show ample bosom. It had startled him so much he'd initially walked directly into a street lamp. And then a few feminine giggles had reassured him that the modern-day women still possessed a wicked tease comparable to those from his time where their wardrobe was concerned.

"Okay, Monsieur Paganini," she said. With a shake of her head to spill the untidy long blond locks over one shoulder, she hooked her thumbs at the back of her slender-fitted trousers that hung low, exposing a slice of skin above the waistband, and rocked back and forth a few times on some odd violet shoes. "So uh…this next question is a doozy."

"Doo-zee. I do not understand that word."

"It means it's going to set you off your feet real good."

He stared down at the bespoke leather shoes he'd been buried in. Treasures to him. For to find a comfortable shoe that had fit his large feet? Not so easy. "Very well then." He crossed his arms and prepared for the remarkable question to set him off his oversized feet. "Serve me your best."

Because really? After climbing up from one's grave, it couldn't get much worse. Or was that better? He hadn't yet decided if he should be pleased or worried about his new *alive* status. He'd been buried for a long time. The world had changed. And he was in a daze from it all.

"Did you just crawl out of a tomb?"

Nicolo's jaw dropped open. And then he snapped it shut. There was only one explanation to her having such information. "Are you a witch? I know witches exist. How did you portend such a fact?"

"Just answer me. I was on my way to the Parma cemetery to see if you were still safely buried. Uh, but I guess you're not."

"I am not. For reasons beyond my knowledge, I have been summoned from death." He brushed his fingers over the velvet coat he'd been buried in. His son had style, indeed. Though it fit tightly across the shoulders. When being resurrected, he'd gained some muscle. It made the coat cumbersome. "Does everyone know about this strange occurrence of my resurrection?"

"No, just me. And I'd like to keep it that way. You'd better get in the car. We have some things to talk about."

"Get. In?" He stretched his gaze along the carriage. There were seats for others inside the compact conveyance, but— "No, I am perfectly fine standing outside on this smooth pavement. Such wicked alchemy you've concocted to make this vehicle travel without a horse is not something in which I wish to partake. I have avoided the devil's work all my life. I shall not soon subscribe to such folly in my afterlife. As it is."

"Your afterlife is because of me, I'm afraid."

"How so? Did *you* summon me from the grave? You *are* a witch!"

She held up both hands, one of which still held the mysterious device containing his image. "Chill, Paganini."

"I am rather warm in this attire. These are my funeral raiments. I've seen people wearing so much less. And you in your odd trousers and shoes. What has become of the gowns the women once wore? Your attire is freakishly masculine."

She bristled at that statement, but then set back her shoulders, proudly. "I may be a freak, but the clothes are common for women nowadays. The world has changed a lot in a hundred and seventy-five years."

"One hundred and..." He gaped. Truly, it was well beyond the 1920s in which Mary Grace had been buried.

"Like I said, we need to talk. I suppose I can't interest you in climbing back into the coffin and letting me bury you again?"

"Are you— That is perfectly ghastly! You are worse than a witch, you—"

"Yes, yes. But since you know witches exist and suspect I am one, I need to set you straight right from the start. Get a load of this."

She grinned widely, and Nicolo watched her upper incisors descend. They were pointed and sharp and— mercy, he knew what she was. He hated that he had such knowledge of the paranormal creatures that existed in this world. But he did because he'd had far too many conversations with the devil Himself.

And he knew what this woman was. "Vampire?"

She nodded and grinned. Surely the world must be overrun with her sort? For the very first person he should converse with would be a blood-drinking vampire? Perhaps crawling back into his coffin would not be such a terrible idea after all.

No. He was alive. And he wanted to remain that way.

"No," he said defiantly. "I will not get into that conveyance with you today. Good day, vampire."

And he strode off down the smoothly paved road, not sure where he was headed, but dearly hoping that his path landed him at the nearest tavern with a kindly serving wench who would take pity on his empty pockets and allow him a drink. Or two. Or many. Drunk seemed to be the only way to handle the day's events.

Quickening his pace, he tried to ignore the vehicle rolling backward toward him. He had walked a great distance from the cemetery, but he was not tired nor were his muscles taxed. In fact, he felt good. Remarkably good. He couldn't remember a time during his first life (that's what he was calling it; how else to term it?) when he'd felt so utterly alive. So vital. So strong.

And he wanted to keep this strength. And figure it out.

The carriage stopped and out jumped the woman. She marched toward him. Petite and very pretty, despite her messy blond hair that seemed to fall in twists down to her elbows, and the terrible clothing that made her resemble a boy. He was surprised at her insistence.

And even more surprised when she grabbed him by the arm and spun him around.

"Take your hands off the coat," he insisted. "It is fine velvet."

"Yeah, yeah, velvet is cheap nowadays, buddy. Get over it. So the fact I'm a vampire didn't freak you?"

"Freak me? You mean, you expected me to run screaming from you? I know of your sort, blood drinker. Have never met one, but I do have knowledge of the occult."

"We call it the paranormal. Vamps, witches, were-wolves, demons. All that jazz."

"I'm not sure what creature a jazz is, but I am aware of the others you listed. Demons." Nicolo stifled a shudder.

"You and me both." She echoed his shudder.

"But I've always thought vampires—" He glanced skyward where the sun beamed brightly. "Aren't you supposed to lurk in the shadows?"

"We vamps can do sunlight for a bit. But we still keep our heads down. But, as it probably was in your time, most humans are not aware of us."

"So you are still not a large part of the population?"

"Large enough. But smart enough to walk in the shadows."

"Yes, shadow creatures. So you are vampire." So opposite of what he'd expected. Completely un-creature-like, this woman of the enticing blond hair and blue eyes. Save for those vicious fangs. Best not to rile the creature. He could play nice to protect his ass if need be. "I don't think you should bite me. My blood may be…off."

"Off?"

"I did just rise from the grave."

"Right. Don't worry, buddy. I'm not going to sink in my fangs. You're a job."

"A job—"

"So tell me how you're feeling after a climb out of the grave? I should probably keep an eye on you. For, uh…possible decomposition."

"Decomposition?"

"Well, yeah." She gestured her hands through the air in exclamation and blurted out, "You could be a zombie."

"A—what? I am not familiar with that term, vampire. What year is it, by the by?"

"2016. So you could be a zombie." She pressed the tiny box a few times, then held it before him to display yet another painting. "Because zombies are dead things that have risen from the grave."

The image was of a person. Maybe. Whatever it had been, it was decayed and—flesh was falling off its face and it oozed gore.

Nicolo flinched and made a disgusted face. "That is not me."

"Probably not. Zombies are usually mindless and gross. They have limbs falling off and look like they just rose from the grave. They also eat brains. You're… hot. So not zombie-like."

Again she did something with the tiny device, then turned it toward him. "Here's the mirror app. Take a look."

He bent to study the reflection in the silvered surface of the device. Indeed, it had changed from showing a painting to a mirror. Marvelous. And diabolical. And yet…

"That is...me? I look...well." He tapped his teeth again. They were white and not wobbling in their sockets. "Such a marvel." His nose, long and with a bend at the middle looked like the same nose. His eyes were gray and clear. His hair seemed longer. As did his face look—well, healthier. Such a handsome fellow, eh?

Realizing he was mooning over himself, Nicolo cleared his throat and stood upright. "Did you say it was you who facilitated my rising from the grave?"

"Inadvertently."

He quirked a brow.

"When I was inspecting my find, the bow slipped across the violin strings. Played a few notes. But I didn't do it on purpose. It was accidental."

"You have the black violin?" Nicolo's heart thumped once, and he winced at the aching remembrance of that vile instrument.

"I do."

Blowing out a heavy breath, he clutched his hair in frustration. "I asked Achille to destroy that monstrosity! Oh, this is most awful." He started to stride away, then turned and paced the pavement back up to her. "Do you know what this means?" He slapped a hand over his chest. "That explains why I feel so alive and strong. I feel as though I could run round the world and not pause to catch my breath. And my teeth." He tapped the perfect teeth in his mouth.

"Oh wow." She peered at his teeth. "I read you had lost all your teeth before your death."

"I did lose them! As well as my voice. I could not speak above a whisper for years before my death. And now it is as if I have transformed into a new version of myself when I climbed up out of that coffin. And you are the reason for it!"

He clutched her about the neck and squeezed. She struggled and then kicked and landed her foot successfully at his hip, just missing his groin. Nicolo dropped the vampire and with a shout, stumbled backward into a swath of lush tall grass.

"We women have learned a thing or two about defense since your time," she said, standing over him. "Let that be a warning. You're strong, though." She rubbed her reddened throat. "Kind of weird for a dead guy."

"I am not dead," he managed as he fought to free himself from the long grasses tangled about his shoes.

"No, you're not. But what are you?"

That was the question, indeed. By all the blessed mercies he prayed that foul brimstone bargain had not been enacted.

"Why did you play the violin?" he asked the vampiress. He had best be cautious for another attack. The next time she could use her fangs.

"I didn't play it," she said. "I was supposed to find the violin and bring it to Acquisitions, but I figured I'd better open up the case and check to be sure it was inside first. When I did, it was almost as if the violin had a mind of its own. I'm sure it played those notes by itself."

That did not surprise him. What he knew of the violin was that it was magic most foul. Diabolical, even.

Truly, had she summoned him by enacting that bedamned brimstone bargain? It didn't seem possible. The condition had been that *he* should be the one to play the violin. Only then would he be granted immortality and immeasurable supernatural power.

Did he have immortality now? He certainly felt...

something. Stronger, and more powerful. Sure. Yet if not immortal, what, indeed, had he become? And how to fix it?

Did he want to fix it? That may imply his going back to the grave, of dying. Again. He rather liked the air today and the soft, sweet grass beneath his shoes. The sky appeared so clear and bluer than ever he could remember. When had he last admired the sky and simply inhaled the crisp summer air?

No matter, he must not rile this woman overmuch in case she might bite and kill him. Perhaps he could play along with her suggestion to keeping an eye on him. Yes, must needs.

A zombie? If he started to decay he would immediately request a second death, because if he turned into something like that thing displayed on her little box then—absolutely not.

"Where is it?" he asked.

"The black violin? It's uh…" Her eyes wandered along the side of the fancy silver carriage, then snapped back toward him, though she didn't meet his gaze directly. "…on its way to the Archives for storage."

"I don't understand that." She was lying to him. Moments earlier she had said she had it. "You played it not too long ago. I *felt* the music. It moved through my veins. And it called out to me."

"Really?" She stepped before him, admiration sparkling in her pale blue eyes. He recognized that look. So many had looked upon him as a literal idol when he'd been at his prime performing on the stage. "You're really him. *The* Paganini."

"Indeed." He set back his shoulders and puffed up his chest. Felt good to step back into the acknowledgment

of his talents. He was a maestro, and he would resume
that status. Because he knew nothing else.

"What is your name, vampire?"

"Summer Santiago." She offered her hand, and he
assumed she wanted him to shake it.

He gripped it and her skin felt warm. Amazing to feel
another being's warmth and life, to be reassured that he,
as well, possessed life. Then a flash burst in his brain,
and he received a series of images as if a manic dream
chased his reality. The vampire was twenty-eight, had
always been a vampire, had a vampire brother named
Johnny, and vampire parents. Her job title was a Retriever, and that had something to do with finding lost
items or magical objects. An image of her lying beneath
a steel carriage such as the one they stood before confused him. She wasn't hurt. It was a place where she
enjoyed being, or rather, working.

Summer pulled her hand from his, and the images flickered out like an extinguished candle. Nicolo
chugged out a gasp as the blue sky and sweet grass resumed his senses. "What was that?"

"That was a handshake. I'm pretty sure they did it
back in your time. Nineteenth century, right?"

"No, those images. I saw..." He tapped his forehead.
"You have a brother who is a vampire, and he sings on
the stage alongside his wife. Why does she have horns?"

"How do you know that?"

"It came to me when I held your hand. Is the woman
demon?"

"No, Kambriel is vampire, but she wears horns as
part of her stage costume. So holding my hand gave you
images of my life? That's some kind of cool power."

"I don't know. It wasn't cold. Your reference to things being hot and cold makes little sense to me."

"Oh, buddy, it's slang, and you have so much to learn. But of course I don't think you'll have much time to gain all that knowledge."

"Why?"

"You shouldn't exist."

"Is that so? Why? Do you believe I am some unholy beast resurrected from death?"

"Well…are you?"

He hadn't an answer to that one. And if he thought about it too much, he wouldn't like the truth. She wanted to put him back in the grave? Never. He was alive, and nothing would change that. And he was strong enough to get one little vampiress off his back.

He shoved her shoulder hard and watched as her body soared through the air a good thirty feet and she landed on the side of the road, tumbling into the grassy ditch.

Nicolo winced. That had to hurt. But he had to protect himself if he wanted to survive this new world.

"So long, vampire Summer. I am off to live my new life."

# Chapter 4

Summer gave the guy a head start. The next town was only a couple kilometers away, and she was in no hurry to slide behind the wheel again for the long drive home. She'd have to take him with her. Couldn't let some dead guy wander around unsupervised. Especially if he had anything to do with the possibility of Bad Things Happening.

Or even, Bad Things that Had Already Happened.

She sat on the hood of the Audi and slipped on her Ray-Bans. Sunlight beamed over a distant swash of chestnut trees, glittering in white over the leaf canopy. Crickets chirped in the grasses edging the road, and somewhere a cow mooed.

It wasn't often she heard a cow moo in Paris. She loved these quiet moments out of the city. It served a different sort of adventure. A mental escape. Much as she sought the fast paced, the always moving, the rush and thrill of her job, times like this centered her. Gave her a few moments to appreciate nature. She wasn't a tree-hugging hippy chick, just a soul who understood she was a part of everything on this planet, as it was a part of her.

So what part of it all had Nicolo Paganini become? He was the furthest thing from a zombie. No body parts falling off. No nasty skin peels or lumbering gait. Hell, the man was good-looking, and she'd noticed the hard muscles beneath the white dress shirt. For some reason he looked fit, beyond what any picture had depicted of his sometimes comically distorted figure in the nineteenth century. According to the history books he'd been tall, gangly and often sickly.

Was it possible he'd been forged differently when rising from the grave? Certainly he must have decayed lying in situ for a hundred and seventy-five years. So he had been renewed. To a marvelous degree. All parts of him were nicely proportioned and muscled. Every bit of him well made.

"But let's hope he's not the Beneath-breaking-loose part of the director's suspicions."

The musician had seemed innocuous enough. No flashing magic or vicious powers. Though when he'd shoved her away from him, she'd been startled at the force that had landed her far from where she had stood. He had never been that strong in his previous life. No mortal man was, for that matter.

"He is different," she decided. And that part worried her.

Pulling out her cell phone, she dialed Acquisitions,

and the director took her call. "You check out the cemetery?" Ethan Pierce asked.

"I uh, didn't get that far."

"I don't understand. That was part of the mission, Santiago."

"I found Paganini. Alive. Wandering the roadside."

The director's exhale spoke so much more than a curse or a few curt, remanding words.

"I can hardly lure him back to the grave," she provided. "Unless you need me to do that?" She winced, hoping the answer would not be an affirmative.

"He's alive. A man from the nineteenth century crawled out of his grave and is now walking the streets of Parma?"

"Yes."

"I'm not sure what the protocol is for this. I'll have to look into it. Does he seem violent, a danger to others?"

"No. Just startled to be in a different time period. It's like he's a time traveler flashed forward to the future."

"Yes, sure. Is he exhibiting any zombie-like tendencies?"

Summer smirked, then winced as she closed her eyes behind the sunglasses. "Define zombie-like."

"Limbs bluing. Necrosis of the tissue. Parts falling off."

"Nope. He's good."

For now. But she intended to keep a close eye on him for changes. She'd never had to deal with a zombie before, and she did not look forward to starting.

"Keep an eye on him," the director said. "Do not let him out of your sight. I'll report back with further instructions." He clicked off and Summer shoved the phone into her back pocket.

"Keep an eye on him. Sure. No problem." Not as if she could look away from all that musician nummi-ness, was there?

Twisting at the waist, she could no longer see Paga-nini's figure walking along the roadside. He'd put some distance between them. But she'd find him. Shouldn't be that hard to track a nineteenth-century musician who had just clambered out of his coffin. Had she just thought of him as nummy?

"You need to get laid, Santiago, if the dead guys are starting to look good to you."

When had she last—? She didn't even want to think about it.

Paganini had said his blood might be off. Meaning, he probably didn't know what the heck he was. Either that, or he had been freaked she was a vampire.

Then again, no one ever really wanted to get bitten by a vampire. At least, no one smart.

Thinking of which… Exhaustion clung to her limbs. She needed to drink blood for a burst of renewal until she could steal a few winks for a true refresher.

She hopped off the hood and slid in behind the steer-ing wheel. She suspected Paganini wouldn't go far be-cause he had to be hungry, too. She had time to find a meal before pursuing the former dead guy.

The tavern was a welcome respite from the sun's sweltering heat that had worked up his perspiration dur-ing the walk along the black road. Nicolo had removed his coat and folded it over an arm while walking, and now he felt as if he'd walked into a different atmosphere. It was as if a thousand fans blew cool air on him, yet he couldn't feel the wind of said fans. So refreshing!

No one sat by the long stretch of bar, and the barkeep nodded to him before asking what he wanted.

"Beer?" Nicolo tried. He wasn't sure what the modern taverns served, but beer had been around for ages. "Have you food, as well?"

"Special is fish-and-chips. Our cook is Irish." He shrugged and set a glass mug of beer on the bar before Nicolo. "You want that?"

Nicolo nodded. "Yes, please."

Fish sounded great. But he had no idea what chips were. He would be surprised. The lure of the golden liquid in the glass coaxed him quickly forward. He slid onto a bar stool and tilted back the liquid. Yes, beer. And quite tasty. He downed half in a long swallow.

Looking about, he marveled at the clutter of paintings on the walls. Yet, they weren't exactly paintings. Done in blacks, grays and whites, they were each framed and depicted people smiling and holding beer mugs. Had they all been composed and painted in this very tavern? Interesting. In the window a sign that said Pull Tabs flashed red light. How was that possible to produce light of such a color with no flames in sight? And overhead, light beamed down from small glass globes. Not in candle form.

"Remarkable."

He finished the beer and asked for another. "Tell me about that device," he said to the barkeep and pointed to the framed rectangle above the rows of liquor bottles behind the bar. On it images moved, as if he were witnessing a scene in real life. Men kicked a small white ball across a green field. They wore similar clothing. It must be some sort of sport.

"The TV?" the barkeep asked. "Where are you from anyway?"

Nicolo shrugged. "I've…been away from things for a while."

"One of those hippies who lives in a mountain for ten years?"

He wasn't sure what a hippie was or why a person would want to live in a mountain, but Nicolo again shrugged and nodded. "Sure."

"You look it. But the women love the long, messy hair nowadays, eh? That's the rugby competition. England versus Ireland. The Wolfhounds are givin' 'em hell. In case you haven't seen a television for a while, it's a big screen, digital, HD, all the bells and whistles. I can get a hundred and eighty channels. Pretty fancy, eh?"

Nicolo had no clue what the man had just said, so he instead sipped the beer and nodded subtly. The bells-and-whistles device was like a larger version of the mysterious box Summer kept on her. Must be some sort of knowledge receptacle. Most likely of the devil.

Yet he could not bemoan this incredible chilled atmosphere. He glanced about, tracking the ceiling and noting the barkeep's odd look. Nicolo shrugged, "Your establishment fascinates me."

"Sure." Jabbing a tiny wooden stick into the corner of his mouth, the barkeep reached through an opening in the wall and yelled thanks to an unseen person.

A plate of hot food was set before him, and Nicolo leaned over to inhale the delicious aroma. Yet, hadn't he ordered fish? Whatever it was on the plate, a long strip of something pale brown, did not resemble fish. And he assumed the thin strips of similar color were the chips? He didn't want to be rude and ask, so he picked up a chip and tasted it.

A salty crunch ignited Nicolo's taste buds, and he quickly finished the first. And the second, and another.

"Amazing," he murmured and finished them all before even trying what would prove to indeed be fish.

"Pace yourself, buddy," the barkeep said. "We've more if you're that hungry."

"Thank you. I find it delicious, and yet strange at the same time. May I ask you how a man might find his way to Paris from here?"

He needed to find that violin that Summer had said she'd sent on to Paris.

"You could take the train, rent a car or hop on a plane."

"Hop on a plane?" Even as he said it, he could only imagine hopping onto something flat. "I don't understand."

"An airplane? You really don't know much, do you? Do you have money?"

Nicolo nodded quickly. He'd figure out some means to recompense before leaving the establishment.

The door behind him creaked, and in wandered two women, chattering loudly. They sat at a table in the dark corner next to a front window, and the barkeep brought them two bottles of wine.

Nicolo turned his attention to them. They wore trousers so short they revealed skin all up to their thighs! And what gorgeous legs that glided a long way down to their feet, which boasted strappy shoes on them. And their shirts were cut so low he saw the crease between their abundant breasts. They must be freezing in this chilly establishment. But when the one winked at him and raised a bottle of wine in a toast, Nicolo's grin grew.

He recognized an invitation when he saw one.

The donor had been dozing outside a quiet cottage that looked like something from a Kimball painting. It had gone down quickly. Summer had taken but a few sips. Enthralling him to think good thoughts and fight the inevitable madness, she had then stepped away. She never stayed to see what results would come of her bite. That was asking for emotional heartache. Once she'd drunk too long and had actually witnessed her donor's descent into madness. He'd beat his forehead against a brick wall. His body had shuddered, and he'd clamped his arms about his chest, crying and wailing. She'd fled, hoping it would be temporary. It had to be, yes?

Her weird ability to change her donors was her dark nemesis.

"Find the dead guy," she muttered, focusing her thoughts as she got out of the car and walked across the street.

The Sneezing Cow tavern was one of those cozy little hideaways at the edge of town that most tourists passed by for the peeling paint on the outer stucco walls and the general lack of signage stating it did, indeed, serve liquor. But the tiny drunk lemon motif in the window clued Summer that inside she could find limoncello, which was her favorite aperitif. She didn't do human food, but the occasional refreshment was always welcome.

Summer walked inside the tavern, eyed the dark corner where two women giggled and noted they were draped over a man who sucked in the attention as if with a straw.

She made way to the bar where, after asking, she was promptly served an icy yellow drink. *"Grazie,"* she said. "He's not giving you any problems, is he?"

The bartender pushed back his long gray hair and winced. He wobbled his hand before her as he said in Italian, "I'm not sure he's going to pay."

She picked out the words *pay* and *not* from his Italian. She knew Nicolo wouldn't, because what man came alive after a hundred and seventy-five years of death with a credit card and bank accounts? Was she going to have to teach him about the world and babysit him until he got his feet on the ground? The prospect didn't sound as awful as it should, considering her list of things she found attractive in a man had apparently grown longer with the addition of "recently deceased."

But the women would have to go.

"I got it," she said and laid enough cash on the counter to cover a good hour's worth of drink. Bottles, not glasses, she guessed, as another side glance spied one of the brunettes tilting back a dark wine bottle to her lips. "He's harmless." She hoped.

With a wink from the bartender, Summer sipped her sour lemon drink, then turned to go corral her new ward. She'd gotten them both into this situation. Now to deal with it.

Paganini acknowledged her with a wide rogue's grin as he spread out his arms to embrace each woman wedged against him. She had to stop thinking of him as Paganini. Nicolo was his first name. It would help her to idolize him less. And right now, that was easy enough with the sluts he'd found casting her shade.

"Summer, you will join me and my new friends for a drink?"

Thank the goddess she'd had that sip before coming in here. It would make dealing with this easier because she was cool and collected right now. "We should get back on the road," she said. "I'm sure you're eager to find your violin."

"But you already know where it is."

True. She'd lied to him about it being on its way to Paris. The guy was newly alive. He couldn't be operating on all pistons yet. Fingers crossed.

Nicolo tilted back a long swallow from the wine bottle, then said, "What's a little stop along the way to renew my memory of humanity?"

"Why are you talking about violins?" one of the women asked in a drunken slur. A shift of her shoulder lifted her double Ds closer to Nicolo's grinning face.

Mercy, his taste in women was— She'd cut him some slack. He had only been alive again for a few hours. And in the short trek he'd taken from the coffin to the tavern, Summer guessed the selection of women had not been overwhelmingly vast or varied. They were tourists looking for a good time with a sexy looker.

"I like drummers," the other woman said as she licked Nicolo's ear.

"Timpani?" He bristled and gave Summer a wink. "I am a violinist, ladies."

"Sounds dirty," the licker said. "You want to violin me?"

Summer rolled her eyes. Enough. She didn't need this kind of torture.

"I'm parked outside," she said to Nicolo. "I'll walk slowly. But I am leaving. Which leaves you to either bone them and walk to Paris on your own—where you'll find the violin—or hop in and ride shotgun."

She'd let him figure out what that meant on his own.

Giggles followed in her wake. Summer did not turn around. A guy like him would probably choose the greater of the two evils. Heck, if she were newly risen from the grave she'd probably want to party it up, too. Who could know how much time the man had before he actually did begin to drop body parts and prove her zombie theory correct?

She wouldn't mind the drive back to Paris alone. Yet she did have an order to keep an eye on the man. And she would. In her manner.

It was misting when she stepped outside. She slid into the driver's seat, fired up the engine and flicked the windshield wipers on to the delay option. A few minutes to struggle with her ultimatum was all the man should need. She really should be nicer to him. Nicolo was like a newborn in this modern age. Everything must be new to him. Women in pants! Who'da thought? Of course, lust never changed. Sluts in bars!

And was she feeling jealous that he'd chosen such low-class choices for his first act of debauchery as a living man?

A man? What *was* he, anyway?

"There's got to be someone who can take a look at him and know. Read his essence. Maybe a witch." She grabbed her cell phone and scrolled through the contacts. "Verity."

Verity Van Velde was a powerful witch who had a thing about knowing other people's souls. Maybe she could touch Nicolo and know what he was? Because if he really was evil incarnate then Summer would have to suck it up and take him out. She would not be responsible for unleashing Beneath on the world.

The passenger door opened and Nicolo, smelling of wine and salty fries, slid inside. His velvet pants were sprinkled with rain droplets. He tested the seat by bouncing up and down, then slid a hand over the dashboard. It must have met his standards because he settled in. "You waited for me? I knew you would."

"How's that?" she said as she shifted into gear. She should have started rolling down the street, just to give him the illusion that she didn't care.

"You like me," he offered.

"Yes, well, I am your only friend. And please don't call anyone who drags her tongue down your face a friend."

"That was pleasant. The women in this age are much more open than I've been accustomed to. Yet still very much the same when it comes to lust. And the clothing! You women wear trousers and leave your shirts unbuttoned to reveal so much bosom. Marvelous."

"I suppose petticoats and corsets were your thing, eh?"

"Those damned corsets did cause some extra effort for a man on a mission."

"I bet." She smiled despite herself. "I imagine bras will fascinate you and lead you on a quest of discovery."

"What is a bra?"

"It's a modern-day corset." She wasn't wearing one, so she wasn't about to lift her shirt for an example. "Holds up the girls."

"The girls? Ah, your breasts? Can I take a look?"

"You're not as smooth as you think you are."

"I would beg to differ. After I told the one woman

that I understood her pain she melted into my arms for a nice snuggle."

"Her pain?"

He turned on the seat to face her, gesturing casually as he spoke. "When I touched her I got a flash of her life. I did not understand the images of her pouting over a mystery device such as you showed me and crying for days on end, but I knew it was painful for her. So, I worked with it."

"You got a flash of her life?"

He nodded. "Same as when I touched you."

"Huh. You never had that ability before? In your previous life?"

"No. Do you think it's a condition of my new existence?"

"I'm sure it is. But whether or not it's good, bad or ugly remains to be learned. How about we head west for the French border? If I drive all night we should gain Paris by morning. You can take a nap."

"I don't feel tired. But I do wish I'd have brought along that last bottle of wine. Might we stop by another tavern along the way?"

"Depends on how nice you are to me."

He tilted a genuinely concerned look at her. "I have no reason not to be nice to you, Summer the vampire."

"True. And I did give you a second chance at life."

"Yes, well, at what price?"

She glanced at him. The guy tilted his head as if to say "You did this to me."

And she could undo it. Maybe. No matter, he'd better be nice to her.

"You said you resisted the offer from the Big Guy?" she asked.

"The Big Guy—oh, er, the Dark One?"

Good. He was on board about not speaking Himself's name too much.

"Of course I resisted. Wouldn't you?"

"Yes. But power is not an easy thing to resist. And playing such an exquisite violin."

"The not playing was the hardest part. But you know, the black violin that raised me from the grave was not mine?"

"That's the part where I get confused. I thought your prized violin was on display in a museum."

*"Il Cannone?"* Summer knew that was the nickname he'd given his prized violin. It referred to the explosive sound he had been able to produce with the instrument. "It is still around?" he asked.

"As far as I know, it's still in a museum in Genoa. The Guarnerius?"

"Yes, made by Guiseppe Guarneri. I played that instrument for decades. It was my beloved. But after I fell ill I couldn't make my fingers move as quickly or hit the right notes. I donated it to the city of Genoa as a means to put that torture out of my life."

"So how does this other violin come into play? The black one I found?"

"It is the one the devil Him—er, the Dark One offered me. He told me I would be restored to health and could play again. Would have all the powers he possessed. Would become a god walking this mortal realm. He made me that offer many times over my lifetime."

"Really? And you always refused? That takes a lot of courage and bravery."

Nicolo shrugged. "I was talented by my own right. I did not need the dark evil. Nor would I ever accept.

I did not want my son to see his father become a monster. But the Big Guy—as you call him—did not relent in his temptations."

"I give you credit for resisting. I had a run-in with him once."

"Is that so? What great temptations did he offer you?"

"None. I was just a baby. He kidnapped me and used me as bait to get my brother, Johnny, to come to him. He was trying to steal Kambriel's soul, and Johnny was in love with her. It's a long story. Suffice it to say, Johnny got me out of there safely. But ever since I've had an allergy to demons."

"How does that affect you?"

"Whenever one is around I start sneezing. It's weird, but kind of handy when you want to avoid the bastards."

"I hate demons."

"Tell me about it."

"Really?"

"Uh, no." She smiled at him. "That's just an expression of agreement. So, I'm sorry. For the bringing-you-back-to-life thing. Because we don't have any clue now if you're going to go evil or—" Best not to make assumptions and make him feel worse than he must already. "I gave a witch friend of mine a call. She lives in Paris. I think if she touches you she might be able to tell us what you are. Would you be okay with that?"

"Yes, I suppose. I don't feel evil. But I do feel as though I have so much to explore and learn now. I want to do it all, Summer. I have been given a new life, and I mustn't waste any time in diving in."

"Such as with the sluts back at the bar?"

"Sluts?"

"Women of ill repute. They were looking for a good time. And I had to pay for their wine."

"I thank you for paying the bill. I ate fish-and-chips."

"I guessed at the chips. What did you think of that?"

"Exquisite. They were crisp and savory. I have never seen a fish cooked in such a manner, but it was delicious. I want to taste all the food. I want to drink all the wine. And I want to hear music again. How I have missed it."

"I can help you with that." Summer tapped her cell phone, which sat in the dashboard holder. She scrolled to the music app. "This might blow your mind."

"Is that similar to freaking out?"

She chuckled. The guy was sweetly innocent. Something that felt so refreshing in her life right now. "Same idea. This is what music has evolved into since your time."

She flicked through the various playlists and decided to take the first song that came up. Thanks to her dad's obsession, she'd grown up listening to a few of the country-music classics. Johnny Cash's "Ring of Fire" blasted through the car speakers.

Nicolo gaped and eyed her, then touched his ear as he tried to comprehend.

"Pretty cool, huh?"

"That's—" He turned his head, checking around the inside of the car. "Where is that coming from? What sort of music is that? Is it magic?"

"Better. It's technology. Let me find some rock and roll. With your background in music I think you might appreciate the head-banging stuff."

"It comes from your tiny box? Surely that is witchcraft. And that thing is a witchbox."

"Whatever works for you." Black Veil Brides blasted through the speakers. "This is called heavy metal. The band actually incorporates a violin in some of their songs."

Nicolo, while touching his ears intermittently and then touching the dashboard in seek of the source, gradually allowed a huge smile to trace his face. And when his eyes met hers, dancing with delight, Summer felt her heart drop.

The guy was a job. And before said job was over, she may need to kill him.

# Chapter 5

The sound—where was it coming from? Nicolo rapped the dashboard of the carriage, then sensed the sound was also coming from somewhere in the door. And the song had changed from one sung by a male vocalist to a female.

"So loud," he remarked. "Yet her voice, it is tortured. What *is* this violent yet delicious music?"

"It's called hard rock or heavy metal," Summer said. "You like it?"

He met her daring gaze with an unsure nod, which then changed to a more positive shake of his head. "I think I do. What is she singing?"

"Song's called 'Welcome to the Gun Show.' The band is In This Moment. I love her voice. So raw and raunchy. But I know something that will be even more interesting to you." She turned down the volume using the radio dial.

"Don't do that! I want to hear this."

"I'm going to switch songs."

"But you are moving too fast for me. I like this song. I want to put this into my brain."

His enjoyment must have given her a kick, for she chuckled at him again. Such a bold woman. He attributed that to her being vampire. Or perhaps the twenty-first-century woman had evolved to a sort of exotically aggressive powerhouse. He liked it.

He liked Summer.

"A little David Garrett might surprise you," she said. Tapping the witchbox, she said to it, "Play David Garrett's 'Paganini Caprice No. 24.'"

"Did you just ask me to—" Nicolo paused when the surprising first notes of the violin caprice carried over the speakers. "*Mio Dio!* This is *my* composition! But it is…"

"Given a hard rock edge. It's awesome, isn't it?"

Despite the fact he'd never appreciated when someone had attempted to play his compositions—because they could never achieve the perfection he had mastered—Nicolo found himself shaking his head to the dashing allegretto scale. "It's different, but I do like it. The violinist even manages the harmonics. How were you able to command it to play a specific song? Does this vehicle know every song ever composed?"

Summer laughed. "No, it's in my, uh…witchbox." She tapped the tiny device. "More stuff you'll have to learn about if you want to survive in the twenty-first century."

"The twenty-first century." He leaned an elbow on the vehicle door and caught his forehead in hand. "Who would have thought? And I am being conveyed in a horseless vehicle with no fear of running off the road. It is a marvel. And such a smooth ride."

"Shock absorbers."

"We had the like in my time. Just those springs were not so smooth as whatever is under your carriage."

"It's a car. Ah, I love this part." She turned up the radio.

And Nicolo closed his eyes to take in the composition. It was well played and even more rapidly than he had once managed. The violinist was an expert. But he could not get beyond the marvel that the music was right there, at the literal touch of the vampire's fingertip. She could call up any song she wished with her witchbox. A song that summoned many wonderful memories. Life had been beautiful when standing on stage. To be adored and respected had mattered to him. He'd had a lovely son and many lovers.

Could he have that again?

"We're driving through a town," Summer informed him.

"Ah." He opened his eyes. "Keep your eyes open for a tavern."

"They are usually referred to as bars nowadays. I see a liquor store. With luck, they might still be open."

After Summer had bought a bottle of wine for Nicolo and explained how money was kept on small plastic cards, he decided he wanted one of those cards. They stood outside the car, and she handed him the wine. He bit the cork out with some difficulty.

He asked after swallowing a good draft, "They issue those plastic cards to everyone?"

"Yes, but you have to pay back the money. It's not free money. And I'm pretty sure you are penniless."

"You said my violin was on display in Genoa? If I sold that I would have thousands."

"More like millions," she said. "The Guarnerius Paganini is worth a fortune."

"Just so?" She nodded at him and took a quaff from the bottle. "Then we should drive right to Genoa and demand they hand it over. It is mine, after all."

"And how are you going to explain who you are? The whole rising-from-the-dead part?"

"I will leave that to you. It seems zombies are common in your modern world. You carry pictures of them in your witchbox."

"I didn't take that picture. It was from *The Walking Dead*. A TV show."

"I know what a tee-vee is!"

"Good for you. I'll have to find a music station for you to watch. Until then, I can do this." She stepped alongside him and held up the device before them. "Smile."

Nicolo could not figure what she was doing, but he smiled on command. Of course, he was distracted by the sweep of her hair across his neck. She took liberties with their proximity. He liked that, as well. The device clicked and after adjusting it, she turned it to him for inspection. Their images had been captured. Just now. The two of them standing together. It was...

"More than witchcraft," he said on a tense whisper. "Is this the devil's magic? Is it you who has come to tempt me this time around and see me play the black violin?"

He backed away from her. Tried to recall the way to hold his fingers to ward off the damned, but making a cross with two fingers was not it, he was sure of that.

"Nicolo, don't worry. And we vamps are not repelled by the holy unless we've been baptized. Which I am not. Anyway, the last thing I want you to do is play that violin. A few accidental notes may have raised you from the dead, but I don't think it was enough to make you evil. I suspect you actually have to play it to get the power promised to you by Himself. You uh…don't want that power, do you?"

"The brimstone bargain." He shook his head. "Never. I swear to it. It is vile. Monstrous. I would become like him. That is the last thing I want. I will not play the black violin, I promise you. But I must know how did you get it to Paris so quickly? If you found it back in Parma?"

"It was in Cella Monte, actually." She shrugged, and Nicolo sensed a lie would follow. She looked away from him when speaking a mistruth. "We have our ways of making things happen."

"We? That's right, you said you worked for some organization that retrieves things." Apparently they could transport items rather quickly. It surprised him, yet it should not, seeing that the world had changed so drastically. "Why was it decided you needed to locate the violin now?"

"I'm assigned my missions. I fulfill them. I'm always off after some kind of magical device or haunted item. Your violin was just another mission."

"Not *my* violin," he reiterated.

"Right. The devil's violin. Yikes. I touched it. Do you think it will have some kind of residual effect on me?"

"You are the furthest from a zombie, my lovely blonde cherub."

"I'm a vampire who sucks blood from people's necks to survive. Cherub will never be me."

"Perhaps not. But a vampire named Summer?" He let his eyes stroll across her soft skin and up to those brightly inquisitive blue eyes. There lived a tease in her look that he wanted to entertain. Might his first love affair in this new age be with a vampire? "Just seems a bit too cheery for a creature of the night. You, with blood drooling out the corner of your mouth, and a pair of white cherub wings stuck on your back."

"Ha! Quite the image. You've got a bit of goth to you, I suspect."

"What does that mean?"

"It means we'll get along just fine."

"Thanks, Brightness. You like that better than cherub? I do. You are bright as summer." He tapped her witchbox with the neck of the wine bottle. "Now command it to play some of that hard metal. I like the tones and wild scales those guitars produce. How is it that they sound so different than the guitar I once played?"

"They are electric. The sound is amplified. Electricity came about after your time, and it's a long explanation. Get in the car and I'll crank the tunes."

They did so, and the car filled with the raucous tones of the female singer and some strange instruments that he guessed might be guitars, but he'd never heard one so...amplified, as Summer had explained. Amazing. It would serve to distract him from the sudden distrust that had risen when she'd paused after he'd asked about the violin.

She had it still. She must. But where had she put it? And how to find it?

About two hours east of the Italian/French border Summer stopped the car at a roadside rest stop and got out. She'd had the music on the whole way and not the GPS. Bad idea. She announced, "I'm lost. I don't recognize this road. I wonder if I took a wrong turn?"

"Why don't you ask your witchbox?" the violinist said with weighted sarcasm as he got out of the car. "It seems to have everything you need in it."

"Good idea." She tugged out her cell phone and asked Siri for directions.

"That is utter madness," an astonished Nicolo said as he joined her in a stroll along the curbed rest area. "Tell me, is it a tiny witch who lives within that box?"

"No. Not even this day and age could invent something so strange. *Are* there tiny witches?"

He shrugged. "You're the one with the fangs."

"Doesn't mean I know everything about witches. I'm going to go with no on the tiny witches. But this?" She waggled the phone between them. "It's just bits and bytes. Of which, I also know little. I only know that all the information I need is contained in here, and it's also great for finding a good vintage car supply store in a pinch."

"Vintage. So you do have an interest in the carriages that once conveyed me from city to city?"

"Vintage is like 1950s and '60s. I own a 1960s Bimmer R65 that I've been tinkering on for years."

"I see. So I must be absolutely ancient to you, eh?"

Summer chuckled. "You are not the oldest of my friends. Trust me on that one."

"Right. Vampires live very long, as I recall. How old are you again?"

"Twenty-eight."

"I remember twenty-eight. I was traveling across

Europe with *il Cannone* and Antonia. Such a lovely voice she had."

"Was she your son's mother?"

"Indeed. I had no desire to marry, but I was thrilled to become a father. My son, Achille, traveled with me on the concert route, as well."

"Did you ever play in Paris?"

"A few times. Took me two weeks to travel the same path we now journey. I must have stayed for months following. Couldn't force myself to get back into that stuffy, wobbly box on wheels. If they would have had that remarkable cold air forced through tiny vents back then. Whew!"

"Right? It's called air-conditioning. Wait until you learn about the shower and toilets. And computers!"

"Is a shower what I think it is? Because I could use some freshening. I feel as though I've gone for almost two centuries without washing."

"Ha. The dead guy made a joke."

"No, the dead guy is merely speaking the truth." He flapped the lapels of his velvet jacket open. "This thing is hot. And…a hundred and seventy-five years old. I need new clothing. But how to obtain clothing and food without money? I require a violin, as well. Then I can play for a living again."

"I've got cash. Don't worry about it."

He walked around in front of her to stop her in her tracks. "Summer, a man does not accept money from a woman. Not unless she wishes him in her bed every night after a concert," he added with the roguish grin.

"Have you ever been a woman's gigolo?"

"There were a few times when the money did not

come in quickly and in such amounts as I had needed. Must needs for hard times. You understand."

"Yeah, sure. You were a man whore."

He caught on to her tease and could play along. "I never stood on the streets offering my wares. Yet before my name became known I had to sacrifice for my art. Now where is that violin? You have to have it with you." He peered over her shoulder at the parked car. "Where did you hide it?" He strode off toward the car.

"I said I sent it to Paris!" But she didn't believe that lie any more than he obviously did.

Summer spun around and went after him. He pounded on the trunk and ran his fingers along the seam opening.

"It is inside this car," he said. "I can hear it. There, within this receptacle. It looks like a back boot on a carriage. Open it!"

"You can hear it, too?" For a moment their eyes met, and she saw his wince before it even happened. "I don't think it's a good idea that you touch that violin. We can't know what it will do to you."

He rapped his chest with both fists and gave her the most incredulous stare. Okay, so they did know what it would do to him. Because it had already done it. It had brought him back from the dead.

"Let me rephrase that," Summer said, trying for the stall.

"Open it," he insisted. "Or I'll—"

"You'll what? Toss me across the field? Shove me so hard I'll fly into the next town?"

"I apologize for my quick aggression earlier. I had no idea I was so strong. It is a new strength to me. But I like it. It makes me feel powerful." He flexed his fingers into a fist. "But I won't allow you to redirect this conversation. You have the violin." He rapped the metal trunk hood. "In there. I'm sure of it. I can hear it. It whispers," he said, feeling it in his veins. The darkness that curdled up his spine whenever he considered his origins and the wicked bargain he'd continually refused in his previous life.

And now he was alive again. Due to the evil contained inside this car. Destroying it seemed the smartest option.

He rapped again. The vampiress crossed her arms and shrugged. Not going to open it?

He gripped her by the shoulders, but she tugged away from him and then, palms to his chest, shoved him back. Such an aggressive female. He wanted to make her do as he demanded. But he would not harm a woman, even if she was a vampire who should be strong enough to fend for herself. So he turned and banged his fist onto the metal. It dented in deeply.

Nicolo marveled over the damage.

"Wait!" she yelled as he raised his fist in preparation to again smash in the trunk. "That's my car, you idiot. Do you know how expensive an Audi is?"

"Not nearly so valuable as the violin within."

He pried his fingers along the seam, but it would not give. Although the metal edge did bend upward in a crunching creak. It wouldn't take long if he persisted...

"All right!" She shoved him back and thrust up her palm between the two of them. "It's in there. You can stop destroying my car right now. And I will open it if I have to. But I think you should seriously consider what might happen should you get your hands on that thing."

"Its music has already summoned me from the dead. What more calamity can it bring?"

"Oh, I don't know, everlasting evil? Literally raising Beneath. Dark and malevolent uprising of all the demons in the world?"

Nicolo winced at her dramatics. "Oh please. The conditions were that should I play the violin I would gain all the power owed to me. There was no mention of demons or everlasting evil. Though, trust me, that alone is terrifying."

"The power owed to you? What does that mean?"

He waved a dismissive hand between them. "Open it."

"You're not telling me something. You were *owed* some power by the Big Guy? Did you...*do* something for him that required repayment?"

"It is completely unnecessary to divulge because I don't intend to play the black violin. I swear it to you. But I must see it. I must..."

"Destroy it?"

He rolled his shoulders back and quietly said, "Yes."

"Because you think if you do destroy it then all chances of you going black, dark evil will be destroyed?"

"There is that hope."

"And what if destroying the violin destroys you? Caput! End of your new life? It brought you into this world, its destruction could take you out."

"That is a chance I shall take." He gestured toward the trunk. "If you please."

She dug in her pants pocket and pulled out a key chain. With a click of a button, the trunk release popped but didn't open. "Idiot. You've damaged it." She pried at it and heaved upward, to no avail. He did like that she tried, though. Such spunk!

Nicolo joined her, shoulder to shoulder, and curled his fingers under the metal. But before lifting, he slid a glance down her blond hair and inhaled her scent. Nothing like flowers or the powders the women he'd once known had worn. She was strong and confident. A certain sweetness lingered about her, but it was more like a calm measure of surety. No, he'd best not harm her. Right now she was the only person he had in this world.

And, odd as she was, he did favor her company.

"I am sorry," he said. With a jerk, the thing popped upward, revealing the inside. "But I have to look at it."

Within sat a violin case Nicolo recognized with an intake of breath. The devil Himself had delivered it to his bedside for one last temptation. A wicked tease when he could barely breathe, let alone speak. In those final moments of life he'd almost taken it in hand and drawn the bow across the strings. But then he'd thought of his son and how he would ever explain his sudden recovery and seeming powers. That he'd gotten it from the most foul evil that existed. That was no way to teach a child about right and wrong. He'd welcomed death, if only to be away from the evil that had stalked him most of his life.

Summer crossed her arms firmly over her chest. "Not even a note, buddy."

He didn't intend to play it. Though the urge to hold a violin—any violin—was strong. To see if he could still play. While it felt as if he'd only expelled his last breath but days earlier, it had been a long time. Had he lost the skill? He waggled his fingers before him, wondering would they have the muscle memory to achieve the perfection he'd striven to achieve. Or with his new-found strength would he crush the neck and strings as he tried a scale or a racing arpeggio?

Nicolo leaned forward and brushed his fingers over the black leather case. It felt cold. Abnormally so. Perhaps the vehicle's air-conditioning had cooled it. Or perhaps it gave off the vibrations of the damned. He hissed at the thought.

Silvery whispers softened his resolve and lured him closer. His fingers trembled over the case. An entreaty to open it, grasp what was his, echoed in his very bones.

Tugging back his hands, he pressed them to his chest. Looking over the trunk cover, he eyed Summer. She wore sun spectacles against the waning sunlight, so he couldn't see what was surely a condemning look from her. He didn't want to disappoint her for reasons that were not clear to him. She meant nothing to him. And yet, as he'd realized moments earlier, she was all that he had in this world. He did require a guide, of sorts, to navigate this future world he'd stepped into.

As well, he needed some sort of connection to all he did not know, a visceral, even emotional anchor to the world. Someone to…hold his hand?

But neither could he disappoint his curiosity.

With a flick of his thumb, he released the one intact leather strap from the rusted buckle. He lifted the case top and pushed it back. Inside, the black violin gleamed like the devil's horns. And he had seen those horns. Too close. Too many times. The smell of sulfur had tainted his dreams many restless nights. The strings were taut, the bow tightened as if ready to play, yet the hairs were not aged and yellowed but rather clean and only slightly dusted with rosin.

He'd never touched this instrument. Had not heard its sound.

Well, yes, he had heard the sound. Just this morning it had summoned him.

How was that possible? The devil's bargain could not work that way. He didn't understand. Unless Summer was allied with Himself?

He again glanced at the vampiress. Still waiting for him with that stern demeanor he could feel in his bones. Or was she simply waiting for him to take it in hand and become the devil's slave? Himself worked that way. He could send others in the guise of temptations to lure Nicolo into doing his bidding. He had once almost rousted with a gorgeous woman who had wanted to hear him play the black violin. Only when her eyes had flashed red did he realize she was demon. He'd encountered many more demons wearing human costumes in his lifetime.

Was Summer another temptation? While unlike any woman he had ever been compelled to, she was gorgeous, in a rough, unpolished manner. More comfortable in men's clothing. Barely a curve on her stick-straight body. But those blue eyes. Not red, thankfully. And that smirking smile as she shook her head when watching him fumble with unfamiliar things. He did admire her.

Was that the point?

Affected by this ponderous query, Nicolo stood back and pushed his hands along his thighs to keep from reaching into the depths and drawing out the violin. Just a note or two? To test the tone? A quick scale could not possibly transform him into something evil.

He shook his head. No. He would not succumb. Not

for all the power in the world. He was alive. He was seemingly more healthy and stronger than he had ever been. What more could he ask for?

On the other hand, why *not* test it? The diabolic whispers seemed to tease at his better judgment. They sounded like harmonics, the very tones he'd invented on the violin.

"Dude, you okay?" Summer asked.

Again he clasped his arms across his chest and took a step away from the trunk. "I'm not sure. It calls to me. And yet I want to run from it. I don't know what I should do."

She leaned against the back of the car and nudged his arm with her fist. "Maybe you should start with an easier play first? I could drive you to an instrument store in Paris and we can get you a real nice violin."

"Something not created by the devil Himself?"

"Yes. And I wish you'd stop saying that name. We just call him the Big Guy if it's necessary."

"Good call. I'm sure the Big Guy is waiting for me to touch that thing. And yet? Who are *you*, Summer Santiago?" He peered deeply into her eyes, and she met that stare with an equally confident stare.

She challenged, "You think I'm working for the Big Guy?"

"Are you?"

She chuckled. "Did you see red in my eyes?"

"No, but—" Nicolo exhaled. "You do tempt me."

"I do? You mean with my sexy tennis shoes and grease-smeared shirt?" She lifted the hem of the shirt to reveal a smudge of grease. "I think you're just desperate for any woman who crosses your path, am I right? I mean, it's been a while for you."

"I am not such an undisciplined heathen that I must grab at any woman before me to satisfy my lust. I am simply disturbed by all of this, Summer. You must allow me my caution. And give me only truth. Do you work for the devil?"

"No. Absolutely not. Never. Nada. Okay?"

He nodded.

"You're thinking about things too much," she said. "You're thinking the bargain has already been enacted by the very fact you are standing here right now. Do you feel any evil running through you? Do you want to do something bad or mean?"

"Actually." He dropped his arms and held up his hands. "What I'd really like is to ask you for a hug."

Summer's eyebrows raised and her jaw dropped open.

"I need something right now," he said, speaking faster than his brain could stop him, but knowing it was coming from his heart. "Reassurance. Comfort, perhaps. Please, Summer?"

She balked, rubbed the back of her neck, then, when he thought she was going to beg off, she plunged into him with a surprisingly generous and comforting hug. Nicolo pulled her to his body and tilted his head down onto hers. He'd never done such a thing as ask for a hug before. It was a moment of strange emotional neediness. Because he was lost. A new traveler in this strange world. Yet old, so very old. And haunted by what he'd once had, and could possibly have again.

He felt her relief and saw images of her relaxing, smiling—yet knew she was trapped, as well. Something about madness? He wanted to know the truth of her, but it felt like a violation to read her too long. So he sup-

*The Vampire's Protector*

pressed it by allowing his focus to stray to the violin in the trunk. He had but to play one note to own his power.

One note.

Summer tilted back her head and smiled up at him. "I bet it's tough. You are a man without a home or personal belongings. You've been thrust a hundred and seventy-five years into the future. And you're not even sure what you are now."

"I don't believe I'm a zombie. A zombie would probably be snacking on your brains right now."

"Touché." She traced a finger along his jaw and then danced it back through his hair. Hair that he imagined could not look so appealing after over a century lying in a coffin. He needed to find some personal grooming time. "I'll help you," she said. "Whatever you need, just ask. I owe you that much."

"You owe me nothing. But perhaps I will ask for your patience and… I will need a place to stay until I can establish a means to earn money and buy my own things. I am like a child now, aren't I?"

"A handsome one."

"You think so?"

"Very much."

He bent to kiss her and landed his mouth against the corner of hers. When he thought how foolish he was being, and expected her to pull away, suddenly she adjusted her position and their lips coalesced in a firm and satisfying connection.

He closed his eyes and slid a hand up her back. Her body melted against his, and where he'd thought he'd had no curiosity earlier now he felt her breasts against his chest and his body reacted. His erection hardened. Excellent. He could still manage that. It was a strange but satisfying thing to confirm. He tilted his pelvis back so she wouldn't notice.

"Wow." Summer stepped back and shrugged her hair over a shoulder. "That was…uh—whew!"

"It was the best kiss I've had in over a hundred seventy-five years." He pushed down the dented trunk hood and managed to make it catch in the clasp. "Let's be on to Paris, then," he said as he swung around and got in on the passenger's side. Mainly to avoid her noticing the hardness that tented his trousers. "Have your witchbox take us there, will you?"

"Sure," she said, perhaps a little dazed. From his kiss?

He still had it. He could seduce a woman. And get it up. Ah, what a life he was going to live.

# Chapter 6

The classical music station currently played Bach's *Symphony in D Major* and Nicolo enjoyed conducting as the moon rose before them and the car rolled into Paris. Much as Summer wanted to drive home, make a beeline for the shower, and then snuggle up on the couch and consider another kiss with Nicolo—her phone rang. Johnny's name flashed on the screen.

"My brother. Give me a minute." She turned down the radio volume.

"You back in Paris?" Johnny asked.

"Just got here."

"We're playing in an hour at La Nuit. Domingos's pickup is buzzing on the violin. I wonder if you could take a look at it? And we've a dead amp. Please, little sister?"

She was always available to fix anything when Bitter/

Sweet played at the local clubs. While the guys in the band were amazing musicians, surprisingly, they hadn't a clue about how to fix a loose solder connection or an amp that might simply have an electrical short. She was the tomboy; Johnny was the goth prince. Their father, Vaillant, was proud his son had taken up the black clothing and silver accessories. Not to mention Bitter/Sweet's grinding heavy renditions of more than a few Johnny Cash songs.

She glanced toward Nicolo, who took in the passing buildings with awe and wonder. Life was no longer the usual. She now had a dead guy to babysit. Former dead guy. Talk about stepping in it deep. Not only had she fucked up the mission, but she may have raised Beneath itself and now it wanted to chum around with her. Be buds.

Why did the man have to be so pretty? So sexy? He smelled delicious, and that was remarkable considering he'd climbed out of a grave this morning. And he was witty and bright. He was a musician, for goddess's sake! As with mechanics and bikers, there was not a single thing about musicians that did not turn her on. And this man was *the* musician. A classical music god.

A makeout session was definitely in their future. She wasn't ashamed to go after a guy when he attracted her. Playing hard to get was for the prim and proper. Both of which, she was not.

And she hadn't heard from the director yet. He'd told her to keep an eye on Nicolo. She could hardly let him loose in Paris with him knowing little about the twenty-first century. Though, he should be able to manage well enough.

Or maybe not. He hadn't a single euro to his name.

And those clothes, while he might fit in with the gothic Victorian crowd, she really wanted to get him into a pair of leather pants and a modern shirt.

"Yeah, I think I can manage that," she said to her brother. "Have to stop by the Archives first. Drop off a retrieval."

"Awesome. See you soon, sis!"

"That was Johnny, my brother," she said to Nicolo. "I need to drop the violin off at the Archives. And then Johnny wants me to stop by and take a look at some of his band's equipment. They're playing tonight."

"Playing? A concert?"

She nodded. "It's a rock band called Bitter/Sweet. Remember the hard rock you liked? The woman with the rough and raw voice?"

"Yes, indeed. Very rousing and intense."

"My brother's band sounds like that. He and his wife both sing lead. Johnny also plays guitar. They have a bass guitarist and a drummer. And Domingos plays cello and violin. It's a cool mix."

"I am eager to hear this collection of musicians play live. Please, we must go."

"I'm not sure. Maybe I should take you home and…"

"And what? Hide me away? Are you worried I'll turn into a monster and slay everything in my path?"

She winced and met his dark gaze. "Would you?"

"It hurts me that you would ask such a thing. But I know you don't know me at all. I don't even know myself. And that is not encouraging. No, I would not slay everything, as you so unkindly suggested. No matter what becomes of me. If evil should overtake me, I'll… control it. But if all that's happened is what I am now, I'm not so terrible, am I?"

He was the furthest thing from terrible. And that could get her in more trouble than she preferred to dive into. Emotional connections? Ugh.

"Not at all," she replied. "Let's hope this is the worst that curse could produce. Maybe the centuries dimmed the curse?"

"Perhaps a person can't become evil unless he really desires it? I've never wanted it. But even if it was given to me, I would refuse it. I have to hope that my moral compass will keep me from becoming like…you know who."

The creature they would not name. Could not. The last thing Summer wanted was an audience with the devil Himself.

"You know, history writes you as a wild and crazy guy. I wouldn't call you evil, but good?"

He shrugged. "I did have my moments. Gambling. Drinking. Whoring." He sighed. "But those were not so much evil as vices. Truly, Summer, evil harms others. The only person I've ever harmed is myself. Not that I'm proud to admit that."

"No, you're not evil. But the world has changed."

"I wager vice has not?"

She sighed. "Still the same."

He picked up her hand and stroked the back of it. "Is this okay?"

"Uh…yeah?"

"I find I get a read on a person immediately upon touching them, but then I can fade it out. Yet when we kissed earlier all I felt was everything in the now. It was something I'd like to do again."

Summer pulled her hand from his touch.

"Sorry." He tilted a look at her. "You were offended by my kiss or the suggestion for another?"

"Neither. I just…" What was her excuse? Why did she need one? She'd take another kiss. A no-strings-attached kiss. Because she wasn't keen on dating dead guys. But again, she wasn't against a fling.

Why did the man have to be so appealing?

"We should probably get going. Too many things to do." She shifted into gear, avoiding the look he gave her, which she felt as a punch to her chest.

Yeah, she wasn't big on romance. So sue her.

Certainly Jones met Summer at the curb out behind the Council headquarters, where the Archives was also located. The Council's vast headquarters was located in the 11th arrondissement tucked amidst businesses and residences, but at only four stories high it remained un-assuming with its red brick walls and lacking signage. The Archives twisted and labyrinthed a good seven stories underground. Though Acquisitions was in the same building, Summer had never been inside the Archives, but CJ's wife, Vika, had told her about it. A fascinating place, for sure.

As she'd requested, Nicolo remained in the car while she walked around to the trunk and met CJ there.

The dark witch was tall, lean and always dressed in black. His long black hair must hang to his waist when not tidily queued with a leather thong, as it was now. Spell tattoos covered his entire left hand. He looked like someone you'd want to walk a wide circle around on the street, yet Summer knew he was kind and gentle, albeit a very powerful dark witch with whom no man should be foolish enough to mess.

Whispering inaudibly, he smoothed the tattooed hand over the dent in the trunk, and with a few metallic pops, the metal rose beneath his palm and reformed into a smooth surface.

"Oh man, you just saved me hours of bodywork," Summer said. "Thanks."

"Who's loverboy in the front seat?" he asked as she popped open the trunk.

"Uh, just a friend." Her missions were confidential. And she didn't want anyone from Acquisitions or the Archives learning about her slipup. "We're heading to the club to meet up with Johnny."

"Nice. Wow." He bent over the violin case, inspecting it without touching it. "Paganini's actual violin?"

She nodded. "Yep."

Didn't want to say too much because if she started talking she'd blurt out all the stuff she didn't want anyone to know about. Like the real identity of loverboy.

"Have any problems obtaining it?" he asked as he lifted it out and carefully held it in both hands.

"Nope."

"The case is exquisite. In perfect condition, save for the buckles."

Summer nodded.

And CJ peered at her curiously. She knew witches could perform a soulgaze on their fellow witches. Stare into their eyes long enough and they could read their souls. But she didn't think they could do it to vampires.

"Something's wrong," he said. Not a question.

"Everything's cool. I'm just, uh... Well, you know this wasn't Paganini's *actual* violin. This is the one rumored to have been used to tempt him by you know who."

"Right. Which is the very reason we've been tasked to retrieve and catalog it. I'll have to put some devil wards on it. Just to be safe. Might have to look those up. Don't use malefic magic all that often."

She certainly hoped not. And if she stood here any longer she'd probably blurt out the truth, so she gestured toward the inside of the car. "New guy. First date. He doesn't really know what I do. So I should be rockin'."

"I see. Got it. I'll tag this and find a place for it in the stacks. Thanks, Summer. Have a good time tonight!" CJ walked by the passenger's side and bent to get a good look, waved at Nicolo, then frowned, but he didn't say anything else.

Summer slid into the front of the car. "Whew."

"You're keeping me a secret now?"

"From anyone who works at the Archives? Yes. Only Director Pierce and I are aware of your rebirth, as it is. You're not supposed to be above ground. And until I can figure out what to do about that, you're just some guy."

"Your loverboy." He tilted his head and his eyes twinkled. Probably a reflection from the nearby street-light. Had to be.

"You heard that? Your hearing is very sensitive."

"Remarkably so. Want to make it true?"

"Are you propositioning me?"

"Sorry." He pressed his hands together before his face and smoothed them down to reveal smiling eyes. "It's a habit."

"I've noticed."

"Apparently I've not changed so terribly much after such a long sleep. It makes me happy to talk with women. Your kind fascinates me. Whores, as well as the good and proper. Actually, I prefer a proper woman. I only ever resorted to whores—"

"Not my circus. Not my problem. Let's get going." She shifted into gear and pulled the car away from the curb.

"Will there be women at this club?"

"There will be. But they'll be a lot different from the tightly-laced demoiselles you're used to flirting with."

"Similar to the ones in the tavern?"

"Hmm, nope. This is a goth crowd. But there are always plenty of sexy goth wannabes in the mix."

"Goth meaning Gothic in style?"

"You'll see what I mean when we get there."

Did she really want to take him along with her? Induct him into the atmosphere of dark sex and seduction that absolutely oozed from the club?

"You sure you're ready for this? It's been a long day. We could go straight to my place and kick back." *Say yes, say yes...*

"No, please, I look forward to the challenge of these gothic women."

Summer rolled her eyes. And then a part of her sighed and pouted. She didn't want her dead guy flirting with other women.

# *Chapter* 7

Nicolo followed Summer down a dark hallway into a vast nightclub booming with sound and flickering lights. It was like nothing he'd ever experienced. The more he looked around, felt the thump of the music in his heart and scented the sage and clove, the more he wanted. The sound was amplified beyond belief. And the energy of the people was also beyond his comprehension. Before them a crowd danced and shimmied and moved to the music, which didn't sound very danceable to Nicolo.

Then again, the last time he'd danced it had been to a waltz.

No one was performing that refined dance. In fact, men and women didn't even hold hands, though they did touch. Everywhere. And all body parts. And some didn't even appear to be paired with another, inclined to dance with whoever moved before them at the moment, be the pairing a male and female, or even male to male and female to female.

And which ones exactly were the men, and which were the women? Many women wore trousers. And those who did not? The shimmer of sparkling clothing drew Nicolo's eye to very low-cut dresses that exposed so much bosom he felt he must have stepped back to—if he recalled his history lessons—the seventeenth century, a time when nipples could be displayed by the daring. Yet, the seventeenth century had never allowed for a woman to reveal so much leg. All the way up to… *there*. It was scandalous.

And marvelous.

Sage smoke and sweetness surrounded him as if an opium dream. Bodies and ice. He and Summer walked under a fan that must be another of those fabulous air-conditioning systems such as she had in her car. And not a candle chandelier in sight to drip officious wax into his hair or onto his skin. Summer had called them electric lights. They flashed brightly in all colors, and erratically, making him blink.

Summer tugged his hand and shouted so he could hear over the noise, "We'll head up to the balcony for a great view of the stage. It's private, but I have access."

As he dutifully followed, Nicolo strayed his hand across a woman's thigh covered with some kind of spangled fabric, and then an arm bare of anything but heat. Scents of fragrance flashed in and out, spiked with whiskey and beer and other liquors he couldn't name. One woman with kohl-lined eyes was drinking something that glowed violet.

Summer had explained before they'd entered that this

was a paranormal nightclub, though humans were admitted. Just a few, and generally they were in the know that demons, faeries, vamps and werewolves danced within.

In his lifetime he'd never interacted with paranormals—beyond his real father and mother and a few demons that had been sent to tempt him—and so he was intrigued to figure who was what sort of creature. But he couldn't begin to look for fangs or fur because— the music.

Oh, the music!

Following the vampiress up a metal stairs that twisted around tightly, they gained the vast balcony, which stretched along the back wall of the club, opposite the stage. Many people milled up here as well, but it was less crowded. Summer bumped her fist against a tall hefty man's fist. He must be the balcony guardian. With a nod toward him, she winked, and the guardian's subtle bow of head granted Nicolo entrance, as well.

"Thank you, kind sir," he said as he passed the behemoth.

They filed to the balcony railing. The place was large, but the decor was hardly sumptuous. It looked like the framework for something that could become grand if only velvets and gilt and decadent frescos were laid over the black, black and more black. Nicolo supposed it represented a certain paranormal theme. Gothic, indeed.

It should disturb him, but fascination shimmied within him.

Summer leaned onto the chrome railing, and her hair brushed his cheek. He inhaled, taking her into his senses. Mmm, he missed sex. Could a man have sex with a vampire and survive without being bitten? It was a disturbing thought, but one he should not disregard. Of course, what fear had he of a vampire bite now that he was undead? Was he invincible? Hmm...

She gestured toward the stage. "That's my brother playing lead guitar," she said in a shout.

Drawn out of his speculation, Nicolo eyed the stage. The man Summer pointed out was tall, lean and wore no shirt, which exposed a well-defined abdomen melded from the palest flesh. Jet-black hair, quite opposite of Summer's ethereal blond, swung over his dark eyes as he attacked what looked like a guitar. The instrument had six strings, a long neck, and he fingered it as if a guitar, but it was quite different than the ones Nicolo had once played. Streamlined, glossy and so loud.

"Johnny also sings," Summer added, "but right now the chick singing is his wife, Kambriel."

Nicolo liked that name. Sounded angelic. But the woman singing was the furthest from any idea of Heaven he'd ever imagined. She had some vocal chords, that was for sure. The song thumped in his body, and her voice growled along his veins, yet it was oddly seductive. Add to that the black, body-tight shiny fabric she wore and the horns at her skull that popped out from thick, coiling black hair. Her breasts were gorgeous, exposed nicely by the bodysuit, and her lips were so red, Nicolo wondered if she had not just drunk blood.

"She's not a demon?" he asked.

"The horns aren't real," Summer said. "Just a prop. She's vampire. The bass player is also vamp. The guy on the cello is Domingos LaRoque, yet another vamp." She indicated the brass goggles he wore with a tip to the side of her head. "That dude is terribly allergic to sunlight."

"The cello he's playing is remarkable," Nicolo said, raising his voice and leaning close to Summer. "How is it so loud? I can hear the instrument over the shouts from the people below, which are deafening."

"Amps," she said. "The instruments are electric."

"Like the lighting? I don't understand that."

"Electricity powers pretty much everything nowadays." She waved to her brother, who waved at her and winked. "I should head backstage. Gotta check Domingos's violin. He might want to use it in the next set. This way."

Nicolo resisted her tug when she started off. Much as the music promised a sensory overload, he felt as if he were in his element. "Could I watch from up here? I'm fascinated with all this, Summer. Those guitars. I have never seen the like."

"Of course. Just don't wander off. I'll get you a drink, yes?"

"Yes, please. A nice absinthe, perhaps."

"I'll have the bartender send one your way. When the set is done, come backstage. The door is down there." She pointed to a door outlined with a red glowing light. "I'll let the bouncer know about you."

She leaned in closer to his ear, and her hand slid across his shirt. Nicolo tensed at that touch. To seek her intimate companionship or not? Her touch did not warrant his caution. "Don't tell anyone who you are. Just try to blend in. Observe. Don't ask anyone questions. Save them for me, yes?"

He nodded and placed a hand over hers to keep the

connection that felt so seductive to him. "Don't worry. I'll take things slowly and with caution."

And before she could slip away, he curled his hand across her back and bent to kiss her. Quickly. A moment of touch. A test, even. Could she allow him this intimacy? And was it acceptable for him, for his own morals, to continue to seek kisses from a vampire?

Yes, most definitely.

She smiled at him, then shook her head as if at a naughty child and walked off.

He'd taken liberty with that kiss. He hadn't been able to resist. Kissing her was divine. Of course, it had been so long since he had shared a kiss with a woman. And he'd never thought that after rising from the dead the first itch he'd feel compelled to satisfy was to have sex. But it was certainly humming about in his thoughts. And lower. He did have a fine new body, after all. No sense in letting it stand around, observing. He wanted to feel the touch of a woman's hands glide over his skin, and the heat of her mouth at his. And to hear the sounds of her desire. Now that was gorgeous music.

He would have Summer. He must.

He nodded in agreement with his lascivious thoughts as he followed Summer's trek across the dance floor and to the stage door. Odd woman, she. And not simply because of her masculine clothing and carelessly untidy hair. She was independent and strong. She wasn't about to shrink back and be submissive to anyone. That vampiress could be a force that he would indulge. But he would remain cautious. Unmoored is how he felt as he navigated this world. He didn't want to risk sinking by losing Summer's trust, and her guidance. A careful seduction must be employed.

When the absinthe arrived, delivered by a pretty blonde with fangs, he smiled widely, but had to dispel a shudder when she ran her tongue along one of the fangs. He was all for testing the modern-day woman in his arms, but the only vampire he trusted at the moment was Summer.

"I thank you," he said. *"Salut!"* And he turned to watch the show, hoping she would leave him be.

He loved women of all sorts. But until today, he'd never included vampires in that mix. His world was growing bigger. Faster. Louder. And all he could do was hold on and take it all in. It felt rather lovely. Empowering, even. Potential beckoned.

He tilted back a few sips of absinthe. "Aggh, this is terrible."

Apparently, the quality of absinthe had not survived the ages. But certainly, music had blossomed into something new and devious. And it made his heart thump with joy. Leaning onto the railing, he watched the band yowl and torture their instruments as the crowd danced and bounced and beat their fists in the air. The musicians garnered a sort of manic following.

He remembered such adulation. How it had fueled his creativity and lifted him on days when he'd felt less than adequate. The clatter of applause, of cheers and cries of "bravo" had never failed to fill his soul with a jubilant desire for more, more and more.

Nicolo gripped the chrome railing. "I need to play again," he said. "It is all I know."

The cello player stepped off stage momentarily, then returned with a violin. Summer must have provided the fix the instrument had needed.

The violinist bumped fists with Johnny and Kambriel, and then the whole crew set off the next song. The singer's booming yet sultry voice invited everyone to jump into the flames and sacrifice their souls. Violin and guitar danced in strange harmony, mixing with the thumping drumbeat. The composition was in standard four-four time. A basic beat. The bass guitar played the rhythm while the brother, Johnny, mastered some fine scales with notes that screamed from the instrument.

Nicolo took it all in. When five more songs were finished, the crowd roared for the last song. He noticed Summer peek out from behind the backstage door. She gestured to him, which he assumed meant to come below.

Leaving the tasteless absinthe sitting on a steel-topped table, he nodded to the behemoth at the stairway and made his way down. Many female hands stroked his body as he pushed across the dance floor. He didn't get any images from them as he had with the women in the tavern and Summer. Perhaps the touch had to be longer, more intentional. A good thing, or he might go mad if every tiny contact delivered him some information about a person's life.

Nicolo turned and eyed one particular redhead clad in black leather horizontal strips that revealed more than they covered. The undercurves of her breasts enticed. He wanted to touch everything. To inhale it all and fix it into his system.

He filed through the crowd and into the backstage area and found Summer in a room cluttered with instruments and assorted stage gear. She stood over a table, violin case before her, cleaning the bow with a cloth. The violin in the case was remarkable. It was violet and...not solid.

"What did you think?" Summer asked as he joined her side and looked over the violin.

"The band is quite remarkable. The music. My God, Summer, how is it that it was so wonderful?"

"I bet it's a lot to take in."

"No, not at all." He stroked his fingers over the outer edge of the violin and then was surprised. "It's metal?"

"Aluminum," she said. "Probably didn't have that metal in your time. It's very lightweight."

"But there's no body. No interior to amplify the sound. It's been carved out. How does it work?"

"The pickup is here in the lower body." She tapped the area of the violin that was solid and had small turnable pegs on it. "Like I said, it's electric. Plug it in, and it rocks. I fixed the pickup for the acoustic violin Domingos is playing onstage now. He likes the deeper tones, he says, and prefers that one over the electric. The amp is crackling, though. I'm going to take it home and tear it apart. This baby is sweet, but she needs a new pickup, as well. Domingos's cracked it when he smashed it against a column at their last concert."

"For what reason?"

She smirked. "Rock 'n' roll, baby." She tapped the violin. "Go ahead. The acoustics still work. Give it a try."

She offered the bow, and Nicolo quickly grabbed it. He hadn't held such in…so long. Anticipation quickened his breath almost as a kiss from Summer had. He must have this. Now.

"May I?" he said of the violin.

Touching another musician's instrument was an honor. When she nodded, he stroked along the inner curves of the violin, where there was no body at all. The metal was sleek and cool. All of it had been cut out, save the neck and the right lower side that harbored small adjustable knobs.

As Nicolo put the violin to his chin and shoulder the band members started filing in, slapping each other across the back and shouting kudos over a job well done. Ignoring them, for all that mattered was the curious instrument in hand, Nicolo pulled the bow over the E string. It sounded exactly as it should, only louder, and perhaps more crisp?

"Lovely." He tried a few notes, then wiggled his fingers in vibrato. It was an easy play, and it felt natural in his hands. Not as if it had been a hundred and seventy-five years since he'd held one. He closed his eyes, allowing the notes to shimmer throughout his system. Music had once been his meditation, his voice, his anger and joy. It still sang to his soul.

"Hey, Summer, who's this?" Kambriel said as she hugged Summer. The woman tugged off the demon horns, which left her long black hair tangled near her ears.

"Uh, his name is…Nick."

Nicolo flinched at that but did not stop bowing. She had warned him not to reveal who he was. Made sense. Until he got his footing, he could hardly go around claiming to be a dead maestro. But maestro he was. And he forgot the others who had gathered round to listen as he segued into a sonnet he'd composed when he had begun to take the stage in Italy. He'd never performed it live because of its simplicity. It was lyrical and yet had a good pace.

"Sounds awesome," someone said.

Nicolo closed his eyes and fell into the luxurious arms of his mistress music.

"Wow, we oughta hire him," the one who played the cello and violin said.

Nicolo slowed his pace, opened his eyes and bowed to the man. "Your electrified cello playing was exquisite."

"Thank you," he said with an astute bow. The man wore brass-rimmed goggles propped on his head of long black hair. Dark shadows smeared under his eyes. Women's kohl cosmetics? Perhaps.

"You like the classics?"

"Uh..." Nicolo assumed that he must be considered a classic nowadays. What a kick. "I do."

"Play some Vivaldi."

"Ah. An easy one." Nicolo segued into the spring concerto from *The Four Seasons* piece, which he had always admired.

"That's amazing," Domingos said. "Believe it or not, I have trouble with that piece. Too cheery for me. Heh!"

Summer hugged her brother. The twosome stood off by the couch, watching, listening. Nicolo could not stop playing. It felt too good. And he did not fear enacting the brimstone bargain by playing this fantastic, electrified instrument.

"Beethoven?" the cellist requested.

"Too easy." He paused. Tightened the G string a twist. "How about Handel?"

"Eh. Too boring."

"Ah! I know a good challenge. Paganini!"

"Oh hell," he heard Summer mutter.

With a grin, Nicolo launched into one of his finer pieces. He barely heard the brother lean over and say next to his sister's ear, "Sounds like you've found a new one, sis."

\* \* \*

Summer pulled her brother out of the dressing room into the outer hallway, where a few of the backstage hands shuffled around gear boxes on wheels. Others were chatting, discussing plans for after the club closed at 3:00 a.m. A violet-eyed faery in a red-and-black mini-dress gave her a sidelong glance that she couldn't determine was flirty or assessing.

Johnny wore black leather pants, no shirt and a wrist full of leather and silver bracelets. Kohl makeup shadowed beneath his eyes and streaked along his abdomen to enhance the cut of his muscles. He leaned against the wall, hand to a hip, and eyes imploring. "Well?" he asked. "Is he your new guy?"

"No. Yes." Summer suppressed a wince. "I met him this morning. We've been on a road trip. I picked him up in Italy. We've…kissed."

"Wow, you've never been one to hook up so fast. Though the guy is handsome. Even I can see that. And a musician. See, I told you the girls always go for the musicians."

"Yeah, whatever. Johnny, I am in so much trouble."

"With what?"

"I had a bit of a hiccup on this mission."

"For Acquisitions? What happened? Are you okay, Summer?"

"I'm fine." She butted the toe of her shoe against the base of the wall, keeping her eyes down from her brother's imploring stare. "But I sort of had an issue with the collection process."

"What kind of issue?"

She gestured a thumb toward the door, behind which

Nicolo was bowing one of his famous caprices in all its nineteenth-century glory. "That issue."

"Your boyfriend?"

"He is not my boyfriend. Just met him, remember?"

"I recall mention of kissing." He arched a villainous brow at her.

"Yes, once or twice. He's—" She turned and grabbed her brother by the shoulders. "Johnny, I was supposed to retrieve Nicolo Paganini's violin for storage in the Archives. Actually, not really *his* violin, but rather the famed black violin with which the devil was once rumored to have tempted him."

"Cool. Did you play it?"

"Of course, I didn't—" She shoved back from his teasing gaze. Enthusiasm was no longer appropriate in the matter. "I'm not stupid about magic and curses and stuff. You know that."

"I do know that. You're very freaked about control. You and your madness shit. So what's up?"

He understood the madness stuff and did sympathize with her, but Summer had come to understand that unless a vampire experienced it for themselves they could never truly understand the visceral fear every time they went in for the vein.

"Well, the violin sort of played itself. I think it enacted something. A curse or bargain."

"What kind of curse?"

"The kind that raises hell. Literally. Although it was supposed to be Paganini playing the violin that activated it, apparently it works when Summer Santiago touches the violin. I did not put the bow to the strings. It happened all on its own."

"Okaaay," he said slowly. "So what are we talking

here? Plagues? Violence? You said something about raising hell? You mean Beneath?"

"Yep." Again she thumbed a gesture toward the door. "And he's it. The guy playing Paganini like a pro? He's the real Paganini. And he crawled out of his coffin this morning after only hearing a few notes accidentally played on the black violin."

Johnny gaped at her.

"I know, right? I don't think it should be my fault. I didn't have all the details. I would have never even opened the case..."

His derisive look stabbed her right in the chest.

"Okay, fine, so I still would have opened it. I had to ensure it was inside. It's my job. But you have to believe it played itself."

"If it's a cursed violin, sure I believe you. So that guy in there is the actual Paganini? The very dude whose #5 we sometimes kick the shit out of?"

She nodded. They really did kick that caprice to hell and back. It was awesome.

"Heh," he added. "My sister kissed a dead guy."

"He's not—well, he probably is. I don't know what he is exactly. He's not a zombie, that's for sure."

"Uh huh." He winked and shook his head.

Summer chewed the corner of her lip, then winced. Fangs were sharp and she'd cut herself. Licking away the blood, she paced before her brother. "What am I going to do? The director told me to keep an eye on him until he determines a course of action."

"Then I'd say you're on babysitting duty. What's so wrong with having him here? If he plays it cool he could have a whole new life. He's not some kind of demon, is he?"

"I'm not sure what he is. I was going to bring him to Verity to see if she could figure him out."

"Good idea. Does he make you sneeze?"

"No, so he can't be demon."

Johnny blew out a breath. "You've always balanced the straight and narrow, little sis. You keep your chin down and do your job to perfection. What the hell pushed you over this cliff?"

"What do you mean? I can be as dark and dangerous as the next vampire."

Johnny eyed her slyly. "Right, because you avoid taking more than a few swallows for fear of turning people mad."

"I have to be careful."

"Too careful," he added quickly. "You gotta let that go, Summer. It's what you are."

"Great. Madness Maker." She dismissed him with a slash of hand. "I don't want to analyze it. And it has nothing to do with Nicolo. I didn't go looking to call the guy up from death. It just happened. And now I can't let him walk the streets by himself. He has no home, no money, no identity. Because he sure as hell can't tell anyone who he really is." She stopped before her brother, hands rubbing her opposite arms. "Oh, Johnny, what do I do? I want to help Nicolo."

"Do you like him?"

"I've only known him a day. And for the first part of the day I suspected he was a zombie."

"I saw him talking in your ear up in the balcony. You two were close."

"Yeah, well, he's sexy. He plays violin for goddess's sake! And you know he is *the* Paganini. A lot to like there."

Summer sighed. As did Johnny.

"Have you bitten him?"

"Really? Can you imagine what kind of reaction I'd get from a dead guy? I can't risk finding out."

"Probably not. But maybe he's different. Like, I don't know, immune to your bite. It's always a possibility. Most other paranormals you've taken blood from have fared well."

"Thanks, but you're assuming the man is some kind of paranormal."

"Anyone who climbs out of a grave can't be mortal."

So just toss the truth out there like she'd never thought about it before. Summer sighed and bumped fists with her brother. "I'm cool."

"You're not cool."

"I will be."

She hoped she would be cool. Because the opposite of cool was fucked up, and she had enough of that in her life already.

# Chapter 8

Summer guided the Audi into the garage that was also her home. The place had once been a six-bay mechanic's shop, and she'd converted half into a living area with bedroom, kitchen and living room, along with an enclosed toilet. The rest of the place was open to the three remaining car bays.

The Audi's headlights flashed on the glass shower walls as she parked in the one bay reserved for the car she was currently driving. To the left was the R65 BMW, of which, she was taking apart the engine. And on the other side of that was a Veyron, one of her dad's cars that required major body work. That man really needed to take Driver's Ed.

"Your home is most strange," Nicolo said as he got out and closed the car door.

The smell of oil wafted like perfume to Summer's

senses. Inside was dark and cool. She rarely turned on the light at night, but did so for her guest's sake. She strolled in and set her cell phone on the kitchen counter, while making a beeline for the fridge to pull out some bottled water. It was the only consumable she stocked.

"It's my home," she said. "Take it or leave it. I like to work on cars. I don't have need for a fabulous living space or decoration bullshit. It suits me."

"I see that it does." He sat on a vinyl-cushioned chrome stool reminiscent of a '50s diner, testing it with a gentle bounce, and accepted a bottle of water. "Thank you," he said, eyeing the bottle curiously. "What is this substance?"

"Plastic. It will kill you, but it is useful. That's plain water in it. Go ahead. Drink it."

He tilted back a swallow and nodded. "Nice and cold. Refreshing. Such wonders that you've a means to water by simply opening the icebox. Plastic. I like it."

"I adore your naivety. I shouldn't, but I do."

"I catch on quickly, yes?"

"I will attribute that to a musician's mind." It seemed to her as though he may have just died and got up to resume life. Lying dead a hundred and seventy-five years? Apparently it hadn't screwed with his cognitive skills.

"You should rest, Summer. I can stretch out on your lovely divan over there and wait until morning."

"You're not going to sleep?"

"I don't actually feel tired."

"Well, then come this way. I'm going to introduce you to the bathroom. I think for a nineteenth-century man this will top all the things you've learned about today."

He eagerly followed. Summer led him through her

bedroom, which was set right next to the kitchen and featured nothing but a king-size bed and a garment rack for her clothes. She kept her shoes neatly ordered below the rack, and the very few items of jewelry she owned were stuffed in a cigar box and nestled in her underwear drawer, which was actually the red toolbox next to the clothing rack.

The bathroom sat between the bed and the garage. Anyone showering could be seen through its glass walls by any other person in the house.

The bathroom light was low, like candlelight, and she gestured Nicolo take a gander. "I bet a shower will feel good," she said, "especially after a climb out of the grave."

"How does this marvelous basin work? And what is that thing in there?"

"Engine part." Summer pushed aside the shower door and plucked out the radiator she'd been cleaning yesterday and set it aside on the floor. "Not necessary to take a shower. Sorry."

She explained to him how to turn the knobs for water and adjust temperature. She'd rigged up a stand for the showerhead because it wasn't common for such in France. She liked to shower freehanded.

Nicolo seemed eager to give it a try. His enthusiasm was cute, but also, charming. And after showing him the water closet, flushing the toilet and explaining how that process worked, she set some towels from the linen closet out for him to use.

"I'll give you some privacy," she said on a yawn. "I'll step down to the mailbox and see if I have any mail. Sit out on the stoop for a bit. Feel free to snoop. Just girl stuff in the medicine cabinet. I'll probably shower in the morning. You can take my bed."

"I will not. I will be perfectly comfortable on that divan. And as I've said, I may not sleep. I'll be quick with this interesting shower so you may return and get some sleep."

"No worries. I'm cool. Good night, Nicolo." She hesitated on her way out the door. "I'm…sorry."

"Please, Summer." He grasped her hand and turned her to face him. "Don't be sorry for giving me another chance to live."

"Yeah, but what if—"

He kissed her, ceasing any protest that he might be evil. Good plan. The guy was sneaky like that. She didn't mind it at all. Especially because his kisses were damn awesome. He tasted like licorice. Must be from the absinthe. And he smelled warm and inviting. She couldn't scent a mortal's blood until it was outside the body, but she expected that Nicolo's would be just as amazing as he was.

Allowing herself to simply receive, because she was too tired for anything else, she snuggled against him as he hugged her closer. He murmured another thanks against her lips and then kissed them once more quickly.

"I didn't need to hear what you were going to say about me possibly being evil," he said. "A kiss seemed to quiet you nicely."

"If you ever need my silence, feel free," she replied.

"Really? You favor me?"

"Yes?"

He tilted his head in query at her unsure answer.

To save herself further anxiety she quickly said,

"Night!" and beelined into the garage bay area and toward the front door.

Closing the door behind her, she walked down to check the mailbox. Nothing. She never got mail. Not that she wanted it. Bills were the only thing that ever showed up.

Tugging out her cell phone, she walked up to the stoop to sit and give Nicolo ten minutes to himself. She checked messages. Nothing from the director. That was fine. Because she expected him to call and order her to do something she probably wouldn't want to do. She texted Verity, hoping to meet up with the witch tomorrow so she could take a look at Nicolo. No immediate response, but she was probably in bed with her lover, Rook.

Setting the phone on the concrete step, she bowed her head forward. She had raised a dead musician. And was starting to fall for the guy. Because those kisses had been something all right. And the way he marveled over everything was so refreshing in this day of jaded consumerism. He was easy with her, and she didn't mind that either. Yes, she favored him.

And she wanted to bite him, to taste his blood and learn if it was as rich and exciting as the man. But there was a certain danger in that. She had no idea *what* Nicolo was. And while vamps could bite just about any creature that walked this realm, they avoided faeries, angels and demons.

Demon blood wouldn't kill a vamp, but it was thick and nasty like tar. Blue angel blood caused a gruesome explosion—from inside the vamp. And faery dust, well, that was addictive, as she well knew. Her father, who had once lived in Faery, used to crave the stuff after he'd arrived in the mortal realm and he'd succumbed to addiction. He was clean now. Though their mother, Lyric, never let down her guard around faeries and her husband.

Summer had never had a curiosity for faery blood. She had enough to deal with, being a Madness Maker. What would she impart in Nicolo's mind if she drank his blood? If he were merely human would she drive him mad?

Couldn't risk it. He needed her. And she wanted him to trust her. She was his only connection to learning the new. She could be everything to him. And if she focused on being that everything then she needn't think about biting him. And yet, Johnny had mentioned something about her bite perhaps not affecting Nicolo as it did mortals.

"Don't let this happen," she muttered.

But it was only words. Her heart had already made a leap. And while that scared her, she was always one to follow adventures. Even the kind she'd never before pursued, like the adventures of the heart.

Nicolo had once a rich patron in Venice who owned a sort of shower system in his palazzo. So this was vaguely familiar to him, save the amazing water pressure, the adjustable speeds (massage!) and the ability to control the warmth of the water with but a flick of the dial. Heaven! He stood in the shower until his fingers were wrinkled and he felt confident he'd washed away any remnants from the grave.

Once toweled off, he found a comb in the glass-fronted cupboard above the washbasin and pulled it through his slick hair. When he'd been dying, his hair had fallen out in clumps, and out of vanity he'd insisted his nurse no longer comb it. Of course, he'd written that command out, since at the time he'd been unable to speak. He had been such an invalid! A fifty-eight-year-old man destroyed by drink, gambling and whoring.

But never had he succumbed to the vice of selfish greed in a quest to be all-powerful.

He narrowed his eyes at the distorted reflection the glass showed and wondered about his casino. Now, there would be a way to make some money so he wouldn't have to rely on Summer's charity. Not that he'd ever refused a gift from a beautiful woman. Such acceptance had come easily to him. He gave the world music; he gladly accepted any gifts the world wanted to bestow in return.

So his ego hadn't changed since death. Yet the thought to rely on a woman now seem repulsive. He had a second chance at life. He must live it fully and as a proud and capable man. He was not one to stand on the sidelines and witness life. He wanted to be in it, grabbing it by the throat and sucking it dry like a…vampire.

Heh. He wasn't sure what kind of monster he was now, but he was probably closer to Summer than to a human being. Such proof was in his strength and the hard muscles that wrapped beneath his skin. What other abilities had he gained upon climbing out of the coffin?

Did he want to learn what they could be? He nodded. Would be ridiculous to not exercise any gifts this new life had granted him.

With the fluffy white towel wrapped about his waist, he strode out to the living area, where the large gray velvet divan did indeed look comfortable. In a home

devoid of color and feminine decoration it was odd to
see a pink frilly pillow nestled on the cushion. But it
made him smile. She wasn't so tough as she feigned.

He should have nightclothes to put on. A glance to
the clothes he'd folded across the chair by the shower
gave him a shudder. They were his burial clothes. He
needed new things. Any bit of fabric *not* a hundred and
seventy-five years old.

He sat on the divan and stretched his arms across the
back, closing his eyes. No, he didn't feel at all sleepy.
But it did feel good to sit and ruminate over the day.
What a crazy day.

He had traveled from Italy to Paris in less than a day.
Unthinkable. He'd learned about electricity and modern lighting and air-conditioning. And the food. And
the women! Goth or sluts (as Summer had termed the
women in the tavern), he liked them all. He looked forward to what tomorrow would bring.

Yet he didn't want to think about the Big Guy because that might bring him to his side. Now that he was
again alive would the devil resume his temptations? If
so, could he resist the brimstone bargain again?

Did he want to?

So much power. And now he had not his son to worry
about shaming should he accept such power. If he was
strong and possessed magical skills, he should not want
for money and would not have to rely on the kindnesses
of a lovely vampire.

Lovely? In her own, particular manner, Summer was
indeed lovely. And if she could be his introduction-
to-the-twenty-first-century woman then he was eager
to learn. Hands-on learning, of course.

He knew Summer had entered the house, not from

the sound of the door opening—she'd been very quiet—but from the smell of her skin. Salty and sweet. His senses were simply that acute now. It was wondrous to indulge in the use of them.

A vampiress. She'd been out in the daylight with him today. And tonight at the club, she hadn't been away from him for long. When did she bite people? How often? Did she drink a lot of blood? What did it taste like? Was it a sexual thing? Did the bite feel good to the bitee?

He could imagine threading his fingers through her lush blond hair and pulling her in close, allowing her to kiss his throat and glide those fangs along the thick vein beneath his skin. Such a drink would give her life. The eroticism of it all made him hard, and he clasped his hands over his erection beneath the towel. He wanted the vampiress who quietly filed into the bedroom and pulled a curtain hung on a wire so they were separated by that thin sheet of privacy.

Though there were no lights on in the home, pale moonlight filtered through the window behind the bed and he could see the shadow of her as she tugged off her shirt and slipped down her trousers. The curves of her body were slim and small, but there was no denying she was a woman.

His erection hardened even more.

Did he simply want any woman to fuck after a dry spell of one hundred seventy-five years? It should not be unexpected. If he were going to live life large he must engage in everything sensual, visual, audible, and drink it all in. Because he may not have much time before evil crept over him and changed him. To that thing likc the devil Himself.

Nicolo shuddered. He would not succumb to the darkness that was his legacy. He must not.

## Chapter 9

Summer woke to daylight filtering through the bedroom curtain and the intriguing strains of a violin piece she'd never heard before. It had a gypsy lilt to it. Fun and peppy. Yet, it crackled. Nicolo must have figured how to plug Domingos's violin into the amp she kept out in the garage and turn the volume to low. Good boy.

Did she just think *good boy*? She needed more sleep. Or maybe a new perspective on this situation. She was merely entertaining a visiting celebrity, right?

A celebrity she wouldn't mind learning far more intimate details about than a few kisses and tender hugs.

She rose and wandered into the bathroom. With the curtain still pulled between the bedroom and living room, she had minimal privacy because standing out in the garage, Nicolo could see her shower if he simply turned around. She didn't care. He could look all he liked.

After a shower and brushing her teeth she found a pair of loose jeans in her closet and pulled them on. A Bitter/Sweet T-shirt featured the red outline of devil horns above the band name which looked as if it had been written with spattered blood.

The gypsy dance changed octaves and increased speed. "That's not one of his," she decided. And when the song suddenly changed to something she did recognize, she was startled. "He's playing Bitter/Sweet's 'Welcome to the Fire.'" He'd managed to pick it up merely by hearing it performed once last night.

"He really is a genius."

In the kitchen, she grabbed a bottle of water and then wandered into the garage barefoot. She wiggled her toes appreciatively on the cool concrete.

Nicolo hadn't turned around once while she'd been showering. Bummer.

Ahem.

The guy wore the same pants he'd been buried in and no shirt. The muscles on his back flexed deliciously as his bow arm moved back and forth, teasing the strings to sing. She'd always been a back kind of girl. Abs and biceps? Nothing wrong with the front side. But a wide-shouldered back with muscles that screamed for exploration? Add to that the lush fall of coal-black hair skimming those muscles? Mmm… Her fingers ached for touch.

He certainly could not have gotten those muscles during his previous lifetime. Beyond their fingering skills, violin players were not known for their physical prowess. And she suspected the concept of working out hadn't existed back in his time. He did have long fingers that quickly danced across the strings. She recalled the history she'd read about him had claimed a doctor who had once examined him had made the statement that his hands and fingers were large but not abnormally so. Nicolo simply had dexterity, flexibility and speed attributed to years of practice.

A glance over his shoulder spied her, and he stopped playing. "I like that composition!"

"I guess you do. You remember it from last night?"

"Yes, but I prefer it in E minor."

"I noticed. I think Johnny would like that version, as well. Keep that up and you'll be a heavy-metal rock god in no time."

"That sounds favorable." He splayed out his arms, which gave her a great view of his hard pectorals and impossibly rigid abs. "I don't mind being compared to a god."

"I imagine not." She didn't mind the view either.

"But it does crackle, yes?"

"Yeah, that's the pickup. Need to fix that. So what was the gypsy dance you were playing before this one?"

"Ah, just something I made up while you were showering. I didn't look. Well, not too much."

She felt a blush rise, and that was so startling she twisted at the waist as if she was looking for something in the kitchen. But really? She wasn't afraid of a little flirtation. And she had been eyeing him up, down and all around. "Nothing wrong with looking."

"Is that so? Then next time I will look longer." He winked. "As for the gypsy tune, when previously alive I was constantly filled with inspiration. I am so pleased my muse has not left me. Though, the whispers are distracting." He twirled the violin bow and pointed upward as if to indicate something coming from above. "Must be your neighbors."

"The whispers?"

He swung the bow before him, pointing all about. "Don't you hear it? Sort of a subtle whisper. I can't make out the words, but it is annoying."

"You must be hearing voices, buddy. I don't hear anything but the buzz from the amp. I need to tear that apart and check out its insides."

And yet. She had heard whispers while down in the storage room where she'd found the violin. Was it co-incidence?

"So are you up for some clothes shopping today?" she asked.

"Oh yes. It was a great struggle to force myself to put on these trousers. I was buried in this clothing, by God. It doesn't feel comfortable but rather like something a zombie would wear."

Summer chuckled. "You know I was just kidding about the zombie thing."

"You were not. And that's perfectly fine. Neither of us knows what will come of me. Let's just keep our hopes up for all my parts staying intact, shall we?"

Summer's eyes strayed to his abs. "Fingers crossed," she said. Sucking in the corner of her lip, she restrained herself from reaching to touch.

"Now you are looking at me."

"Huh? Uh…that I am. Lots to admire."

He straightened, preening a palm down his abs. "I thank you for the compliment."

Yes, well, if she didn't turn and find something better to do right now she'd probably have to touch him.

And then all thoughts would turn to biting him. Deeply, and for a very long time. Mmm...

"I got a text from Verity this morning," she said, fleeing the sensual thought. "The witch I told you about. We can stop by her place after we suit you up in some new clothes."

"I am hungry, as well. You don't have any food in your fancy icebox with the light that flickers on when you open the door."

"Yeah, well..." She pointed toward her chest. "Vampire."

"Tell me about that," he said as he set the violin in the case and loosened the bow before also placing that in the case. "Do you bite people every day?"

"I need blood about once a week." More so really, because of her small drinks, but she didn't like to reveal that terrible anxiety to others. "It tastes great. No, I don't kill people." Not anymore, if she could help it. "Don't have to take that much blood to survive. And, no, you can't watch. Anything else?"

"Touchy," he muttered, and he slid his eyes down her for an assessing summation. "As a matter of fact, there is something else I am curious about." One hand stroked up his chest to rest over his heart. His eyes met hers in a stunning fix of smoldering connection. "Is drinking blood a sensual experience for you?"

She raised a brow, seeking truth in his eyes. Was he asking for himself or purely out of curiosity? Because she got the questions all the time. That's why she quickly rattled off all the answers to get it over with. But something in the glint dashing his pupils made her wonder about his intentions. And she wanted to entertain those curious thoughts.

She cautioned her tone to not touch a tease. "Do you want me to bite you, Nicolo?"

"If it is a sensual thing?" He glided a palm down his bare chest. Man, oh man, did that move make her heartbeats stutter and her skin grow warm. Such a fine piece of man flesh. "I'd give it a try."

"But if you're not going to get off then it's not worth the pain, eh?"

"Get off?"

She shrugged. "Get hot. Get aroused. You know."

"It's been a while," he said. "I do have…needs."

"As do I. The first of which is—" Not getting emotionally involved!

He held up a finger to silence her. His eyes traced the ceiling then down around the room. "You don't hear that?"

Was this a side effect of him rising from the grave? Or would she have to face the realization that whatever she'd unearthed down in the Italian cellar might have followed them here? Because she didn't have the violin in her possession anymore. Yet if he were still hearing those same silvery whispers she had heard…

"No, I don't hear anything. What's it saying?"

"Nothing distinguishable." He shook his head yet tilted it as if seeking the source. "Odd. It seems to trail about inside this carriage parking area."

In the kitchen, Summer's cell phone rang. "Don't follow it," she said as she went to answer the ring. "It could be something you don't want to meet. Hello?"

"Summer, this is CJ."

"Oh hey." She had expected Director Pierce. "You get the violin tagged and tossed?"

"Is that what you Retrievers call it? We don't toss

the objects you collect. We handle them very carefully. And in fact, I did tag the black violin last night after you handed if off to me. I set it in storage and then went to look for some heavy-duty wards. Still hadn't found any until this morning. When I intended to ward the violin, and notify the Director of Acquisitions the mission was complete, I found the spot on the shelf empty."

"What?"

"The violin is gone. I've searched the stacks, thinking I might have misplaced it. We do have a large storage room. Nothing. I know where I had placed it because the dust is disturbed. Now it's gone. Have you seen it?"

"Why would I…"

Her vision wandered into the garage, where Nicolo paced around the Veyron her father had driven into a street pole. What was whispering to him?

She didn't have to wonder very long.

"I don't know," CJ said. "Sometimes the objects we store have a mind of their own. I should have put a basic ward on it to hold it tight, though I doubt that would have been sufficient. You might take a look around to see if it's returned to you for some odd reason. Otherwise, I'll take a look through the entire Archives. It's got to be here somewhere. Then again, if it was created with diabolic magic…" His sigh rifled over Summer's shoulders in a chilly warning.

"Sure, CJ, I'll look around. Let me know if you find it."

He rang off, and before she could click off, Nicolo rushed toward the Audi. It was as if he were being called toward the car by an unseen force.

"Nicolo!" she called. "What are you doing?"

"I'm following it," he hastily said over his shoulder.

The silver Audi needed a wash after her adventure through Italy. He stopped before the trunk and pressed his palms to it and then leaned down to put his ear to the place where CJ had performed remarkable auto-body magic.

"What is going on?" she said, coming to a stop beside him.

"The whispers. They are inside this vehicle," he stated. "Open it, if you please."

"But. That's impossible. There's no one in my trunk. And the violin is gone. You saw me hand it to CJ last night."

Though, after talking to CJ…

He splayed his hands toward the trunk, indicating she open it. "Humor me?"

"Hang on. The keys are in the kitchen." She quickly retrieved the keys.

Nicolo leaned against the car, hands on the trunk behind him. The pose showed off his ripped abs. And she could not look away. Nor did she.

"It's odd, isn't it?" he said as she realized her gaze was glued on his midsection. "I've never had such toned muscles. I like this new life."

She sucked in a breath and steeled herself not to stare. "Move aside."

He did so. Summer clicked the trunk release, and it popped open. They both gasped upon seeing what sat inside.

# Chapter 10

Summer watched Nicolo's hands move toward the violin. She grabbed his wrist, wrenching him away from the trunk. "Do not touch that thing."

"How did it get in there? I saw you hand it to the dark witch last night." He rubbed his bare arms, then reached toward the trunk again and recoiled. Yet his hands shook and his breathing had increased.

It was as if he was compelled, and Summer feared that compulsion. It had been activated when she had discovered the violin. It may not stop until the instrument was destroyed.

"Yes, we've got to destroy it."

"No!" Now he was the one to grab her by the shoulders and pull her away from the trunk. "Bring it back to your Archives. Just get it away from here."

"It has to be destroyed or it will continue to whisper

to you. I've heard those whispers, Nicolo. It wants you to play it. Don't you understand that?"

"Yes, I understand that. Do you realize how difficult it is for me to stand here and *not* grab that abomination?" He shoved a hand through his hair, clenched his fingers and then shouted. Slamming a fist on the trunk edge, he cursed. "I have to play it!"

She struggled with him as he grabbed the case. He was strong, but she was, too. An elbow to his ribs forced another curse out of him.

"Summer, it is mine!"

She managed to jam her foot against his knee, bringing him down, and he released the case. Summer slammed the trunk shut with the violin inside. He lunged for her, gripping her around the throat. But he didn't squeeze. Eyes wild, he shook his head and released her as quickly as he'd grabbed her.

"I'm sorry! The cursed thing wants me! Please, get it away from me!"

"I'll take care of it," she said.

He stood back, nodding resolutely. Fingers clenching and unclenching by his sides, his jaw tightened. He was not defeated, but she sensed he would not harm her to get to it. Unless the compulsion grew too strong. Then what would he do? He was capable of defeating her; she had felt his strength.

"Go...play Domingos's violin. Maybe that will satisfy the weird compulsion you feel," she said. "I'll be back in a bit and when I return, I'll take you shopping for some clothes."

He slapped a hand to his bare chest, nodded, then silently turned to the kitchen. But he paused a few steps away and looked back.

Summer shook her head at him. She had brought this black violin up from hiding; it was now her responsibility to put it back into hiding.

"Thank you," he muttered. "I truly do not want to harm you, Summer. I admire you. I…I desire you."

She gulped hearing that statement. They were both on the same page—when they were not at each other's throats.

"And while I am smart enough to realize it is the violin that unleashes my wicked temper," he continued, "I also know I can't fight that compulsion."

"I get that. I'll get rid of it. Just stay here. Okay?"

"Yes, I will pick up the violet violin." He staggered toward Domingos's violin.

And Summer saw then how helpless he was to fight the compulsion. It spoke to him in ways she could never imagine. It had been connected to him, since the nineteenth century.

She jumped in the car and shifted into Reverse. As she backed onto the street she knew she had to drive… somewhere. Where? If she brought it back to the Archives the violin would return here, she felt sure of that. It had to be destroyed. And buried.

"Yes," she muttered and steered toward the vast city park, the Bois de Boulogne.

Nicolo paced the floor. He repeatedly passed the violet metal violin, glaring at it. It was an abomination. Electrified?

"No," he muttered. Not an abomination. The violet instrument produced exquisite sound. Nothing about it was wrong, if he overlooked the crackles that Summer said she could fix. It was a veritable work of art for this new age in which he found himself.

The abomination was the black violin Summer had found in Cella Monte. Why had Achille not destroyed that violin? Had his son tried? What dark evils had kept his son from accomplishing that task? He didn't want to know what Achille might have suffered to accomplish the task he had asked of him.

Who owned the home in Cella Monte and had taken care of the horrible thing all these years? Would knowing provide him a clue?

If it did, what would it matter? It still called to him— he could sense the wicked lure rushing through his veins—yet the whispers had faded. Thankfully. Still, he worried about Summer alone with the thing. It was pure evil. Would she be safe? She had been alone with it once already. And that event had brought him back from death.

Perhaps he should have gone along with her.

No. He turned and paced a line before the gray divan. He wanted to go along only to get his hands on the thing and play it. Because he must. His fingers yearned to hold the neck and glide the bow across the strings. It was all he could think of. It was as if he had been resurrected only for that purpose.

Had he been? Had his resurrection merely been the first step? And then to play the thing would grant him the power he had denied so adamantly all his life. Sure, he was strong now, and he had some strange ability to read people by touch.

He'd seen Himself. Had witnessed the creature's dark, ineffable powers. And...now he felt those very same powers as a seed within his own body. Just waiting for germination via melody.

Yelling in frustration, he turned and punched a fist into the wall. It dented inward, and the thick layer of white paint cracked under his fingers. Drawing back the fist, he rubbed his knuckles. Foolish. He was a musician. He hands were his greatest asset. And the punch had done little to alleviate his aggravation.

Summer had been gone over an hour. Where was she? He should go looking for her.

Yes, he would go out and find the violin—er, Summer.

He paused on his route to the shower area, where his shirt and shoes waited. Shook his head.

*Just sit. She will return. Without the evil thing. Play the electric violin. Get lost in that feeling. And all will be well.*

The garage door glided upward, and Nicolo jumped and turned about.

Summer parked and got out with a smile on her face. "Just me. Didn't mean to give you a fright."

She shoved blond strands from her dirt-smeared face and wandered toward the kitchen. Nicolo followed on her heels, noting her jeans were dirty and her hands, as well. With a glance to the wall he'd punched, she turned to give him a lift of brow.

"Sorry. I'll see to the repair of that."

"Don't worry about it. I know you're frustrated."

"Yes, well, what have you been up to?" he asked.

"I buried it," she said without fanfare. "In a big wooded area."

"You—" Offended that she take such a fine instrument and bury it, Nicolo stopped himself from protesting. Much as his heart pleaded against the travesty, she had done what she felt the right thing. "Your Acquisitions will not be upset?"

"I tried to contact the director, with no reply. He's in meetings with some bigwigs all day. So I had to take matters into my own hands. That violin is dangerous."

"What if someone were to dig it up?"

She paused before the shower and slid her fingers down the glass wall. "I made sure it would be unusable. I need to take a shower. If you don't mind giving me a bit of privacy by maybe taking the violin over to the corner of the garage?"

"Yes, but—Summer." He touched her arm, pausing her again. He smudged her cheek with a thumb, wiping off some of the dirt. Could he find the instrument? If he followed the whispers—no!

Forcing himself to accept what she had done, and knowing it was what was right, Nicolo nodded resolutely. "I thank you again. I know you are trying to protect me. It means very much to me that you care."

"I got you into this mess. I should probably do my best to get you out of it."

"I can keep myself out of it by refusing to play the violin."

"But do you have a choice?"

"I'm not sure." He took her hand. Images of her life started to assault him. He could see her digging a hole in the park, and he swiftly pushed that away. Yes, he could control it. Good. "I don't like to feel so ineffectual. I've always taken charge of my life, be it good, bad or mistakes made I lived to regret."

"Like gambling?"

"You know about that?"

"History records you opened a casino right here in Paris."

"Yes, what a fabulous failure. I do love the thrill of a wager. Does it still stand? Are there yet casinos in this new age?"

"Everywhere. If you're nice to me, I might even take you to a modern one."

He straightened. "I would like that. Something to distract my mind from other things."

"Like wanting to play music?"

"Oh, I always want to play. It's just I've to be careful which violin I do play. That electric one seems safe, yes?"

"Yes. Play that one all you like. But I'll have to get it back to Domingos soon. They have another gig next weekend."

"Yes, you must return it to its owner. Perhaps I could purchase my own? Though I haven't any money. I'll have to make due with listening to others perform. I'd love to see the opera."

"We could do that this evening. They usually offer last-minute ticket sales on cancellations. But I'm a mess. If we're to get you some new clothes none of the shops on the rue Royale would allow me in looking like this. Give me twenty minutes and I'll be a new person."

Nicolo asked, "Might I...join you?"

He looked around the shower wall to see she had paused from lifting her shirt and turned to look over her shoulder. The tiniest smile curved her mouth. And then she said, "Yes."

# Chapter 11

Watching the man remove his clothes while she stood beneath the shower spray was a lesson in, oh yes, give me some of that. Summer wasn't a prude, and she wasn't one of those women who needed to have a relationship before she could have sex with a man. If she wanted to get some, she fed that need with a shameless and empowering jump in the sack with a man she trusted (no strangers, please).

And what better way to really get to know the man who had just dropped his trousers to reveal a very healthy, upright, hard cock. No zombies here, folks.

He smiled at her, flipped his hair over a shoulder and stepped into the shower.

"This is good for you?" he asked.

"It will be. Come here. Let me show you how the modern woman takes her pleasure." She captured his wet penis with one hand and pulled him closer. Gliding her fingers along the shaft, she met his approving gaze with a raise of eyebrow. "No love necessary," she said. "We both get what we want. From someone we know and, hopefully, trust. And I know you want this."

"Uh, oh...yes," he growled. Clutching her hand to stop her strokes, he leaned in and kissed her mouth. "But allow me to show you how a really old man takes his pleasure. Yes?"

"You like to be on top? I'm going to have a problem with that."

"Is that so? Doesn't bother me. But we are standing, and I..." He slid his fingers up her stomach and circled her nipple. Summer bit her lip and closed her eyes. "I like to be the one who gives pleasure."

"I'm cool with that. Oh yeah. That. Is. Good."

"It's much like learning a new instrument," he said, moving closer to nestle his nose against her wet hair and ear. His fingers slipped over her nipple. "Just the right touch, for the right pressure and right amount of time."

She sighed as an erotic zing flashed through her system and burst in her core. A giddiness curled her mouth and she sighed.

"Slowly and curious, yes?" he whispered.

"Curious is good." She tilted her head back, and he bent to take her nipple into his mouth. And her world rocked in the best way possible. She wrapped her hand over his shoulders, gliding them along his slick skin and prompted him forward. The man could take all he wanted.

Thankful the glass walls were heavy-duty and secured with steel corner beams, she laughed when her back hit the slippery glass and dislodged his suctioning kiss from her breast.

"Oh yes?" he said on a tease as he knelt before her and kissed the inside of her left knee. "We'll see if you laugh after I try this."

A lash of his tongue tickled at her inner thigh. He glided higher until a tender kiss to her labia whispered out another sigh from her. Summer raked her fingers through the man's wet hair and did not so much guide him closer as she followed his lead. He opened her with his tongue and tasted her. A long taste that teased and promised, then delivered as he kissed her clitoris and gave it due attention.

She hadn't realized men of the nineteenth century were so educated regarding a woman's pleasure, but—mercy—he knew what he was doing. She almost lost her footing, so she gripped for the top of the glass wall and held firmly as she allowed her thighs to relax and her core to surrender to the sweet, demanding lure of his motions.

When his fingers slicked over her pulsing button she knew exactly how it felt to be played by a skilled musician. And it didn't take him long to bring up her song in a throaty, hoarse shout of pleasure. Her body shuddered against his fingers as he kissed his way upward, over her mons and stomach and to her breasts. She gripped at his skin, digging in as she rode the orgasm to its final, whispering tingle.

"Nicolo," she gasped.

"Not so bad for an old man, eh?"

She chuckled then and pushed him against the opposite wall.

After a remarkable round of sex in the shower they had moved to Summer's bed, still wet, but not minding

that the sheets got a little moist. Nicolo had been flab-
bergasted that the modern woman was so at ease with
the male anatomy. In the shower Summer had knelt before him and taken his cock into her mouth. Of course
he'd had women do that for him before, but they had
been bought and paid for. No respectable woman would
even think to do such a thing for her man back in his
time.

But Summer was respectable. And talented with her
tongue. He did appreciate the forward movement that
women had made over the years. And the up and down
movement. And that part where she'd taken him in both
hands and had gently twisted—mercy. Maybe it was a
vampire thing?

"What are you thinking about?" she asked. Rolling
up to hug him from the side and crossing one of her legs
over his groin, she bit playfully at his biceps. "You think
a few orgasms for each of us was enough?"

"Oh most certainly. I was thinking how much I favor
your talents."

She chuckled and rolled to her back, so he adjusted
to his side to look over her naked body in the muted
afternoon light. Small breasts with tight nipples. Sleek
waist and hips and the longest legs he'd seen in—well,
almost two centuries. She was a work of art.

"Do you ever have sex with those you bite?" he suddenly asked. The mystery of her blood drinking ever
nudged at him. He was a curious man. And he wanted
to know everything about her. This seemed a good time
to ask the intimate questions.

"Rarely. I can't drink a lot. It's a weird thing with
me. So it's usually poke 'em, suck 'em, get the hell out
of there." She turned her head, eyeing him with a fall-

ing smile. "I…" A heavy sigh preceded "…do things to those I bite. I'm not like other vampires."

"What do you mean by that?"

"It's not something I've ever had someone explain to me. My family and I have sort of figured it out over the years. My dad was the first to notice because he went along with me when I started drinking blood. I change the donors I drink from. They go a little mad."

"Really? Like…" He tapped his temple. "…touched in the head?"

She nodded.

"That's quite remarkable."

"Not in a good way. I think…" She sighed, then trailed her fingers along his thigh. "I've never told anyone this…" She closed her eyes, and he sensed her reluctance.

"Tell me," he whispered. "Give me your confidence. I won't spoil it. Promise."

"No, you wouldn't. You are an honorable man." She tapped her lower lip with a hematite-beringed thumb. And then a fang lowered, which he marveled over. So sharp, and yet it fit nicely against her other teeth and didn't seem to cause her a disturbance. "When I bite a person, I think I do something to their soul. I can feel the soul shiver when I pull my fangs from their neck. It frightens me. So that's why I try to take a quick drink, with hopes I won't leave them permanently damaged."

"I can imagine it must be difficult, seeing that it is something you must do for survival."

She nodded, turned her head away from him. And Nicolo swallowed back a rise of compassion that loosened tears in his eyes. She may be considered a creature, but she was a real, living, feeling being. And she had such an awful handicap with which to deal.

"If there's anything I can ever do to help," he whispered, then leaned over to kiss her shoulder. "You are an exquisite being, Summer Santiago. I am glad it was you who found me walking along the road. I believe we were meant to meet."

"Maybe. All that destiny crap is supposed to be true. But right now, I believe we should get dressed and go out and do a little shopping. You in the mood for some new clothes?"

"You don't have to convince me to dispose of the funeral garb. Lead on, my bright and delicious vampiress."

The modern-day shops were a marvel to behold. Nicolo was attended by a female shopkeeper wearing shoes with heels so high she looked to topple if she made a misstep. But they did make her gams look shapely and slender. And her red dress was so tight it emphasized everything, including her hip bones. The cultured women from his time had never been so emaciated, and yet, nowadays it seemed it was a preferred condition by both the men and women. But he stole those glances because it felt wrong to do so in front of Summer. He respected her and didn't want her to think unkindly of him.

The sex they'd shared had been beyond words. A symphony of flesh and sighs. And afterward when she'd confided to him about her condition of giving madness to humans he had felt blessed to have her trust. He was quickly growing enamored of Summer, and that sat

quite well with him. Who would have thought he would
have an affair with a vampire?

*"Trés magnifique!"* the shopkeeper announced as
Nicolo stepped out of the changing room to display the
black velvet pants and white shirt. The cuffs sported a
narrow ruffle around them, and the shirt was just loose
enough to be comfortable. Reminded of his bohemian
days when he'd luxuriate in a salon discussing with his
fellow composers the merits of opium as a useful cre-
ative device.

"What do you think?" he asked Summer, who leaned
against the wall, arms crossed. The loose jeans hung
low on her hips, and the T-shirt was snug, revealing a
slash of taut tummy that he could only imagine licking
and then kissing.

Did she beam? She seemed to beam from her eyes to
her skin to her smile. Must have been the sex. Of course
it had been the sex. He certainly had not lost his prowess. Thank whatever bloody god or demon had granted
him that boon.

No, forget the demons. He would not invite that evil
with a single thought.

He splayed out his arms. "Do you think it makes
me look like a modern man yet still allows me a bit of
my past?"

"Definitely. Very retro romantic. Grab a couple of
those shirts, and be sure to get the leather jeans he
tried on previously," she said to the shopkeeper. "What
about shoes?"

Nicolo extended a foot to display the Italian leather
shoes he had worn—literally—since the nineteenth century. "Much as I abhor wearing er, funeral garb, these
shoes are comfortable. My feet are so long it was always

difficult to find a fit unless they were bespoke. I cherish these shoes. Does that make me odd?"

"Not at all. Keep the good-fitting shoes. That will save us a trip to Louboutin. And my bank account won't scream because I'll be tempted to buy my own shoes while there. Not that I need a pair of swanky high heels." She tapped the rubber toe of her violet sneaker against a mannequin's red-shoe-shod foot. "I like comfort."

"Are you not going to purchase some things for yourself?" Nicolo's shoulders fell. He needed to start playing the concert circuit so he could make some money. Then he could treat her as a lady should be treated, by showering her with gifts. "I should wish to cover you in jewels and pretty things in thanks for your generosity."

"Eh. I'm not much of a jewel girl. I like a nice pair of leather boots and some sexy underwear and I'm good to go."

"Sexy underwear?" And leather boots? Just those two items? He waggled his brows at her. "Did you point out a lingerie shop just down the Champs-Élysées?"

"I did. It's called George V."

The shopkeeper handed Nicolo the check and he looked it over. "That's very much. Do you still use gold francs nowadays?"

Summer snagged the bill and tugged out a small black card from a back pocket. "I got this. And I got the macarons that we'll stop for at Ladurée on the way to George V. I have a craving for a bite of something sweet."

Nicolo leaned in and kissed her below the earlobe. "I have something sweet in my arms."

"You're such a rake."

"Guilty as accused. But you like me?"

She nodded in a resolute sort of acceptance. "I do."

"So why did I hear reservation in that agreement? Do I not clean up well? You are still worried about me suddenly wanting to eat your brains, aren't you?"

Summer laughed and tugged out her cell phone. "Not at all. Just...taking things slowly, I guess."

"Do you call having sex with a man you've only known a day taking things slow?"

They stepped outside onto the busy sidewalk that paralleled the bustling Champs-Élysées roadway.

"I call what we did in the shower hooking up and meeting my needs." She looked aside for a moment. Regretfully? He wouldn't judge. If she said she was happy with what they'd done, he would believe her. "I recall you were pretty pleased with the results, as well."

"*Hooking up?* What an odd term for a most delicious coupling. What are you doing on your witchbox? And why is it everyone seems to have one of those?" He looked about at the passing tourists, and at least half of them had their attention diverted by one of the witchboxes.

"I was just checking for messages from the director. Johnny left me a note on Facebook. I don't know why he can't email me. Facebook is so public."

"What is the face book?"

She flashed him a brief view of the witchbox, but Nicolo didn't have a chance to make out the tiny images. "It's a massive gathering of people across the world, sharing things about themselves, posting silly stuff like cat pictures and hooking up."

"Really? You can have sex with that thing, too?"

"Well." She tucked the thing back in her pocket and

hooked her arm through his to direct him down the sidewalk and avoid an onslaught of tourists. "You can, actually. But it doesn't involve touching or the senses. Watching another person get off on screen? Not my idea of a good time."

"But people do that? Communicate via those things, and in the process, have sex? Where is the intimacy? The sensual experience?"

"Exactly."

"The world has changed so much. I remember when it took weeks to receive word about anything, for the post moved only so quickly as the horse or train could manage. And now everything is—"

"Instantaneous. I know. It rocks."

"When you say something rocks is that a good thing as opposed to a pile of rubble?"

"You got it."

Nicolo dodged a young man focused on his witchbox. Was he having sex right there in the open? "I would like you to show me how to work the book of face when we return to your home."

"Why? You want to hook up?"

"No. I prefer a woman in my arms not on some screen. But perhaps there is a means to find fellow musicians? You said it connects people?"

"It's possible. But let's start small with you and technology. You have to own a phone first. And in order to do that you have to earn an income."

"And in order to do that, I need a violin. Or a guitar. I wonder, would your brother allow me to sit in on some of his concerts? Play the guitar?"

"Really? You would want to do that?"

"It would be a pile of rocks!"

Now her smile showed no reluctance. And when she leaned up to kiss him he felt as if this new life could not get any better. So long as he could protect Summer from the evil that ever simmered within him.

Summer did not try on the lingerie for him in the shop, but Nicolo could already imagine the pink lace caressing her slender hips and tiny breasts. She didn't need one of those fancy brassieres for support, but she pointed out that it would be a crime to break a matched set of bra and panties. He had to agree. But he also believed when he finally did see her in the set it likely wouldn't remain on her for long.

Three cheers for the modern woman and her spare items of clothing!

They strolled down the street, bags in hands, dodging tourists. Summer sported sunglasses, and Nicolo desired a pair for himself. The esthetic value of looking "cool," as she'd explained, appealed to him. She pointed across the street where they could purchase a pair of the dark spectacles, and next to that stood a shop that sold cell phones.

"A witchbox of my own. Then it's home to see what those pretty nothings look like on you?" he asked eagerly.

"I thought you wanted to go to the opera. I checked tickets. There's a will call an hour before the show. If there are any cancellations we can get the tickets then. There's a symphony orchestra performing twentieth-century composers tonight."

"Really?" All thoughts of exploring lace on skin vanished. "I should like to hear the new composers. We must attend!"

"Hold your horses, big boy. We're headed to Verity's place after we fix you up with some technology."

"Verity is the witch?"

"Yep."

"From vampires to witches in less than two days. Truly this new life is not without wonder."

# *Chapter 12*

**V**erity's place was on the way home, and when Summer called while Nicolo had been in the dressing room, the witch had encouraged her to stop by. She was home alone this evening. Her lover, Rook, was tending hunting matters.

Vampire hunting. Rook was a knight for The Order of The Stake. But Summer didn't fear him. He was an okay guy. The Order only went after those vampires who presented a real threat to human lives. Summer was ever polite when drinking blood. Just a small sip. Because anything more… She didn't want to go there. And Rook would never know about her bite imparting madness into her donors.

Though she bet Nicolo's blood would be an interesting taste. First, she wanted to ensure he was not a zombie. For as little as she knew about zombies she figured their blood could mess up a vampire. But if he was anything else, and not a human, he could be a possibility.

She was trying to think of anything and everything besides that hot sex in the shower. And on her bed. It had been as if she were making love with the only man who existed for her. She'd had her share of men. Never had the sex made her so melty and mindless. And made her forget everything around her. And want to tear his clothes off right then and there. Which she had. And then he'd wanted to give her pleasure. Which he had.

Whew! Her skin was prickling with heat thinking about it again. She flicked the air conditioner up a notch.

And what was with her inability to mark it off as just another hookup? The fact he was still there, right beside her, was one thing. She could smell him, earthy and aged like a prize whiskey. He wasn't like any other man. And that made her want to keep him, to clutch him to her and see if he would stay. Because…

Because the idea of him staying felt right.

"The city has grown large," Nicolo commented as she navigated a street between business buildings and restaurants. This outer arrondissement was not such a tourist trap. Only a few people walked the sidewalks. "The buildings are all so, hmm…inelegant. What has become of the exquisite architecture?"

"It's around." Yay, a conversation not about sex to distract her thoughts. "Haussmann, at Napoleon's command, tore down a lot of the original architecture and put up his own designs." That was about as much as she knew about the Paris city design.

"Yes, I recall a lot of construction going on in my time. I wasn't so curious about it, though, since I did not spend a lot of time in Paris."

"The city has managed to preserve a lot of its history. But, yes, the newer buildings are kind of boring. I'll have to drive you by La Défense. The Grande Arche is pretty cool."

"What is that jutting up on the horizon? Is that a lighthouse?"

Summer thought back to his date of death: 1840. She had to smirk at him calling it a lighthouse.

"They erected that up in 1889 to celebrate the World's Fair. It's called the Eiffel Tower. It's remarkable, but is constantly clogged with tourists. If we drive through the inner circle of the city I'm sure you'd recognize a lot of monuments."

"Does the Opéra still exist?"

"The Palais Garnier? Yes. There's the Opéra Bastille, as well."

"The Bastille was torn down when I was a toddler. The site boasts an opera house now?"

"Yep."

"What about my casino? The Casino Paganini?"

She eyed his gesture, which indicted they move forward. "That one didn't survive the ages. Did you ever play there?"

"Violin? No. I was rather sickly in my later years. Unable to stand on stage for so long. But, because of my fame and sheer number of patrons who merely wished to be seen with me, I was paid to make appearances at the gambling tables. It was a swell gig."

"I bet. You may have been one of the first Kardashians."

"A what?"

"Celebrities who are famous merely for being in the right place at the right time, popular because people simply want to see them. I think I read you weren't such a lucky gambler."

"Indeed." He shrugged. "I cannot be a master at everything."

Summer smirked at his ego. No, indeed, he'd been a maestro and a handsome man who had a way with the women. Of course he'd require a bête noire such as gambling.

"Let us visit the Opéra," Nicolo said. "I want to listen to music played live and not through the car."

"Fine, but let's see what Verity has to say about you first."

"Ah, yes. You think she will know something about me?"

"Let's cross our fingers."

Verity Van Velde was a violet-haired fire witch whom Summer had met when she was a baby. Not exactly *met*. More like, Verity, along with fellow witches Libby Saint-Charles and Zoë Guillebeaux, had helped Summer's brother, Johnny, to get her away from Himself's clutches. She'd stayed in touch with Verity over the years, and the Santiagos always invited the witch and even her vampire-slayer lover over for summer parties at the family mansion. Rook, her lover, rarely accompanied her. Summer assumed it was because he'd rather not attend a party populated by vampires. But he was a good guy. Polite, and incredibly sexy. And as her father, Vail, often said, there was nothing wrong with having a vampire hunter in your pocket.

Thinking of sexy, she turned to the darkly gorgeous man who stood behind her on the stoop before Verity's home and gestured to him as she made introductions, "Verity, this is Nicolo Paganini."

"Very pleased to meet you." Nicolo bowed gracefully. If he'd had a hat, he might have pressed it to his chest so elegant a move it was. The velvet jeans were perfect on him. The touch of lace at his cuffs? Romantically masculine. "I take no offense to witches. Or vampires, as you can see from my lovely assistant here."

"I'm your assistant?" Summer asked with as much doubt as she could muster.

"You are assisting me through this new world."

"Whatever."

"Come in, you two. I've been waiting." Verity stepped aside. The light in the hall fell across her hair, highlighting the brilliant violet tones that wove through the dark brown strands. That was no hair dye; she had faery blood in her family.

Summer stepped in, followed by Nicolo, and as Verity closed the door behind them, she exhaled and then announced, "Well, that didn't tell me much."

"What do you mean?" Summer asked.

"Before you arrived, I warded the threshold for every species possible—save vampires, of course. If you would have been repulsed, Nicolo, I could have read which ward had done so and we could have determined your nature."

"So maybe I am just a regular human," he said. "Not a thing wrong with that."

"Not at all. Or you could be vampire," the witch offered with a thoughtful tap of her finger to her lip. "Follow me. I've tea."

They filed down the hallway, through the kitchen and into a living room, where Nicolo would not sit until he was allowed to help Verity carry in the tea tray. He set it on the coffee table, and only after Verity and Summer had sat did he take a seat on the couch beside Summer. He sat close enough that their legs touched, and Summer resisted running her hand along his thigh.

"This is a lovely home," Nicolo offered. "I don't feel so out of place in time here." Verity had a decidedly art deco decorating esthetic, with some older pieces in dark woods that surely might have been in vogue during the musician's time. "Though I suspect that large box on the wall is similar to Summer's witchbox? What did the barkeep call it? A televisor?"

"Television." Summer tugged out her cell phone and waggled it as Verity laughed. "He's most impressed with the music that comes through my witchbox," she offered.

"Wow," Verity said, "I can't imagine stepping forward in time as you have, Monsieur Paganini. You'll have much to learn."

"So I've been told." He sipped the lavender tea. "Exquisite. As is my hostess." His wink only made Summer stifle another giggle. The man did like to flirt.

"Summer tells me you've been summoned from death?" Verity asked over a sip of tea.

"I heard the sound of the violin's song, and I rose. I cannot explain how or why. I only know that I emerged from the top of the grave, turned and saw a bust of my head carved out of stone. It was a nice likeness, really," he said to Summer. "And then, well, here I am."

"I'm familiar with your history. That you made a deal with the devil. Was that true?"

"I never accepted the deal. But it was offered. I used to call it the brimstone bargain. Though I consider it more a curse than an advantage gained through a bargain or deal made."

"What was the bargain, exactly?" Verity asked. "It might help me to determine what's happened to you."

"It was issued to me more than a few times throughout my life. By the devil, er...the Big Guy. You know who I'm talking about?"

Both women exchanged looks. Had it not been for Verity, Himself might have killed Summer when she was a baby. They certainly knew who Nicolo was talking about. "Yes, go on."

"He always put forth the black violin and said should I play it I could have the power I was destined to own."

"Destined?" Summer turned to him. "You never said anything about destiny. What does that mean?"

Nicolo shrugged and splayed out his hands as he offered, "Have you heard the term *hexensohn*?"

"That's German for witch's son," Verity said. "Was your mother a witch?"

Nicolo nodded. "It was something I was aware of but never wanted to fully accept. She kept it very under the table. Is that how you say it? And my father—the one I'm sure the history books note—was actually my stepfather. My mother died when I was a teen. I know there were some who knew what she was because they used to whisper *hexensohn* when I would walk through town."

"I read about that in your biography," Summer said. "I thought it was merely hearsay. An epitaph. Something they didn't believe but pinned on you as a means to explain your incredible skill with the violin."

"Well, there was that, too. The news sheets and gossips spoke often of my making a deal with the devil. I always thought it ironic that they spoke of it as if they believed it. I mean, who believes the devil is real and appears before people to make deals with them? I took great pleasure in feeding those rumors, actually. It was easier for me to make play of it than to face reality. If they had only known that it was true, or at least, partially true. The bargain was presented to me. I just never accepted that deal."

"Which was?" Verity prompted.

"If I should play the black violin then I would have all the power."

"Yes, right, your destiny," Verity confirmed. "I don't really understand that. Are you a witch like your mother?"

"No. I've always and ever been human." Nicolo stood and paced the living room between the couch and the wall where an original Mucha lithograph in emeralds and gold hung. "Instead of destiny, I should use the word legacy. Of course, the legacy thing does apply to my father."

"He was a witch?" Summer asked.

"No." Nicolo turned and shoved a hand at one hip. "You've told me that you've met him," he said to her.

"What?"

He splayed up a hand and said, "He's the devil Himself."

# Chapter 13

Summer gaped at Nicolo. And then she switched her gaze to Verity, who looked equally as shocked as Summer felt. Her fingers curled into claws before her stomach. She should speak. Say something to the man who had just casually announced he was the devil's son. Words didn't form.

Maybe running out the front door would be a better plan.

No, she wasn't a runner. She was a stand-up-and-face-it-no-matter-the-situation kind of woman. Hell, she was responsible for the guy. She couldn't leave him on his own just because...

The devil's *son*?

"Summer?" Nicolo prompted.

"Holy hell," Verity said under her breath. The witch settled onto a nearby chair arm and caught her forehead with a slap of her palm.

Summer exhaled. Closed her eyes. Counted to two, and then got lost in the mad realization of what she had done. She had summoned the devil's son from the grave.

She really had raised Beneath.

"It can't be," she blurted out. "No, no, no. That's impossible. You're not—"

"I am. Unfortunately." Nicolo sighed heavily. "I know this because he told me every time he visited me to make the bargain with the violin."

"Maybe he lied to you."

"For what reason?" Verity asked as she stood and approached Nicolo. "For real? You're...?"

Nicolo gave her a wincing nod. And Verity touched him over the heart. She recoiled with a hiss and backed up so quickly she stepped on Summer's toe. "Sorry."

"What is it, Verity?" Summer asked, hooking an arm about her friend's arm. "What did you feel? Is he telling the truth? What is going on? Nicolo? Tell me you are joking, because I am freaking out here."

"Could you refresh my memory on what freaking out means?" he asked calmly.

Summer stomped the floor and did a frustrated shuffle of her feet as she slammed the air with her fists. She pinned him with a wide-eyed freaked-out stare.

"Ah," he said. "How could I have forgotten? Trust me, I did a lot of freaking out myself when... I was first alive." Again he winced. After being dead for so long this whole new existence had to be beyond difficult for him. "I am his son, but trust me when I say I am completely human. Neither witch nor devil nor demon. Or at least, that was so in my former incarnation."

"You're not human now," Verity said. The women hugged one another closely as they stood before the man who could be evil incarnate. "I felt some crazy power in you."

"As I felt your flames," Nicolo offered.

"He can read people," Summer provided. "Since he's risen."

"Interesting. You sensed my fire magic. You couldn't do that before?"

"No, completely mortal then. The only explanation I can offer for my enhanced strength and senses is that the bargain was enacted when she played the violin."

"I'm not following," Verity said to Summer.

"I was supposed to retrieve Paganini's violin. It was a Retrieval job. But I did not play it. It sort of…bowed itself."

"And the devil—er, the Big Guy," Nicolo corrected, "cursed that violin. If I should ever play it I would be given the power I should have received as my birthright. But the bargain has always and only ever been offered to me. Something must have gone wrong for it to have been enacted. For me to be standing here before you now."

"If Himself is your father why weren't you born a demon? Or witch, for that matter?" Summer hugged Verity's arm closer to her.

"I think I can guess that one," Verity said. "Sometimes when two paranormal souls create a child their genetic gifts and powers can pass right over a bloodline, leaving the child completely human. That is if there are humans in their bloodline. Perhaps Nicolo's mother had humans in her family?"

"She did. She was the lone witch alongside her four siblings. But I've never had magical abilities. I am human." Nicolo splayed his arms out. "Or rather…was?"

"Such skipping of the bloodlines happens with vampires more often than you would expect," Verity confirmed.

"This is not cool." Summer unhooked her arm from her friend's arm and began to pace. "I was supposed to claim the violin. Not raise a dead guy from the grave. And now look what I've done. I've brought the freaking devil's son to ground. And—ohmygoddess—I had sex with you!"

Verity smirked and tapped a finger against her curled lips.

Nicolo shrugged. "I thought you liked it?"

"I did—but no! I would never—do that!—with the devil's son. Never. Not. Ever. Me and the Big Guy go back. I told you that. I am so not getting near anything related to him ever again."

"Too late," Verity offered. "I don't think a little skin time is going to harm you, Summer. As well…" She approached Nicolo and this time carefully laid her fingers over his chest. She tilted her head, eyes closed, taking things in for a moment. "I think he's in the process of becoming."

"Your fire. It is very strong," Nicolo said with a kindly gaze into her eyes. "Becoming what?"

"What you were destined to become with the bargain. Demon? Devil? Witch? I can't be positive. But we know you are not human."

Nicolo strode toward the patio door that looked out over a lush green backyard. He slapped a hand over his chest and turned back to the woman with a fierce look. "I have developed remarkable strength since hopping out of the coffin. I feel healthy. And look at me."

Both women nodded, in awe of the handsome specimen standing before them basking in their adoration. And then Summer shook her head and made a frustrated growling noise. "Don't even think it," she muttered to herself.

"If you give me a few days," Verity said, "I might dig up a spell that can read Nicolo. Tell us exactly what we're dealing with."

"Sounds fair enough. I would like to know what, exactly, I am now. Though I should not care to be a zombie."

Verity looked to Summer, who shrugged. "He did rise from the grave. To explain I showed him some pictures from *The Walking Dead*."

Nicolo held out his hand toward Summer. "Are you frightened of me now? You, a mighty vampiress who put me in my place at the Sneezing Cow and who can command me to my knees in adoration of your beauty? I am just a man. Who needs your help to find my way in this world."

When he put it that way Summer felt guilty for her little freak-out. But seriously? The last person in this realm she—any smart paranormal being—wanted to deal with was the devil Himself. And Nicolo being his son did not give her warm fuzzies about dating into the family.

Not that she was dating him. But she had slept with him. And—oh man, what had she done? This guy could go über-evil on her. And she had enough issues as it was avoiding the dark side.

Nicolo stepped before her, not touching, but she could feel his heat, his utter need to connect with her on a level similar to the intimate moment they'd shared earlier this afternoon. She forced herself not to flinch away from his soft yet assessing gaze. The remembrance of the times she had smelled sulfur, the scent of demons and Himself, prodded her to inhale. She couldn't scent the acrid odor on him.

"Sorry. I should have handled that differently," he said. "I assumed since you were in the know about all things paranormal…"

"Yeah, well, it's not every day the handsome man a girl has been mooning over tells her he's the devil's son."

He stroked the hair from the side of her face over her shoulder and tugged her earlobe. "I am honored to be admired by one so lovely."

Oy, but the man had the words. And the moves. Her ear tingled under his gentle touch.

"Are you still okay with hosting me at your home until we figure things out? What about the opera tonight?"

She'd forgotten about that date. Hell's bells, what to do?

"Yes. I brought you into this world. I—" Yeah, she wasn't going to say she could take him out. She probably could. But what sort of crazed vengeance would that bring upon her when his father came looking for the woman who put his son back in the grave? "We should go. Thanks, Verity. Do call me as soon as you've figured a way to read him, okay?"

"I'll text you. Nice to meet you, Monsieur Paganini!"

Should he have revealed that small detail about his paternity? Not so small. Nicolo could still recall the day Himself had told him. For one moment he had doubted, and then, he had known. Just *known*. A visceral knowledge had inhabited his veins and made him shudder. Such a vile thing to learn about oneself.

Yet he had been determined not to follow in his father's footsteps. He believed a man made his own way, his own life. And he had done so, rising to a fame he'd earned through hard work and persistence. Never because of a skill bestowed upon him by playing that bedamned violin. He did not have to become what legacy or an accident of paternity dictated.

He glanced at Summer navigating the car toward her home. She'd been repulsed to hear he was Himself's son. The only reaction he could expect from anyone. For had she thrown her arms about him and giggled he might have questioned her sanity. She was a smart woman, and she would use caution henceforth.

He did not fault her that caution. But he needed her. To navigate this modern world. To imbue him with passion and emotion that could easily be overwhelmed by the wonders of this new world. And as his only connection to the black violin. It wasn't finished with him yet, as he was not finished with it. He would not rest until he had seen the thing in ashes and knew with certainty the devil Himself cared little for the son who had never respected him.

And yet, what reason had he to refuse the brimstone bargain now? He no longer had a son to worry would see him succumb to such evil.

What had become of Achille? Had he married? Fathered children? Perhaps Nicolo had ancestors? He'd missed so much. And yet he had led a good life. A man should only be granted one life. And that he had been given another he couldn't fathom whether it was good or bad.

"Can your witchbox tell us anything about my son, Achille?"

Pulled from her intent focus, she cast him what seemed like a forced smile and nodded. "Yes. The clerk set up your phone account as part of mine in the store. When we get to my place I'll teach you how to do an internet search."

"I will find Achille on this internet? What of the book of face you had mentioned?"

"It's all live people on Facebook. Mostly, anyway. You should be able to find a history on him and your family."

"Thank you. That will serve to put my mind and heart at ease."

Nicolo settled into the passenger seat. Yes. He would start anew. Rise to fame. He would do it all again. Only this time, he would embrace what little power he had been resurrected with and use it.

And if Himself offered the bargain again?

He didn't have an answer for that one right now. He knew what the answer should be. But his life had changed. How to resist so much power and a promise of immortality?

# Chapter 14

They'd stopped by her home to drop off their shopping booty, and Summer had changed into a slim blue wrap dress. Out of the ordinary attire for her, but she knew jeans and a T-shirt wouldn't go over well at the opera house. She did own two dresses. Not out of necessity, but rather, they'd been gifts from her mother and sister-in-law.

Sitting in the balcony box now, she didn't mention to Nicolo that beneath the dress she wore the pink set of lace La Perla. He'd find out later if he was lucky. And he probably would find that luck, if she had her way.

Maybe.

Hell.

Literally. She couldn't resist the guy, even knowing what she now knew about him.

While the orchestra played a Dvorak piece Summer could only think about sitting next to Himself's son. The devil had fathered a child, and he sat right beside her. Of course, the Big Guy could have hundreds of progeny walking this earth. Was the devil a man whore, or did he choose his lovers with care, ensuring his offspring were only raised by a few and the finest?

But why had Nicolo not been born with such powers as the brimstone bargain would give him? Why hadn't Himself simply bestowed those fabulous yet evil powers upon his son? She didn't get that.

Unless such powers had to be accepted? For wouldn't the burden of such evil destroy someone kind and innocent like Nicolo? If he'd had even an ounce of greed in him, he would have taken the bargain and perhaps embraced his powers. Yet he'd been a gambler and had other vices. Greed was certainly not new to him.

Which meant he really had tried his best to refuse. So the man was admirable. Honorable, as she'd already decided about him. She liked that about a man. Even a man whose heritage was dubious and his current physical and/or paranormal state was unknown.

So she'd give him a chance. Because he deserved it. And because she liked him. Much more than she would have expected. Generally, Summer clicked with a guy on the first date or said so long, don't get hit by the door on the way out. Nicolo felt right to her. And while that should trouble her more with this new information about his paternity, it did not.

What did that mean when a woman overlooked the obvious in favor of an infatuation? She didn't want to know. Really. Because in her heart she already did know, and the answer involved walking away at first sign of adversity.

She wasn't a walker, nor did she favor turning and

running. She prided herself on serving Acquisitions, and she would treat this personal affair the same.

But what about her job? Protecting Nicolo was probably not what the director had in mind when he'd told her to keep an eye on him. Was she jeopardizing her job by engaging with Himself's son? Or course she was. The question was, was it worth the risk?

A clash of cymbals tugged her out of the troubling thought.

While Summer loved a great symphony, she was more interested in her date. Nicolo was enraptured by the performance. Elbows propped on the balcony railing, eyes glued to the stage, he'd not once leaned back into the plush red velvet seat. Though sometimes he would close his eyes, falling into the music.

She knew exactly why he had been such a lady-killer in his past. He was gorgeous. An amazing lover. A classic male, yet he had the extra gene that turned her on: he was a musician.

She slid her hand up the thigh of his black velvet pants and over his lap. He hadn't learned about underwear, so everything against the fabric was tangible to her touch. And growing harder. She gave him a squeeze.

That stirred him out of his reverie. He turned to her, but when she expected a lascivious suggestion he instead said, "I want to be on that stage."

And here she'd thought her hand play might have turned him on. The only thing that seemed to get this man's blood hot was music. But she could work with that.

"Want to go home and compose a duet?" She tapped her fingers along his erection. She could play that.

"Do you have two violins?"

Deflated by her less than successful attempt at seduction, she didn't let that stop her. Leaning in, following his innate cedar scent, she kissed his jaw, then nuzzled her nose against it. "I mean a different kind of composition."

He pulled her onto his lap and his hand slid over her breast. "I know that. Music stirs me to a heightened sense of awareness. What of you?" His fingers pinched through the thin fabric, tweaking her nipple.

She leaned in to kiss him again so she could purr into his mouth. Didn't want anyone else to hear her pleasure but him. Hooking a leg up higher at his waist, she forgot she was wearing a dress and probably a stylish woman wouldn't be caught dead hiking up a leg and making out with her boyfriend at the opera.

But she wasn't that woman. And Nicolo's hand gliding up her thigh enticed her to kiss him deeper. He tasted like the wine that sat in the goblet to his right. And when his fingers slipped aside her panties and found her clitoris she was thankful for the dexterity of a musician's hands.

Wrapping herself about him so he could yet view the stage, she rocked her hips against his hand, finding they subtly matched the rhythm that filled the theatre. What a kick, getting off to the classics. Ha!

Nicolo nuzzled his face against her breasts and licked before biting softly as his finger just found…that spot. The music raced. Summer's heartbeats dashed faster. Body tensing, she buried her face in his hair and gripped a thick hank of it to smother her moan as she came in the first movement of Dvorak's *Symphony No. 9*.

After the opera, and a rousing make-out session, the twosome strolled under the midnight sky down the rue des Pyramides. The city never slept, which made for brightly lit streets and tourists still exploring this late. But it was the same as Nicolo remembered it. A lively city.

He threaded his fingers through Summer's hand and smiled at her. He was having a great time being alive again and didn't want it to end. Remarkably, Summer did not appear offended by his paternity. In proof, he'd gotten an exquisite hand job during the third movement of the symphony. Could he ask for a more understanding woman? She truly wanted to be with him. He felt that.

And she was doing everything in her power to make it possible for him to remain alive and in this realm. Yet if she'd really buried the black violin...

"What if it kills me?" he suddenly asked, stopping at a corner across the street from the Tuileries. The huge carnival wheel lit with red-and-blue lights spun slowly before them. Such a marvel that the intangible substance called electricity was everywhere!

"What if what kills you?"

"You said you destroyed it," he said "How, exactly, did you do that?"

"I stepped on it and smashed it."

He cringed at the thought of destroying such a precious instrument. Even if it had been born straight from Hell. "You...?" He gestured in a crushing motion with his fist.

"Had to be done. You know it."

He did know that. But. "What if it brings *my* end? The violin's song brought me to life. What if now it's gone...so am I?"

Summer crossed her arms and assumed an assessing pose as she looked him up and down. "You look pretty alive to me."

"Well, yes. Now. But—"

"But I think if it was going to have the reverse effect on you, you would not be standing here right now talking to me. Yes?"

"Perhaps so. Of course, devil's magic could never work so logically."

"True. But I would think it to the Big Guy's advantage to keep you alive."

Such an idea startled him. "You think he'll offer the bargain to me again?"

"I don't know. Why can't he just give you the powers? Why does it have to be accepted by you? Is it as I suspect? That you have to take the power?"

He nodded. "Such evil must be assumed of my free will. That was how it was originally explained to me. But what if I did accept?"

"You would? Of course, you've no reason not to now."

"Summer. My Brightness." He clasped her hand and tugged her into his embrace. "We may have known each other a short while, but do you really believe I could do such a thing?"

"I hope not." Her gaze fluttered from his, unwilling to make contact for too long. "But after you've had time to think about it, you might change your mind. I mean, do you believe you would not accept the deal? Really believe that?"

"It may have been almost two centuries since I died, but little has changed regarding my moral values. On the other hand, I can't know what I would do should the offer be presented. This new world has changed.

As have I, in ways even I cannot fathom." He tapped her chin to force her to look at him. "I want to resist, if it comes to that. But I do wish to have as wondrous a life as I can now. Like playing on stage again. I simply must stand before the spotlight again."

"I'd like to see that. And I think with some clever name change and maybe even a fashion change, you can do it." She tugged at the clingy dress, which hugged her tiny curves.

"A dress is not your comfort, is it?"

"Just tried to fancy things up for the opera, but it makes me crawly. I hate feeling a breeze on my knees."

He eyed the knees in question. "They are too pretty to cover. I should kiss them—"

She stopped him from kneeling. "Save the PDA for—wait. I know. Want to go for a ride on the Ferris wheel?"

"Is that the spinning monstrosity right there? The one glowing with so much electricity?"

"Yep. Come on." She grabbed his hand and led him across the street. "You can see all of Paris when you're at the top! And, I'll let you kiss me. And my knees."

Twenty minutes later they indeed sat at the top of the world. Nicolo stretched his gaze around the City of Lights. He'd never been up in the sky higher than the bell towers in Notre Dame. Now the city glittered as if stars had fallen to earth. Such beauty!

Summer's warmth hugged his arm and thigh as she snuggled closer. "What do you think?"

"This new world is a marvel, Summer. I can't go back. Please make sure I won't go back?"

"To your coffin? Nah. You're here. You're breathing. But we will have to figure out your new life. You can't use your name anymore. You could still be Nicolo. But Paganini has to go."

"Hmm, I suppose." The wheel shifted into movement again, and they started their slow descent, pausing every length as a new car arrived at the top. "Yet what am I without my name? I am Paganini!"

"You *were* Paganini. And you made an incredible mark on the musical world. You can still perform. But not as Paganini. Besides, I suspect your musical style might change a bit if you listen to Bitter/Sweet often enough."

"I do like the hard-metal stylings."

"Heavy metal. Rock and roll. But there are so many genres of music. You'll want to listen to them all."

"I will. Can I ask my witchbox to sing for me?" He patted the inner coat pocket where she'd told him to keep the device. It wasn't turned on, though. Still, he felt like he belonged carrying it around with him. He had become one of the people in this new age.

"Yes, I'll teach you tomorrow how to use the GPS so you can navigate the city. And if I ever need to find you, that'll help."

"Yes! My first initiation into the modern world. Now, about that promise to kiss your knees? It did take us a while to reach the pinnacle. I imagine we've some time while going down. And I do use those words going down in a manner on which I hope you'll pick up."

"Yeah, I got that, Nineteenth-Century Guy with the Slick Hookup Line." She inched her dress up her thighs. "I'm all yours."

# *Chapter 15*

Summer had never been overly romantic. Though she'd grown up watching her parents make out and canoodle (yes, her dad, the fierce vampire Vail, called it canoodling) every chance they got. As well, her father was an extreme romantic, always with flowers in hand and a serenade for her mother. Apparently, when Summer had been born, the romance gene had been exchanged for the freaky madness-making gene. Her relationships tended to be one-night stands, hookups or friendly with benefits. But no gushing or cooing or making moon eyes at one another. That was uncalled for.

Now, she highly suspected the way she was staring into Nicolo's moonlight-spattered eyes could be construed as making moon eyes. And against all she believed in, she didn't care.

After getting off the Ferris wheel—and *getting off*

on the Ferris wheel—they'd walked to the river to check out the beach. A live band featuring accordion, mandolin and a singer performed a classic Parisian love song while couples danced on the shipped-in sand beside the broth-colored Seine. Bonfires lit up the area. Partiers drank wine straight from the bottle and tossed horseshoes nearby.

But she was lost in a man's eyes. And in his arms as he held her gently but firmly, leading as they slow danced. He had her. And she wanted him to have her. She felt a silly teenager swoon coming on. Could she be his girlfriend? Could they go steady? Exchange rings? Do romantic dating stuff like make out under a blanket and tickle each other until one of them begged for mercy?

It was a startling realization. And when she figured she should pull away from Nicolo's irresistible warmth and instead go join the game of *pétanque* nearby, she settled her head onto his shoulder and melted against the powerful strength and delicious scent of him. He smelled like cedar, with a touch of leather. Like a finely preserved artifact. She inhaled deeply, wanting to fill her pores with him. To, just for a moment, be the silly girl with a crush, and not the vampiress with a penchant for making people mad.

Nicolo spread a hand across her back, and her skin prickled with desire. Her nipples tightened. She hugged up against him closer and felt his erection nudge her belly. She pressed tighter, teasing.

"You modern women are quite bold," he whispered. "Careful, Summer, or I'll have to throw you down onto the sand and have my way with you."

"Again? I'd love it."

"With an audience?"

"No. I'm not much for PDAs."

"What does that mean?"

"Public displays of affection. Just hold me. This feels great. Kind of romantic."

"Why do I suspect you are not much for romance?"

"You figured that one out, eh?"

"It may have been the mud smears on your cheek this afternoon or even the engine part in your bath. Maybe even your exquisitely ever-untidy hair. No laces or frills for you. Of course, one doesn't require frills for romance."

"Maybe there's not much in this world to be romantic about anymore."

"Standing on the beach in the arms of a lover seems romantic to me." He looked up. "And with the stars overhead—well, the artificial stars from the nearby buildings. And the music? I am befallen with romance."

"I like that. Befallen with romance," she singsonged out. "Mmm, nothing can make this night better. Achoo!"

Nicolo held her away and studied her gaze. "Summer? You mentioned your propensity to sneeze earlier. When demons are in proximity. What does that mean?"

"I uh…" She glanced around, seeking demons in the shadows. Anything out of place. "Not sure. Could just be summer allergies."

"Do you *have* summer allergies?"

"No." She was a vampire, for heaven's sake. The usual human maladies didn't apply to her species. "Could just be some friendly demons dancing in the mix. Doesn't always mean something bad is going to happen."

Yet her heartbeats thudded. She never liked being

around a demon, friendly or otherwise. She mustn't let down her guard.

"Right." He hugged her close and cast his gaze about the party area. "We'll keep our eyes out for anything amiss, just to be sure."

"Yes." She nodded and hugged him tightly, wanting it to be nothing. But the brief thought that her sneeze could be because of Nicolo disturbed her.

Would he become like his father? How would she know if he did, beyond the telltale sneeze that alerted her to a demon presence nearby? And would she know what to do when that did happen? Because she was falling for this guy. Hard. And she didn't want to lose the best thing that had happened to her.

A thin line of sunlight teased the horizon. After the beach had closed, Nicolo and Summer had strolled the rue de Seine paralleling the river. No demons had caused a disturbance at the beach, and Summer hadn't seen any glowing red eyes in the vicinity so had decided the sneeze had been a fluke. They hadn't wanted to go home as they walked hand in hand, and hadn't needed to. But now she did.

"I should get inside," she said to him as he bowed to kiss her. "Morning sunlight coming right up."

"Ah, yes, the vampire thing."

"I'm hungry, as well. Maybe you should head on to the house and I'll follow close behind?"

"I'm not sure where it is exactly. You haven't given me training on how to use the witchbox, and there are not many landmarks I can recognize. Can't I come along with you? Are you going to find someone to bite?" He tugged her hand, bringing her into an embrace. Drawing a finger along the V of her neckline, he asked, "Why not me?"

Summer snorted. "Please."

A querying brow tilted above his serious gaze. As if to ask *what is so wrong with me?*

Hmm… Why not him? Because—well, just because.

But really? She did want a taste of this luscious specimen. A long, languorous drink that would further imbue her body with traces of him, just as inhaling his scent had done. And she hadn't taken blood since right after she'd found him walking alongside the road in Parma. She needed to drink more often than the usual one to two weeks because her sips were so small.

But if she did drink from him she feared taking too much, for it would quickly turn erotic. And with that she risked making him mad. If he was human, that is.

Human or not, this guy had been through a lot already. The last thing he needed was to lose his mind.

On the other hand, he hadn't been a live, sentient being for a hundred and seventy-five years. And she didn't sneeze around him. He couldn't be demon. But Verity had suspected he wasn't human. Could she be safe with this one?

The Tuileries was bare of anyone that she could see. Majestic lime trees formed aisles as she led him down one paved with crushed stone. She'd have to search the alleyways on the way home for a bite. Or… Answer the call to indulgence with the closest thing to hand.

Again, he asked, "Summer, you could bite me, yes?"

It was dark here, for the rising sun was hidden behind the massive Louvre museum. And in a moment of silence she jumped into the unknown. But not really unknown, because she knew what she wanted.

Luring Nicolo beneath a lime tree trimmed high to expose the trunk so a man could walk beneath, she pushed him against the smooth-barked trunk.

"Why not you?" she said with a tease as she licked her lowering fangs. "Okay. Why not you. I haven't been able to summon a reason against it beyond the very obvious driving-you-mad part. Like I told you, I'm not like most vampires."

"Because you are bright and don't hide in the shadows?"

"The madness thing."

"Yes, right." He took her hands in his, reassuringly rubbing the backs of them with his thumbs. "You fear driving me mad. But you said that only occurred with the humans you bite, yes?"

She nodded.

"And we're not sure what I am, exactly. I must be more than human. Even the witch suspected as much. I feel quite in control of my mental faculties and don't believe a little bite should change that."

She raked fingers through her hair as she glanced aside.

"Summer?"

"I *am* hungry." And ever willing to take risks. Unknown mysteries? She was so in. She met his smiling gaze. "I need blood."

"And I am willing. Let me take a look?" He touched the tip of one of her fangs, and the sensation strafed through Summer as if he'd stroked a fingertip over her bare breast. She shivered. Always sexual to have her teeth touched. "What did *that* just do to you?"

"Turns me on to have my fangs touched."

"I see that. You want me to stop?"

"Never," she said on a sensual gasp. Leaning against his long, muscular shape, she bent a knee and hooked her leg high at his thigh. Pulling his interest down with a bend of her finger, she whispered, "This is going to be good for me and you. But I might have to stop abruptly if I feel this is going wrong, so don't hold that against me."

"I won't. So long as you don't mind if I feel the need to push you away. This is a new and out-of-the-ordinary experience for me."

"More out of the ordinary than rising from the dead?"

"You have me there." Again he stroked her fang. Mercy. "Do it then. Drink from me."

She traced a fang along his skin until it moved over the pulsing carotid. Nicolo moaned and hugged her close, tilting back his head to give her better access. Clutching his shirt with one hand, and running the fingers of her other up through his hair, she then shoved his head back against the tree trunk and pierced his skin with both fangs. Hot blood oozed onto her tongue. She retracted her fangs and sipped his thick, delicious life.

Again he moaned and stretched his head back farther, clinging to her while his fingers curled into her hair. "Oh, Brightness."

Yeah, she knew he would get off from this. So would she. This man's blood was amazing. Bright, thick and vital. It coursed through her system, seeming to enliven every nerve ending. It was as though she were drinking his power, his skill. Could she feel the music within him? Yes. Oh yes. It was grand and full and danced with her soul.

And she greedily took more than she needed only

because the taste was so sweet, so magical. She had not ever tasted such blood as his, nor had she enjoyed a drink more. And yet, she remained cautious for that telling soul shiver she always felt from her other donors. Minute, it often jittered only briefly, just enough to alert her.

"Mercy," she said on a gasp as she managed to stop drinking. "You will get me drunk."

"That good, eh?" He pulled her closer and caressed her breast. "Your bite is like sex. Just a little more?"

She nodded. "You...feel okay?"

"I feel all of my senses."

"Really? And I haven't felt your soul shudder yet."

Maybe drinking from a dead guy was a good thing for her? She hadn't considered it until now, but did he even have a soul? Usually the soul exited the body with death. Then again, he wasn't a usual man.

She wasn't about to question such fortune. Not when the thrill of taking a longer drink coaxed her to indulge.

Summer sucked out more, gorging herself on the treat. And when her body shimmered with a similar feeling to orgasm (but not quite) she licked the bite marks on his neck to seal the wound. As she stroked her tongue over his skin, Nicolo shuddered and cried out, his fingers gripping at her breast and the tree behind him.

His body sank before her until he sat at the base of the trunk. Then he moved forward onto his knees and, looking up at her, clasped her hands. "My mistress of decadent desires."

Yeah, the swoon always served them well. Gave them a nice orgasm and left them riding a sexual high for a while after. Usually she used the thrall to ensure the human did not recall her bite and then quickly walked away. But not this time. No need to hide from this beautiful man.

"Did you…" he gasped, still enjoying the sensual high "…have an orgasm?"

"I usually don't. But I feel something even better. I've never felt so…clear after taking blood before." She squatted before him and studied his eyes. The pupils were large and dark. "You're different. Together, we're different."

"That's a good thing, yes?"

"Yes," she said on a wondrous gasp. Had she finally found the one person she could drink from without endangering his soul from the volatile attack of madness?

She bowed her head to bump foreheads with him. "Let's head home before the sun beats us."

"As you wish."

Once at the house, Summer walked through the front door, her lover dutifully following. Turning, he pulled her close and kissed her deeply. He was still in a bit of a swoon. They walked together, she backward, toward the kitchen, but as her foot stepped onto something squishy, he pushed her aside and charged into the kitchen.

Summer lifted her foot and inspected her shoe. "Mud? How did that—"

In the kitchen, her lover swore. Summer followed a trail of mud blops into the dimly lit kitchen. Nicolo stood before the steel counter, arms spread out as if to prevent himself from rushing forth.

On the counter, amidst mud and grass, sat the black violin. Intact.

# Chapter 16

Nicolo approached the counter, hand outstretched. The violin gleamed like polished ebony nestled amidst muck and dirt. The strings were clean, the bow seemingly tightened and ready. The body of the instrument could not be wood but perhaps carved from the devil's very horn.

And at that thought, he retracted, pressing his palms against his chest. His heartbeats thundered, but beyond that inner timpani he heard the seductive whispers. The silvery voice did not speak in Italian or French. He did not know the language. A diabolic babble?

And yet, he understood what it wanted.

Him.

"Nicolo, please don't," Summer said softly. Her hand touched his shoulder, and he flinched. The sexual high from her bite had dissipated. If he could feel that way all the time, he need never desire what gifts this wretched instrument could grant him.

"I thought you said you destroyed it" came out in hissing syllables.

"I did. I stepped on it and crushed it before burying it. It was shards and string. I don't understand—well, yes."

Well. Yes.

They both knew how it had been restored and now sat before him as the temptation it had been forged. So many times he had resisted. He had died a frail, sickly man who could no longer lift the violin to his chin for his staunch refusal to accept Himself's offer. He'd left Achille to survive in the cruel world at such a young age.

And now he was being given a second chance.

To do what? His son was no longer alive. He could no longer claim his fame as Nicolo Paganini. He did not exist in this new age. He was lost and without a home. He had to rely on a woman's kindness for clothing and food.

He could make his own way. He must. Without this wicked power. Because he still had the skill. He could play the violin as well as he once had. And with practice he would again rise to fame. But to what value?

What did he need now in his new life? And what was it worth to him to again resist the temptation? He had nothing. Would not such power make his adjustment to this world smoother?

Summer wrapped an arm across his back and stood beside him.

He had nothing? Change that. He had Summer. For now, at least.

"Do you want me to take it away again?" she asked. "Burn it to ash?"

"You don't believe that will have any consequence on it reforming and returning to me yet again?"

She sighed. "If you play that violin, you become—"

"A monster? A devil? What if I merely become stronger, more powerful, my skills honed to an exquisite point?"

"You know that's not what will happen. You'd be like him."

"My father."

An all-too-cheery bell rang in Summer's pocket. She pulled out the witchbox and stepped away from Nicolo, yet she remained in the room, her eyes on him. "Yes?"

Nicolo could hear the conversation easily.

"It's Ethan Pierce," the caller said.

"What's up? Got another mission for me?"

"Summer, there's an issue with the Paganini violin. Certainly Jones reports it is missing and that you might have an idea about that. Are you still watching the man? We've made a decision regarding his incarceration. I'll need you to come in. Immediately."

"Sure." Incarceration? She winced and turned away from Nicolo. "Now?" It was seven in the morning.

"What part of immediately do you not comprehend?"

"Right. Be, uh…right there."

The phone clicked off. Nicolo cast her a wondering gaze.

She waggled the phone before her. "Work stuff."

"That was your director. Asking after me. Are you going to turn me in?"

"Never."

He clasped her hand. "Maybe you should? If you take me away from the violin then I can't ever play it, yes?"

"I'm not sure what plans the director has for you. But I don't expect they'll be 'Buy him a place to live and welcome him to this new age.'"

"I suspect not."

"Nicolo." She bracketed his face with her palms. "I want you here. As much as you shouldn't be here, you do have a new life now. And I'm not going to let anyone take that away from you."

"You are most kind. I feel the same. I rather enjoy the new now. And you."

She kissed him. Too quickly. Did she really believe what she'd said to him? How could she possibly jeopardize her job to protect him?

"But what to do?" he asked.

"I'll bring the violin to the Archives. CJ can bespell it. He did find a warding spell after it had disappeared the first time. I'm sure we can take measures to secure it properly this time. Okay?"

He nodded. "Go quickly. I want to feel that thing in my hands."

"Right." She collected the violin, and as she did so the mud slipped from it, leaving not a trace on the glossy instrument. The case was not to be found, so she slipped the violin and bow under an arm then set it down. "I need to put real clothes on first."

She slipped out of the wrap dress and into jeans and a T-shirt, then grabbed the violin and rushed toward the Audi.

"Wait!" Nicolo met her at the car's hood. He reached for the bow, fingers shaking. Every bit of him needed to know the feeling of that bow in his right hand and the neck of the violin in his left.

"Kiss me," she entreated.

Nicolo nodded. She had a plan, and he liked it. His hand slipped along her neck, and he fell into the sensational connection of breath, heartbeats and desire. A delicious foray that led him away from the call to darkness. So surprising, considering she had bitten him earlier and sucked out his blood. But she wasn't darkness. Summer was brightness and joy. And he needed her if he was to resist temptation this time around.

"You are my brightness," he said, bowing his forehead to hers.

She shoved him away and got inside the car. Nicolo closed his eyes, listening as the garage door rose and she backed out.

He'd give her a head start and then follow. He would not let that violin out of his sight. It demanded he play it.

And he would.

He was following her. Summer could feel him in the air. Not a scent or even a sighting. She'd had sex with him, skin against skin, mouth over mouth, heartbeats thudding against heartbeats. And she'd drunk his blood. He was inside her. And he had made her feel so clear. Because he wasn't human? Likely.

Now she could *feel* him nearby. His heartbeats. The volume of his being occupying this realm. This thing between her and Nicolo had gotten intense. Fast. What was up with that?

She was heading to the home office to hand over the man's violin and probably give up classified information about where to find him. Hell, she wouldn't have to reveal his location; he was less than a hundred yards behind her. But she couldn't not hand over the information. Her job depended on her alliance to Acquisitions.

Would she ultimately have to choose between being a Retriever and protecting Nicolo? She hoped not. Her job meant everything to her. And Nicolo…he meant more than she could fathom.

The Council headquarters housed the Archives, Acquisitions and Hexes & Curses, and various other departments, all under the Council's supervision. The Archives library was vast, and while Summer had never been a stickler for studying and books, she often wondered what an afternoon in one of the Archives' stacks might stir up.

"Probably something evil," she muttered as she turned down a narrow passageway paved with uneven cobblestones. The violin was safely tucked under an arm, the bow in her other hand.

She paused and decided to backtrack. Best to get Nicolo out of the area before she went inside. As she stepped out of the alleyway and looked both ways, she didn't see her stalker anywhere. Not even a stray tourist out on this overcast, cloudy morning. Had she actually lost him? She hadn't been trying to.

Closing her eyes, she transferred her focus to sound. No footsteps, nor the subtle cadence of his breath. Yet their bodily connection—it existed.

Turning, she walked right into Nicolo. So maybe they weren't as aligned bodily as she had thought. He gripped the bow and wrenched it from her hand. The violin slipped away without her realizing it.

"No!" She made a grab for the instrument, but he

held it high above his head in one hand. "Nicolo, you can't touch it!"

"I am touching it, and I haven't turned into a wicked demon."

"It doesn't work that way!"

"How does it work?"

"Just give it back to me. You don't want it. You know that. You're a smart man. You have to resist its call to you."

He lowered the instrument until the wide black body of it rested against his ear and shoulder. Eyes closing, he hummed in appreciation. "It feels so good. Like a part of me."

"It's not a part of you! But it will be a terrible part if you so much as draw that bow across a string."

"Hmm. Shall we give it a go?"

"No, Nicolo. Please." She knew all the begging in the world wouldn't stop him, so she'd use force.

Summer pushed the man against the brick wall, not caring if the violin took on damage. With one hand he shoved her backward, but she didn't have far to go with the opposite wall but three feet away. Her shoulders hitting the wall took the breath from her. He didn't comprehend his immense strength.

"I don't want to hurt you, Summer," he warned. "Let me have this. It's not something I can control."

"Then let me help you." Again she lunged, trying to grab the violin, but he held it out of her reach. Stepping back and taking a leap, she managed to grab it by the chin rest, and he let it go. She landed, crouched over and protecting the violin. Nicolo's hand gripped a hank of her hair.

And then he shouted, and the bow dropped to the ground.

Summer twisted, still in a crouch. Nicolo stood surrounded by a crackling green electricity. And commanding that weird magic was a man who held his heavily tattooed fingers together to activate the spell, the dark witch Certainly Jones.

"You okay, Summer?" CJ called.

"Yes, fine. He can't stop himself from trying to play the violin. He wasn't going to hurt me."

"Didn't look that way to me."

"What is this?" Nicolo tried to scrub off the green light with no success.

"A binding spell." CJ approached Summer. "It won't hold for long. I can feel a malevolent power fighting my own dark magic. What the hell is this guy? Who is he? I...I don't think he has a soul."

Summer sighed and clutched the violin to her chest. "He's Paganini. I raised him from the dead when I found the violin and it accidentally played itself."

"Accidentally played itself?"

"I know. But I didn't do it. No soul? How do you know that?"

"I feel it. Or the lack of it. Vika, who you know has a sticky soul, has taught me to be sensitive to souls."

Vika was the light witch Certainly had lived with for years.

"Wow," she muttered. Was that why Nicolo didn't seem to be affected by her bite? Why she hadn't felt his soul shiver when she'd sunk her teeth into his vein? That could mean...so much.

"Summer?"

Dragging her thoughts away from what could be the

most remarkable thing to happen to her, she gave CJ her full attention. "I'm on my way to talk to the director now. I know. I'm in deep shit."

"About as deep as it gets." CJ eyed the musician, who struggled as if bound. "Let me take the violin. This time I'll bind it securely."

She picked it up and handed it over to him. "You might want to use devil's traps if you can. It's cursed by the Big Guy."

"We had our suspicions." He shuddered as he received the instrument. "I'll take this below to the Archives. You have a meeting."

"What about him?"

"I'd estimate another five minutes before the binding is depleted." The witch strode away.

"Get me out!"

Summer studied the green spell covering Nicolo as if an exoskeleton. "I'm sorry, Nicolo. It had to be done. CJ said it would wear off in a few minutes."

"You've chosen your job over me. I knew it!"

"Not exactly. Unless you consider a meeting to get my ass kicked my choice. I'm not going to stop protecting you, Nicolo."

"I don't need your protection! I need...aggh! This is like sticky biting insects!"

Much as she wanted to rescue him from the irritant, he was right. He didn't need her protection. And she needed to focus on her job right now. He'd be fine. "You can either wait out here or go back to the house."

"I refuse! You will give me that violin."

"I guess that means you'll be waiting out here. I'm truly sorry. If there was any other way..."

"You do not care for me."

So he would appeal to her emotions? Tough luck, buddy. Maybe.

Ah hell.

"I care too much. That's the problem." She sighed. Thankful, for once, that her emotions never did lead her to silly female dramatics. "If you wait for me I promise I'll make it up to you. And maybe if you get away from the violin the call to it will be not so strong and you'll start thinking straight again."

"Summer, you wound me!" he called as she walked away and turned the corner.

It was tough leaving him there like that. But the binding wouldn't hurt him, only cause humiliation. He was a big boy. He could handle it.

And if he really was without a soul? Now that could prove fortuitous.

# Chapter 17

Once she'd wandered in to the Acquisition's reception area Summer didn't get a chance to say "hi" to the receptionist before the redhead gestured for her to head immediately into the director's office.

She stepped onto the metal grate surrounded by a biometric scanner and waited as the machine read her stats. Vampire. Retriever for two years. Thirteen successful retrievals. Marked for termination? She hoped not.

She exhaled as the scanner flashed green, signaling she could walk forward through the tall wood doors that opened into Ethan Pierce's office.

Pierce was also a vampire and kept his office dark and cool. She liked that. And he was an amiable man, always welcoming with his bright smile. Tufts of gray peppered above his ears in otherwise brown hair, so she'd often wondered how old he was. If vampire since birth it would take a long time to gray naturally. If he was a created vampire he could have been gray when it happened.

The man behind the desk gestured she sit in the leather chair before the desk, and she did so. "Good morning, Santiago."

"Director Pierce."

She smiled and crossed her legs, clasping her hands over her knees. Then changed her mind and put both feet on the floor, straightening her back. And then— hell, she hated being nervous. She wondered if CJ had already secured the violin? Was there magic strong enough to contain something the devil Himself had created?

She looked to Ethan to start with a battery of questions, but he merely stared at her. Not assessing or judging, but waiting. Mercy, just out with it!

Finally, he said, "Talk to me."

Shoot. She would have preferred a drill of questions. Not free speech. She tended to ramble. And even when she wasn't talking, her thoughts rambled. Like now!

"Santiago?"

"Ah, yes. Er. So do you have a new mission for me?"

"Santiago," he said more sternly.

"Right. Current mission discussion. Where to start?"

Ethan tapped a few keys on the keyboard and eyed the laptop screen to his right. "CJ just checked in Paganini's violin. Let's see if it stays put this time, eh?"

"We can certainly hope for that."

"And the musician?"

CJ had probably sent Ethan a note about the alley snafu.

"He's…contained."

The director leaned forward, pressing his palms onto the granite desktop. His eyes now looked into her. Summer's neck muscles tightened. Again, he silently nudged her to speak.

"I brought you the violin. That should be all you need. Please don't ask me to turn Paganini in," she began her argument. "He's…alive. Renewed. He looks a man of thirty and not the fifties he was when he died. And he's cognizant, learning new things consistently. Did you actually expect me to shove him back in the ground? We Retrievers don't take lives unless that life presents a clear and immediate danger to innocents. He hasn't harmed a soul!"

"But he will, should the curse be enacted."

"You don't know that."

"CJ reports Paganini was mad to get his hands on the violin just now out in the alley. Santiago, that violin is cursed."

"It's more a bargain than a curse."

Pierce lifted his chin, not caring for her petty semantics. "A mere few notes raised him from the dead. Can you imagine what will happen if he plays a song on it?"

Certainly she could. Destruction. Chaos. Beneath rising. Probably Nicolo and Himself getting together for a good ole father-son reunion. Diabolic magic would abound. Things would go wild. People would probably get hurt. Should she tell the director he was Himself's son?

"Exactly," Ethan said. "He has to be contained."

"For how long? He's a living, breathing person. It's not as if we can cage him up forever."

Ethan's raised brow alluded that perhaps that wasn't such a ridiculous suggestion.

Summer leaned forward, hands clutching the chair arms. "Don't tell me Acquisitions has imprisoned people?"

"We do what is necessary to prevent chaos."

"Nicolo is not chaos."

"Nicolo?"

She looked down at her hands and slumped back against the chair. Oops. That had been a little too much information.

"Have you had sex with him?"

"What? What kind of question is that? I just found him a few days ago."

A tilt of his head and he delivered the classic stern father's reprimand. And Summer felt it as an admonishing wag of the finger.

"What does it matter if we've had sex?" she tried to save her humiliation. "The man is not a danger to innocents. I can vouch for that."

"And what are you going to do with him? Babysit him? Start dating? Keep him from the violin for decades? Aeons? It's not a task I believe you are up for, Santiago."

Thanks for the vote of confidence. Not. And she could date whomever she wanted to date. This man could not tell her otherwise. But the issue wasn't about her relationship with Nicolo Paganini. It was about what he was or could become.

"We can destroy the violin, and then he'll be free of its whispers," she offered.

"Whispers?"

Shoot. "He says it whispers to him. I heard it myself when I first located it. It's not any language I've ever heard. I suspect it's…" She shouldn't have brought that up.

"Summer, you know what that is. If it's been cursed by the devil—"

"Yes, the whispers are likely demonic."

"Diabolical," Ethan corrected.

"Sure. But all we have to do is destroy the violin to set him free of those whispers. I'm sure of it."

Ethan sat back in his chair. She suspected he was pondering her suggestion. She hoped he was. Nicolo needed a chance. To be free from the violin. And from there he could start a new life. With her. Perhaps even play the professional circuit again. And she wanted to help him with that.

Her feelings toward him aside, he did not deserve death. No job was worth that to her.

"Summer, I'm sorry."

She wasn't going to like what came next.

"As the director of Acquisitions it would go against protocol to allow the man to remain free. He presents a danger to any and all."

"But after the violin is destroyed?"

"Why would we destroy such valuable magic?"

"What? But— It's the darkest magic there is. It's diabolic! It's the devil Him—" She paused when Ethan put up a hand.

"You've stepped out of line, Santiago. You will be reprimanded severely if you do not turn over Nicolo Paganini."

Summer sat back in the chair. Her legs wobbled, and she slapped a hand onto her knee. "I don't know where he is."

"I thought you were just with him?"

State the obvious then?

"If CJ's binding spell has depleted, I'm sure he took off. Paris is new to him. He has no way to navigate the twenty-first century."

"Then you have a new mission. Find Paganini. I'll give you until tomorrow morning to bring him in. If you do not, you will be taken into custody until we can solve the dilemma of the undead musician. That is all."

Mouth hanging agape, she didn't rise. Taken into custody? For what? Refusing to imprison an innocent man? What kind of organization was this? Okay, a secretive one maintained to keep order. No matter the emotional cost.

Emotional?

No, she would not go dramatic on the guy. It wasn't her style. She was strong. And she always followed orders.

"You may leave, Santiago."

Standing, she quickly exited, fists balled near her thighs. She raced through the scanner and out the door that opened into a long underground hallway that twisted and finally ascended two flights of stairs to the surface. She stepped out onto cobblestones, deep in the 11th arrondissement. Only then did she let out a frustrated shout and punch the air with her fists.

Following orders had never felt so wrong to her before. And caring about someone took a lot more out of her than she'd expected. Was that a tear wobbling in the corner of her eye?

She swiped a fist aside her eye. She was acting like a stupid girl.

The house was cool and shadowed. Summer returned just before noon. She didn't expect to find Nicolo because he probably had no idea where to find the place. Had she lost him? She needed to train him on the witch-box. And make sure he was still here. *In her life*. She needed a hug from him, actually.

She got out of the car and strode into the kitchen, where the new iPhone sat on the counter. The store had set up an account for him on her tab and given him an email so he was ready to go.

A breeze from a window fluttered through her hair. She smiled at that, then realized—the only window that ever opened far enough and was positioned to get a breeze was the one between her bedroom and the shower. Turning, she spied Nicolo standing by the window, arms across his chest and head bowed. His silhouette entertained a regalness that made her gasp.

He smiled at her. Extended his hand for her to take. So she did. And he pulled her into a hug that surprised as much as it released her apprehensions. He was still here. In her life.

"I am sorry," he said. "It was the violin making me act so cruelly toward you."

"I know that. Don't worry about it. I'm good." If not a little emotionally off balance. Why did she have to care about him?

"Did you get sacked?"

"I'm under evaluation. The director insists I bring you to him for safekeeping."

He pulled back and stroked a dash of hair from her eye. "Safekeeping?"

"I assume that means in a cage in a dark dungeon. I had no idea that Acquisitions secured living beings, but the director alluded there may be others in captivity. Dark, dangerous beings."

His eyes found hers, and in them she found a welcome place in which she wanted to stay. "Am I so dark and dangerous?"

"You're dark." She stroked his hair. "Mysterious. Sexy. A man out of time. But I don't think you're a danger to me. Or others, for that matter. At least not...yet."

He raised a brow, but didn't need to question that one. They both knew his future balanced on a violin string.

"And did you hear when CJ said you don't have a soul?"

He nodded. "I've been thinking about that. Does the devil have a soul? Perhaps when I rose from the dead I returned soulless? But what does that imply?"

"I'm not sure, but it may be why I can bite you without you going mad. That's a good thing."

"That's a very good thing." But his expression did not match the positive statement.

"I'm not going to turn you in, Nicolo."

"But your job...?"

"It means nothing to me if it requires I harm an innocent man. I think if I can destroy the violin then you'll be safe from its wicked control over you."

"And how did that go the first time you crushed and buried it?"

She sighed and dropped her head against his shoulder. His hair smelled great. She wanted to twine herself within it and snuggle there. Forget the world. Just...be.

Kissing his neck, she nuzzled into his skin, drawing in a deep breath. She noticed the bite mark and tapped it. Should take a couple days to heal completely.

"Were you marking your territory?" he asked.

"Yes." But she sighed, despite his light tone. Because it was forced. They were both attempting to walk around the huge elephant in the room. "I've been given until tomorrow morning to bring you in."

"Then you must."

"No. I'll figure something out."

"Indeed. Then we must create a plan." He smoothed a hand down her back. "They've taken the violin into custody. With no intention to destroy it?"

She shook her head. "Surprises the hell out of me. Then again, I imagine the Archives is a dark and foreboding place."

"Can a person simply walk in and out of that building with it?"

"Probably not. CJ has warded it securely this time."

"That witch's magic is powerful. It hurt."

"I'm so sorry. But you shouldn't have followed me."

"I was lured by the whispers."

"Right. Which means we have to act fast before you are unable to resist. I might pay CJ a visit in the Archives to see that he's properly stored the violin. Get the layout of the place."

"So we can then break in? Do you think you, a vampire, have the skills to stand against one so powerful as the dark witch?"

"Stop stating the obvious. I just want to keep you safe. Is that so wrong?"

"It's rather sweet. I think you favor me."

"I do favor you."

"And I you. But you mustn't think I will stand aside and allow you to do the protecting. I am the man. I will take care of you. And in the process, myself."

"Sounds good to me. So let's figure this out."

\* \* \*

Summer sat at the counter, talking on the witchbox with various friends. People, she told Nicolo, who could help their situation. She'd given him what she'd termed a crash course in using the witchbox. He understood the GPS app. And the book of face app intrigued him. Summer told him she'd set up an account for him later, after he'd established himself with a new name. (Though he still didn't understand what an *app* implied.) And she put her contact number in so they could communicate. She'd called him, and it had been oddly remarkable to hear her voice in the little box. But more remarkable? She'd fixed the ringer to play the first notes from his *Caprice No. 5*.

Now he studied the violet violin, running his forefinger along the inner curve, finding he favored the unique, fantastical design. Why *not* make changes to the traditional wood instrument? This one was not only visually appealing, but it also put out incredible sound. If he had the money he would buy it from the owner. Alas, he needed to find work.

But to do that while fleeing possible captivity? And who could know what Himself had planned for him?

"A warlock," Summer said as she joined him on the couch.

"A warlock can help us?"

"Maybe. Verity suggested we visit Ian Grim. He owes her a favor. And while he travels the world a lot, she thinks he's actually in town. I left a message for him with his partner, Dasha. Cross your fingers."

He studied her crossed fingers and then made the gesture himself. "Is that not a devil's sign?"

"No, it's a hope for good luck."

"Hmm. I suppose I should not care if it is also the devil's sign, eh?"

"It's not, Nicolo." But he didn't miss the worried tone of her voice.

"If you say so. I've been thinking…" He leaned back, setting the violin aside. "What if I appeal to the Big Guy? Call him out and say 'here I am. Let's do this. For once and for all.'"

Summer gaped.

"It might afford me a better chance than a dungeon."

"No. I'm going to keep you out of the dungeon. Or maybe the warlock can. Don't you dare call on You Know Who. He'll have you then, Nicolo. You know that."

He nodded. "Yes. Or who knows? Perhaps I will be so clever as to change his mind about me. He wanted my soul back in the nineteenth century. But now? If I am without a soul what value do I present? Surely, he has set his sights on more substantial, and perhaps even *modern* prey."

"Maybe. How many children does the man have?"

Nicolo blew out a breath. "I have brothers and sisters? Don't make me think too hard on that one, Summer. It was difficult enough accepting who my father was so long ago."

"Sorry. It is possible, though."

"Sure. But let's focus on what we've to do. How much time do we have?"

"Kiss me."

"What?"

"I know that will keep your mind off things."

"Yes, but I just said we need to keep our mind *on* things."

She delivered the proposed kiss, running her hands up his chest and pushing her fingers into his hair. She straddled him, and he pulled her in close as he surrendered to the kiss. Keeping his mind off things? It did. And it kept his hands on better things. Like the curve of her bottom as he cupped his fingers about it. And the scent of her skin, and sighs that whispered into his mouth.

There was something about Summer that he'd never known before with a woman. Not that she was a vampire and the piercing of his skin with her fangs was the most incredible experience. Nor that she was rough and unfeminine. She accepted him, and not because he was a star on stage. Did she feel responsible for him? Certainly. And yet, she allowed him his own way. Wanted to help him survive to start a new life.

And he wanted her in that life.

Summer's phone rang. She answered and said to Nicolo, "It's Ian Grim, the warlock." She pushed a button on the witchbox, and Nicolo was able to hear what the man said.

"Verity Van Velde told me you owe her a favor and she'd transferred that favor to me," Summer said, holding the witchbox between the two of them. "I need to steal a violin from the Council's Archives."

Grim whistled. "The Archives are virtually impenetrable."

"Virtually, but not completely."

"What's up with the violin?"

"It's the black violin that Himself used to tempt Nicolo Paganini with untold power." They exchanged glances. Just calling it as it was.

"Interesting. Tell me more."

"Well, Paganini is sitting beside me right now—I have you on speaker—and we think if we can destroy the violin, the temptation will pass, making him a free man. And that will keep him free from imprisonment, as well. I'm a Retriever. My job is to bring Paganini in because he's a suspected danger to society."

"Is he?"

"He could be if he plays the violin."

"So the man is alive? Fascinating. And I imagine that black violin is calling to him?"

"You got it. Can you help us?"

"Perhaps. There's always a universal price, you are aware?"

"Verity said you owed her a favor."

"Oh indeed. But the price for using malefic magic to destroy something created by the Dark Lord could be very grave."

Summer glanced to Nicolo. "Let's give it a go," she said.

Grim gave her his address, and they agreed to meet immediately.

Nicolo accompanied Summer to the warlock's house because he needed to take charge. To protect her should the warlock try anything untoward.

And he wanted to know exactly what the warlock's plans were for the violin. Destroy it? He could not fathom such destruction. Nor could the subtle whisper that never seemed to leave his ear. It wasn't an audible sound, more like a subconscious entity that would poke him if he considered not playing the violin.

He knew it was Himself. Could that monster know he was alive and walking about Paris? He had to. But it did surprise Nicolo that he'd not yet paid him a visit. The devil generally appeared to a person in the guise of their greatest temptation. Or so Nicolo had learned. He had seen Himself in the form of an elder gentleman (not a temptation) and in his true form with horns and black leathery flesh. Perhaps being the son he was not akin to the creature's display of such physical temptations?

Then why must he fight the compulsion to play the violin so desperately? Why could he not be immune to that?

"What are you thinking about?" Summer asked. They'd taken the underground Metro (fabulous conveyance) and now walked in a quiet neighborhood populated with houses in the Victorian style (or so Summer had explained to him). The style of Victoriana had followed after Nicolo's death. "Penny for your thoughts."

"Is that all they are worth?"

"It's just a saying. I don't have a penny. Just credit."

"I marvel over that plastic card of yours. If I began playing the circuit and earning a living could I get myself one of those cards?"

"I'll help you fill out the application."

"Excellent." He patted his back trouser pocket where he'd tucked the witchbox. So quickly he was adapting to the twenty-first century! "As for my thoughts, I was wondering why the Big Guy had not yet paid me a visit. Doesn't it seem inevitable?"

"It does. Maybe he's biding his time. Which gives us time to destroy the violin. You cool with that?"

"Uh, sure."

No. But no sense in starting an argument. He was going to meet a warlock. And on the scale of the few paranormals he'd met—which wasn't very many—

meeting a warlock gave him the nerves. Why, was beyond him. Hell, he was the devil's son. Nothing should scare him.

Summer clasped his hand and she squeezed, flashing her pale blue irises at him. Her smile coaxed him out of the worrying thoughts and into her world. A sunny, happy world that ever boggled, for she was the classic creature of the night.

Indeed, vampires had changed over the decades.

She turned into a yard and pushed open a wrought iron gate. The sidewalk was narrow, and Nicolo walked on the grass beside her. The dark gray house was trimmed in black. A pepperbox turret rose on the upper right side, and he could see inside the tower's curved windows clung climbing green vines. The one spot of color was the red glass doorknob on the front door.

Summer clanked the gargoyle door knocker. "Dreary, eh?"

"I'd say so. You've never met this warlock?"

"No, but I'm not afraid of him. Neither should you be."

"I'm not. Did you think I was? Please." He crossed his arms and assumed a proud stance. But there was no denying his stomach did a flip-flop.

The door opened to a short man sporting tousled blond hair and black spectacles perched at the end of his nose. "Summer Santiago? And, I presume the maestro Nicolo Paganini?"

They nodded.

"Excellent! Come in. I am most pleased to make your acquaintance, Monsieur Paganini. My partner and I listen to your music all the time."

Heartened by the warm welcome, Nicolo stepped behind Summer, but when his foot touched the threshold his body was forcefully thrust backward. He landed on the narrow sidewalk, arms and legs splayed.

The warlock popped his head out the doorway. "Interesting. Knowing you'd arrive soon I'd let down all my wards, save for one."

"Which one was that?" Nicolo said as he stood and brushed off his pants legs.

"The one against the devil Himself."

# Chapter 18

Summer's shoulders tightened at the announcement that the ward against Himself was what had repulsed Nicolo from entering Ian Grim's home. Then again, she knew he was related to the guy, so it made sense.

But really? He was just like the devil Himself? Did he have powers he wasn't aware of? Had he been like this always? Even in his former life? He had to have been. Yet Verity hadn't sensed what he was, had been sure he wasn't demon. And Summer had yet to sneeze because of him. Maybe the wards were reading some kind of genetic remnants in Nicolo? Or perhaps dormant genes waiting for the brimstone bargain to be enacted?

The musician stepped up to the stoop and waited with entreating eyes.

Ian Grim, arms crossed and a finger to his lips in

thought, didn't say anything as Summer stepped around him and joined Nicolo's side.

Finally Grim asked, "You think destroying the violin will do what, exactly?"

"I think it will remove the curse of his legacy," Summer offered. "Himself offered the violin. If he plays it, he's supposed to receive all that his legacy will offer. Unless he's already gotten some of it."

"You keep saying legacy," Grim said. "Are you telling me this guy is *related* to the Big Guy?"

Nicolo answered more proudly than Summer thought he should, "He's my father."

Grim cringed. "You didn't tell me that, Miss Santiago. It's a good thing I did have that ward activated. I know I owe Verity a favor, but dabbling with the diabolic is asking a lot of me."

"What if it means preventing unleashing something evil upon the world?"

Nicolo cleared his throat.

She squeezed his hand. "Sorry."

"I am not evil."

"Apparently," Grim said, "not yet." He narrowed his eyes on Nicolo. "Shouldn't he be under a guarded watch?"

Summer's shoulders deflated. "I'm trying to prevent that by destroying the violin. Look, can you help us or not? Because if your magic isn't powerful enough—"

"Fine," Grim said. "I've never been one to fear the diabolic." He glanced hard at Nicolo. "Or the soulless." He stepped back and muttered some Latin words, sweeping both hands before him to take in the doorframe. A gleam of emerald framed the door, then blinked out. "Come in. Let's see what we can do."

* * *

The warlock's home offered exactly the atmosphere Nicolo would expect from one who had been banished by his own race of witches for using magic most foul. Dark woods and gray-and-black wallpapers in flocked damask made it difficult to navigate through the dimly lit home. A stuffed octopus reached out a tentacle from the foyer ceiling. A collection of avian bones sat sorted on a stone kitchen counter. An overall feeling that some-*thing* was watching him from the shadows kept Nicolo's heart pounding.

Summer and Ian strode ahead into a sitting room where the horn of some long-dead creature marked the mantel. Nicolo walked slowly. They kept mentioning diabolic magic. And that he was like Himself.

He was not. And never would be. He couldn't be.

Could he?

"No," he muttered and turned to find something staring at him. He gasped, drawing in a choking breath.

Only when he realized it was not a creature from the shadows did he drop his shoulders. Petite and dark, the woman wore a long gray dress that reminded him of something from his time, with the cinched waist and proper lace about the wrists. He startled at the sight of the red ribbon around her neck, for it was a shock of color in an otherwise dismal setting.

"I am Nicolo Paganini," he said, offering his hand for her to shake.

The dark-haired beauty fluttered her lashes, and as she shook his hand he immediately knew what had happened to her. Why she wore the ribbon. Always. How terrible. Yet how fascinating.

She offered a sweet "I know who you are, Monsieur

Paganini. I am Dasha. I love your music. We listen to it often. Are you like me now?"

"Back from the dead?" he said with knowing. "Yes, but my death was natural. Unlike..." He rubbed his forefinger across his neck so he wouldn't have to say what he knew about her.

She touched the red ribbon. "Ian saved me. Gives me life."

What Nicolo had read about the woman's life during that handshake was that she had been beheaded during the French Revolution, shortly after he'd been born. Yet a dark menace had sown her decapitated head onto a new body. She now survived thanks to life-giving blood. Though he couldn't be clear on how she received that blood.

He didn't want to know. Some mysteries were best left unexplained.

"My partner is a kind man," Dasha said. "You mustn't think because he is warlock that he is terrible. He did it for me. For love."

"I will try not to make judgments," he said honestly. "I suspect there are far worse things to be in this world."

Like the devil's son.

"Will you have tea?" she asked.

"I'd be delighted."

Summer checked that the spell paper she'd shoved in her back pocket was still there. Ian Grim had copied out a spell using blood ink and handcrafted paper. He'd lit it aflame and then doused it in the tears of a newborn. Dramatics. But probably not. Witchcraft disturbed her. Best to simply trust it would work and leave the worry over the process to others.

Merely tear it in two and it would activate, Grim had explained. Seemed too easy. But right now she'd take easy.

It was a little before sunset. She'd suggested Nicolo stay at her home while she was out and had made him swear he would not follow her again. He'd taken it as an admonishment, but had picked up the electric violin and began to play as she'd backed out in the Audi and the garage door had closed.

Once in the Archives, she took an elevator ride down two stories and passed the guard with a nod. He was werewolf, she sensed. Some wolves gave off a wolfie scent of wild.

She smelled mint tea and followed that into the dimly lit Archives office, which was so vast it stretched farther than she could see left and right and was cluttered with bookcases and storage cabinets fashioned from varnished old woods. A scatter of massive wood desks fronted the room, and behind one of them, sitting beside a flickering oil lamp, sat Certainly Jones, his feet up on the desk, eyes closed and head tilted against the seat.

"Surprised to find you here, Summer," he said without opening his eyes. "Tea?"

What was it with witches and tea?

"Uh, sure." Best to humor him. Would he suspect she was about to unleash a spell? "I wanted to check in with you to make sure the violin had been secured. We've been having such a time keeping that darned thing secure."

"You could have called."

Yep. And she was so not good at the stealth around someone she knew. Out on a retrieval? No problem.

But she knew that CJ would probably be suspicious of her visit.

"I was in the area and thought I'd stop in." She shoved her hands in her front pockets. "I've always wanted to see inside the Archives. Can I take a look at it? I do have a stake in this one, CJ. Let me make sure it's safe."

He pulled his feet off the desk and set down the teacup with a clink of cup to saucer. The hand that was heavily tattooed pointed toward her hip. "Is that when you're going to use that spell you've got tucked in your pocket?"

"My—what?"

"Summer. I can smell the malefic magic. You've been consorting with Ian Grim, I suspect. He's the only warlock in town at the moment. We do keep tabs, you know."

No, she had not known that. Now what to do? She'd thought this would be easy. Get a look at the violin. Tear the spell in two. Voilà!

CJ got up and walked around the desk to stand before her. He was taller by a head and imposing. Like a goth king nightmare. But she knew he was kind. Mostly.

In a panic, she gripped his shirt. "You've got to help me. I'm supposed to hand over Nicolo Paganini to Ethan Pierce in the morning. You know they'll lock him away and toss the key. He doesn't deserve that. He's only been alive three days. He's not evil. I know him! Trust me, CJ."

He carefully removed her grip from his shirt and held out his hand, palm up. "Give me the spell."

She shook her head. "I brought him into the world. It's now my duty to protect him."

"Seriously? Summer, the man is the devil's son."

"How do you know that? I just found out— Were you talking to Verity?"

"She did give me a heads-up on the situation. Did you neglect to alert the director of this most important paternal link?"

She sighed and looked aside.

"I thought so. I shouldn't discount the disruption that a fierce attraction can produce, but I would expect a Retriever to keep her job separate from her personal life."

She'd expect as much, too. But the man was soulless. No one could have any idea what that meant to her.

"He may appear harmless to you now," CJ said, "but once he plays the violin—"

"Exactly. This spell Grim gave me will destroy the violin. Why does the Archives need to keep it, anyway? Why not destroy the thing that is capable of bringing a monster to life? Acquisitions would rather imprison a man than destroy the violin. That makes little sense."

"I am not a part of Acquisitions. I merely receive the items you Retrievers bring in and do not question."

"Yes, you receive the items we retrieve. So you *are* a part of this, like it or not."

"Summer, give me the spell."

"Don't do that, Summer."

CJ looked over Summer's shoulder to where Nicolo stood in the doorway. "How did you get in here? I can feel the diabolic magic waving off you."

Really? He had followed again? What did she have to do to make him stay put?

"I've no magic," Nicolo said, holding his palms splayed as he entered the room to stand beside Summer. "I simply walked in. And I don't appreciate you speaking to Summer in that tone. You have something that belongs to me, dark witch. The black violin. And I will thank you to return it."

CJ moved his fingers, and Summer knew he was accessing his magic. She had no defense against magic, so she could but close her eyes and pray this wasn't going to hurt.

With a gesture from CJ, Nicolo was flung backward to land against the stone wall. Nicolo, in turn, thrust out his hand defensively—and some force lashed CJ across the chest and pushed him backward to land across the desk on his back.

Summer twisted a look toward Nicolo. The man looked at his hand and shrugged. "It just happened."

"Don't do that here," she warned. "Seriously? You followed me here? This place wants to take you into custody. And you just gave them good reason to do so. We need to get out of here."

"I couldn't stand to the side and let you do this alone. I feared you might get hurt."

"Admit it, Nicolo. You don't care about me. You wanted the violin."

He was about to answer when another lash of magic from CJ forced him back against the wall.

"CJ, please," Summer pleaded. "I'll give you the spell!"

"Hand it over—" the dark witch held out his hand, maintaining the hold on Nicolo with his other hand "—and I'll let you both walk out of here. But I won't be responsible for what Acquisitions will do to you, Summer Santiago. You know this is out of line."

"That's fine," she said, hoping to appease him so

212 The Vampire's Protector

he would release Nicolo. "I have to face that one on my own."

She shoved a hand in her back pocket and tugged out the slip of paper. But the end of it got caught on the seam, and she heard paper tear. Before she could fathom what was happening, she pulled up her hand. Only half the spell paper was pressed between her fingers. "Oops."

"Ah shit. Was that a destruction spell?"

She nodded and added a guilty swallow.

CJ dashed around her and down the hallway. Nicolo stepped away from the wall and grabbed her by the shoulders. "We must follow him!"

And so they did. Taking a turn in the passageway that had stopped being walled in brick and now was but bare limestone, Summer shivered as the chill air grew noticeable.

"CJ, I didn't mean to do that!" she called after him.

He swerved right ahead at a T-turn. She took the turn and Nicolo followed as they ran down five stairs, where CJ punched in a code on a digital lock.

"I don't even know what to do with you," he muttered. "Summer, your family and mine have been friends for years."

"I'm sorry, CJ. I wanted to help Nicolo. He's not deserving of imprisonment."

"I understand that. You are infatuated."

"Ahem," Nicolo said.

"She is," CJ reiterated. "And at the risk of her job. Do you really care about her?" he asked Nicolo.

"I do."

"Hmph."

"I know him better than you or Ethan Pierce do. He's worth giving a chance to."

"Well, if the violin is gone then I guess he gets that chance, eh?"

"If Acquisitions doesn't lock him up. Will you let him leave here with me?"

The door clicked, and CJ pulled back the thick vault door and eyed Nicolo carefully. "I don't know yet."

The threesome entered the vault, which was lit all around with small blue LEDs and gave enough light to reveal the room was vast. The walls looked like steel as Summer took everything in. The floor was some kind of perforated metal, as was the ceiling. A weird juxtaposition of high tech amongst the ancient stacks and libraries that made up of the rest of the Archives.

"Remarkable," Nicolo said. "I have never seen the like."

"Where did you put it?" Summer asked the witch.

He didn't answer, only walked quickly down an aisle of items set upon steel blocks about waist high. Contained under glass, each had a digital keypad at the fore of the block.

"This time I bespelled it and fixed a warding lock on it before putting it in storage," CJ called back. "Ah hell."

He stopped before a glass case about the size that could easily contain a violin. Hands pressed to the glass, he then beat the clear surface with a fist. Summer arrived at his side. Inside lay a pile of black dust. Sulfur teased at her nostrils.

"The spell worked," she whispered in awe. "It really worked. And yet…achoo!"

They met one another's stares. CJ swallowed audibly. "What the hell?"

"I don't know." She felt another sneeze tickle her nose, but winced to suppress it. She looked at Nicolo and he shrugged, giving her an "it wasn't me" look.

"You two should probably get moving if you had any idea to make a great escape," CJ said. "You know Pierce will track you."

Yes, with the tracking chip all Retrievers wore. It was designed as a means to locate them if rescue was necessary.

"Thanks, CJ. Just give us five minutes before you call the director."

"I'll give you as long as it takes me to return to my desk and pick up the phone."

"Let's go." She pushed Nicolo ahead of her, and he raced back toward the main office. But as they arrived, she didn't expect to find another visitor. "Achoo!"

Nicolo gasped. And standing before them, in all his demonic glory, was the devil Himself. And he held the black violin.

# Chapter 19

The devil Himself turned his great horned head toward Summer. His eyes glowed red. Long fangs jutted from the upper corners of his leathery black mouth. Horns glinted as if hematite sheened by the oil lamp nearby. He shook his head at her. "I don't like you, vampire." His voice was sepulchral and icy. To Nicolo he asked, "Why is she here?"

"She raised me from the dead by finding the black violin."

As he shook his head Himself's horns swept the air, and Summer could almost see the cut marks in the atmosphere.

"What's he doing here?" she demanded loudly. So she was panicking. And another sneeze was necessary. "Did you call him here, Nicolo?"

"I did nothing of the sort!"

"Take a care for greeting the old man, will you?" Himself said. He appeared in his natural guise before the two of them, black musculature, hooves, talons at his fingers, and those massive, deadly horns. His red eyes narrowed as he spoke. "I felt the disturbance in the universe when the violin was played a few days ago."

"It wasn't played," Summer insisted. "The bow accidentally slid across a few strings."

"If that is what you wish to believe," Himself said cryptically. "I knew the violin's voice would bring you back to this realm, my son. The bargain still stands. Won't you finally accept your legacy and play?"

"Never," Nicolo spat.

Behind her, Summer sensed CJ striding toward the office. His voice echoed down the hallway when he must have sighted them standing before their wicked guest. "Ah fuck."

"This does not involve you, dark witch." Himself gestured with one long black leathery finger. CJ was shoved out of the doorway threshold and into the hallway. The door slammed behind him.

Summer had not ever seen Himself in the flesh—that she could remember. She'd been a baby when he had kidnapped her to use against her brother, Johnny. He must be over seven feet tall. The horns gave him another two or three feet. His skin was leathery and muscled. A little Incredible Hulk-ish, but sleeker and black. At the ends of his fingers grew long ebony claws. He wore leather pants, and his feet were hooves.

His red eyes with snake-like pupils took her in. "So we meet again, Summer Rosanne Santiago."

That he knew her middle name made her sick to her stomach. So much magic could be worked against a person with their full name. Not that she had any protection against diabolic magic one way or the other. It just made her shiver to know he knew things that others did not.

"I'd say it was a pleasure," she offered, "but I've never been a good liar. Achoo!"

Himself sneered at her bombastic reaction to him. She didn't know if it was the sulfur or just his overall horribleness. Whatever it was, it tickled her nose.

"Let her leave," Nicolo said. "She is not involved in this."

"I am," Summer defended.

"Yes, you should go." Himself gestured toward the door, but Summer stepped up beside Nicolo.

"I'm not leaving. And you're not going to take his soul."

Himself chuckled. A deep, rumbling tone that she felt stir in her gut. "Why would I want something my son does not have? And you know he is soulless, don't you, Soul Piercer?"

"Soul P-piercer?" She'd never heard her condition named like that. But as she repeated the moniker in her head, it felt real and…she owned it.

"You pierce souls and give madness," Himself said. "All while feeling guilty for it. Pitiful. You are of no importance to me. I have come for my son. I want to endow him with those gifts with which he should have been born."

Nicolo stepped up to Himself. Even with his height he had to crane back his head to meet his father in the eye. "You have no right to direct my life merely because you bear some small part in my conception. Takes less than a moment to get a woman with child. But it takes a lifetime to be a father."

"You are an insolent." Himself tilted his chin up.

Nicolo's body flung backward. His shoulders hit Summer's chest and she was pushed back, but they didn't collapse to the floor. Together they managed to stand upright. Keeping her behind him, Nicolo held one hand back to touch her arm, and the other out before him. He splayed out his fingers in an intentional move.

The movement didn't even disturb Himself, though the dark lord did smirk. "So you've some magic. Excellent. Your rebirth infused you with that gift, and you came into it with your rising. But it's just a taste of all that you can become. Take what is yours, Nicolo."

"And why would I want to become demon, such as you? To wield such power as to harm others, to maim and destroy them? I am a musician. My talent was natural. I can survive just fine with those skills."

Himself shook his head. "You honestly believe that was a natural talent?"

"It was not from you! I practiced. Daily. Every day. Often for ten hours in one day. I practiced until my bloody fingers formed calluses and I could play a complicated composition on but one string!"

"My doing."

"No!" Nicolo protested. "Never. If I did not accept what you had offered why would you give me a gift unknowing?"

Himself had no answer for that one.

"Mine." Nicolo beat his chest with a fist. "All I have had was because of natural skill and determination. Nothing from you! Never!"

Himself pointed at Summer.

Nicolo stepped before her protectively. "You will not harm her. She is…" He swallowed, perhaps stopping himself from saying things he did not want to reveal to the opposition.

"I see." Himself nodded. His wicked gaze dripped over Summer, and she shivered and clutched Nicolo's shirt from the back. "I misjudged the timing. Perhaps you need a little more time before you can be properly compelled to your legacy. But you know, Soul Piercer, the more blood you take from a soulless being the quicker madness will befall you. Such a delicious pairing. And now a dilemma." The devil actually affected a pout. "We will meet again. I promise you that. Good day to you, my son."

Once there, filling the air with his monstrous form, the next moment, Himself shimmered to but a flicker of light. A tiny spark ignited in the air then lit out. The sulfur left the room and the air even seemed to lighten.

"Are you all right?" Nicolo turned to face Summer. He looked her over, touched her cheek and brushed the hair from her face. Worry teared his eyes.

"Yes, I'm fine. But what about you?"

"I'm okay, as you say." He kissed her, then kissed her forehead and held his mouth there. Holding her. Making contact. "Can we get out of here?"

"Yes, definitely. But Nicolo…"

"What?"

"He called me Soul Piercer. It's true. Will I…" If she drank more from Nicolo would she be the one to turn mad?

"Lies," Nicolo said. "Now we must leave."

They found CJ standing outside the door, arms crossed and a grim look on his face. He didn't say anything until Summer remembered she had made a deal with him that he wouldn't call the director on her until he returned to the office.

"We're leaving right now," she reassured him. "Don't call Pierce yet!"

Keeping her eyes peeled for Himself as she navigated the city in the car, Summer didn't expect to see the horned Dark Lord out in the middle of a tourist crush. But she wasn't thinking rationally, and her heartbeats still thundered from their encounter in the Archives. That had been a close call. Twice now she'd been in that bastard's presence.

She did not want a third time to ever occur. Had she initially thought this retrieval mission would be easy-peasy? Mercy.

"Let's go to Italy," Nicolo said as she turned and drove down the street toward her home. "I crave to walk the earth of my home country. And we do need to get out of the city, away from your Acquisitions."

"Sounds like a plan. We'll hop on a train tonight and spend a few days crossing France and into Italy. Maybe it'll put Himself off your scent, too."

Nicolo offered her a doubtful glance.

She shrugged. "You never know."

"I have noticed you are an optimist, Summer."

"I live in a world where my kind have to walk in the shadows and not reveal themselves to anyone for fear of persecution or even getting slayed. I'm a minority, and we tend to carry a heavy burden merely by existing. So what else is there to do but try to see the bright side in things?"

"Will your director sack you?"

"I hope not. I really need this job."

"Why so? Are you financially challenged? Summer, if it is difficult for you to afford my staying with you—"

"No, it's not that. I'm well-off thanks to my parents' setting up an account for me when I was a baby. The Santiagos are rich. We don't have to work. But if I don't have a purpose then what is there to do? Most vampires just…do the vampire thing. I don't know how they can handle not having a job or hobby or something that gives them a feeling of purpose and accomplishment."

"I understand. A purpose is important to a man's sanity."

"Right. I need the Retriever job because it does that for me. And I do my job well." She sighed. "When I'm not screwing it up by hoarding a dead man away from the Big Guy."

"If you had not found the violin I would not have been given this second chance. I know that we all should only have the one life to live. But what has happened must have happened for a reason."

"Everything happens for a reason. I believe that. So you here, in my life? It was meant to be."

"Destiny?"

"For sure. I like the idea of the train ride. We'll get a sleeper car."

"We don't sleep."

"We don't, but we do other things in a bed." She winked.

"Can we bring along the electric violin? I want to practice."

"Uh, sure. I'll give Domingos a call and make sure he's cool with it. He owns other violins. I know his girl-friend, Lark, is a violinist as well."

She pulled into the garage and clicked the door button to close it behind them. Getting out of the car, she grabbed her cell phone. "I'm going to find us some train tickets. You hungry?"

"Terribly. After you've told your witchbox where we wish to travel, can you tell it to bring us some food?"

"I can order in or you can run out and look for something on your own. Try out the GPS on your witchbox."

"I can do that. You get us tickets for the train. Might I borrow your plastic card as well?"

She pointed to her wallet on the counter. "Just slash and sign. You can sign my name. They won't look."

He kissed her. "I admire you, Brightness. You stood strong before Himself."

"Maybe I'm too stupid for my own good. I need to know more about the soul-piercer thing. I'm going to call Verity after I get us tickets." She kissed him. "Bring back pizza."

# *Chapter 20*

Summer was able to purchase train tickets, take a shower and fix the pickup in the violet violin by the time Nicolo returned with reasonably warm mozzarella-and-basil pizza. A half a slice was more than enough for her. They ate without mention of their encounter with Himself earlier. Yet that elephant had joined the other elephant, and while they weren't necessarily walking around it anymore, they both knew if they poked it with a stick, it would rage at them.

Verity called to confirm that Soul Piercer made sense in Summer's case. It was not necessarily a vampire, but could be almost any sort of paranormal who had the ability to pierce a living soul and alter it within the body. For good or for ill.

That news should have devastated her, but oddly, Summer felt relief in finally having a label for her strange condition. But that didn't mean she had to embrace it. Still she must remain cautious when taking blood from humans.

Verity did mention that a Soul Piercer's bite would do no harm to the soulless. And she reiterated that Summer believed Nicolo was a safe bite for her.

Safe, but at what risk to herself? Himself had said she would go mad by drinking from the soulless. She didn't want to think about it.

An hour after the empty pizza box had been trashed, they boarded a night train to Milan. Summer lay on the down-filled duvet, listening as Nicolo experimented with some harmonics and pizzicato on Domingos's electric violin. It had an adjustment to play acoustic, so it didn't matter that she'd fixed the crackle. A few notes here. A bowed scale there. A jumpy allegretto run, and then a smooth and lingering dance between two strings.

Genius creating. She could listen to him constantly. How lucky was she?

"You'll need a new name," she said.

Without stopping bowing, Nicolo said, "I know. But I am attached to the one I currently have."

"You can still be Nicolo. Maybe just the one name? Single-named entertainers have always been popular. There's Beyoncé and Cher, and Madonna and Usher."

"I could live with that. And for my identification papers?" Violin between his chin and shoulder, he adjusted the tuning on the E string.

"You could take any last name that interests you."

"I'll think on it. Nicolo and Summer, touring the world."

"And Summer? I don't think so. I mean, I'd be thrilled to play with you, but I am not on your level by any means."

"I can match my playing style to yours."

The man could make a dig about her lacking talent sound so sweet. "That's okay. I feel the stage isn't big enough for anyone but you."

"I have not so much an ego."

"I think you do."

He shrugged. "Perhaps." Then he lilted into a delightful scale that combined bowing and pizzicato. Abruptly, he set the violin on his lap. "I should like to play with your brother's troop on stage."

"It's called a band. And really? Hmm…"

"Yes, but I'd like to give the electric guitar a try. I know their songs."

Of course he did. He had the ability to recall the complete song after only one listen.

Summer put up her feet on the wall at the head of the narrow train bed. She'd gotten a single sleeper, knowing that the double sleepers had bunk beds. And she wasn't about to sleep alone—or sleep, for that matter. She smoothed a hand across her stomach, beneath the T-shirt, and sighed.

Nicolo tapped her thigh with the bow. "I want to play you."

He moved onto the bed beside her and glided the tip of the bow along her hip and up to lift her shirt. He was careful not to run the actual bow hairs over her skin. They would be rough with rosin. Summer lifted her hips as he pushed up her shirt higher to reveal her breasts, and then he flipped the bow so the glossy wood back of it slid over her skin and just under her breast. The sensation of the sleek wood touching her skin heightened her desire. Not that it needed heightening. She was horny, no denying it.

The surprise of his tongue to her skin just below her naval made her shudder and grip the duvet. "Yes," she moaned, wanting him to reply to that sentence with a long and lingering answer that needed no words.

He unzipped her jeans and tugged them down. But before following the denim downward, he glided up to nudge her shirt up as he kissed the underside of her breast. His tongue lashed just a breath away from her nipple. He straddled her with his knees, the brush of his leather pants against her mons luring her hips upward to seek the friction, but too quickly he moved.

Summer closed her eyes and focused on the heat trail of his tongue as it tasted her skin and twirled curves and ended here and there with kisses that seemed to read an imprint of her very pores upon his mouth. He moved lower, yet just when she thought he would kiss her apex and wet her clitoris with his mouth, he instead moved to the side. His nose softly coasted over her. Kisses there and then there gave her giddy shivers.

Fingers curling, she wanted to push them through Nicolo's hair and direct his attentions, yet at the same time the visceral cry of yes shimmered across her system. His not touching those key pleasure spots was proving even more erotic than if he'd simply went straight for the orgasm. But an orgasm was building within her, slowly, with a maddening promise.

"Brightness," he whispered as his tongue teased the crease between thigh and mons. His crotch rested on her shin, and he pressed down, grinding his erection against her. His next utterance was more a moan than actual words.

His hand clasped her ass and he squeezed. Breath heated her labia. She exhaled and the shimmer of orgasm fluttered through her body. With a sigh, Summer came quietly, gently, yet she had never felt pleasure envelope her so fully, so easily.

"Exquisite," Nicolo said against her leg.

Snuggled together on top of the duvet, the twosome watched the passing countryside out the window. It was around 2:00 a.m., and yet the sky was bright with starlight.

The violin lay on the bench, the bow deposited on the floor. Summer reached over to stroke the body of the instrument. Nicolo matched her strokes, drawing his fingers up her back and then down to the divots that marked the top of her buttocks. His touch melted into her, tracing her within and shivering sweetly in her soul. Was this what it felt like to be bitten and feel the orgasmic rush of the swoon?

"If we are successful in destroying the black violin," he said quietly, "I'll have a new life to look forward to. And the first thing I want to do is visit *il Cannone*."

That was the nickname he'd given to the violin made by Giuseppe Guarneri, which he'd treasured when last alive in the nineteenth century. "Why not do it on this road trip? What town is it in?"

"I had gifted it to the city of Genoa."

She grabbed her cell phone from the floor and checked the map app. "That's not a long trip from Milan. We can most definitely give it a visit."

He kissed her bare back, and his hair tickled her skin. "Thank you. I would like that very much. Do you think they'd give it back to me? If I asked nicely?"

"Considering you'd have a challenging time convincing them you are Paganini risen from the grave? Not a chance. You know, it's been played in concert since your death."

"By whom?" He leaned up on an elbow. "That is *my* violin!"

"A handful of violinists through the decades have been allowed to perform with it. Not a lot. I'm sure they took good care of it."

Nicolo lay back on the duvet, staring upward. Summer could sense his outrage. It made him human. And for some reason she needed that reassurance. Especially since the vision of Himself was still vivid in her memory. And yet she was the farthest thing from human. *Soul Piercer.* The title haunted her.

"I had that violin for twenty years," he said. "It was my closest friend. It was— the Big Guy hated it. Said it was innocence. My balance. I was never sure what he meant by that. But that's probably why I held it to me so fiercely. Perhaps I thought it a means to protect myself from his influence."

"Maybe it did? We'll go see it," she reassured. "Let me rest an hour before we arrive, will you?"

"Of course. Can I hold you?"

"I'd love that. And then when I wake…"

"Yes?"

"I'll be hungry."

"Mmm, I'll be waiting for your bite."

Yes, but now she had to decide whether or not a bite was the best for her. Truly, would drinking from a soulless creature drive *her* mad?

Nicolo wanted to visit the Duomo, Milan's magnificent Gothic cathedral, the largest church in Italy. It had taken six centuries to build and was completed some time in the twentieth century. Summer suggested they head to the cathedral immediately to avoid the tourist rush. It was early, and the sun had just risen. The cosmopolitan city had awoken, but the hubbub still slumbered. They took a cab to the piazza in front of the cathedral, and before Nicolo could tug her toward the entrance, she pulled him into the shadows beside an arriving tourist bus.

"Hungry, remember?" She kissed him. "Will you give me a few minutes to, uh…?"

"Are you going to snack on a tourist?"

She shrugged. "Not much else around right now. Unless I wander deeper into the city and find a homeless guy. Ugh. Forget I said that."

He embraced her and kissed her quickly. "Take from me. I love your bite. In fact…" He stepped back and held her hand as he looked over her from head to toe. The twinkle in his eye matched the curve on his mouth— playful.

"What?" she said, patting her hair subconsciously.

"I think I may be falling in love with you, Summer. Is that okay to say nowadays? Do people declare their love so openly and quickly?"

"Are you sure it's not lust? I mean, we make a great pair in bed. I lust for you."

"No, I believe it's something more. And not simply my being alone in this world and needing you to guide me. I feel it here." He thrust a fist against his chest.

"That's sweet. Really. I could love you. But…"

"But you don't dare because of what I could become? Or is it your soul-piercing thing? Are you afraid to bite me after what Himself said?"

She tilted her head, offering a shrug, unwilling to

come out and admit it was probably a little of both. "What if it's true about me going mad?"

He sighed. "So you must use caution. And I must fight the evil I could become. What about *il Cannone*?" he suddenly said. Standing straight and tapping his lip, he then tapped the air between them. "If it really was innocent, something You Know Who was actually fearful of…? Maybe it could defeat the black violin?"

"How do you mean? You can't pit two violins against one another. Well, in a duet sort of duel you could, I suppose. They made a song about that. 'The Devil Went Down to Georgia.'"

"Really? They sing about the devil and a violin? That's troubling."

"You entertained the rumors back when you were alive. I mean, your first life."

"Yes, but to this day they sing about it?"

"I'm sure it's a different story. The Big Guy is always tempting people. Seems a violin is one of his more popular instruments of temptation. But about your other violin. The one in Genoa."

"Yes, a thought just occurred. What if I played the Guarnerius? I might send the devil packing."

"Sounds too easy."

"But worth a try?"

"Anything is worth a try. But again, I don't know how you'd convince the city of Genoa to let you take it for a spin."

"We'll figure it out. I think we have a plan. A sort of plan, anyway. And what if when I do defeat the black violin I might get a soul?"

She didn't know what to say to that one. With a soul, she could never bite him again. And if she did, he'd succumb to madness. Without one? She could be the one singing for her Fruit Loops.

"Let's go for a walk," he said.

"A walk? I thought you wanted to go inside the cathedral? I was going to show you the gargoyles. They put them up for adoption a few years ago."

"Is that so? That one will definitely require an explanation. But I thought you were hungry? We'll find you a candidate. A donor, as you call it."

He wasn't sure what it said about him, but he enjoyed watching Summer bite a young man. Nicolo wasn't going to overthink things. They had found a tourist wandering a dark alcove at the end of a pretty tree-lined street. A nearby olive tree shushed in the breeze, and the sounds of pounding from construction down the road would muffle any noise of struggle.

But there was no struggle. The man grinned widely at Summer's approach. And now he groaned loudly when Summer pulled her fangs from his neck and began to draw out his blood. Was she the very evil Nicolo had tried to avoid all his life? Summer was bright and good, and he really did believe he was falling in love with her. And he wanted to be the one under her fangs. The madness bit had to be a ruse concocted by Himself to wedge them apart. Though, if he considered it, Himself would benefit more from a mad vampire.

Perhaps his destiny was closer to hand than he'd care to admit? Maybe the evil he'd avoided all his life was already germinating inside him. Himself had said it had begun. And with the playing of the black violin it would be complete. He would be—what?

The tourist pulled Summer tight against his body

and rocked his hips. Nicolo's erection hardened. Summer dropped the man and then pressed her hand to his forehead and told him to sleep and wake only with memory that he'd gotten lost. She turned to Nicolo, licking her lips.

He pulled her into his arms. "Take off your pants," he said. "I want to be inside you as you've been inside him."

"That turned you on?"

"Don't speak, vampire. Just do it."

She shoved down her pants. The T-shirt fell below her buttocks, concealing her modestly if anyone should walk by. She unbuttoned his trousers, and her fingers wrapping about his cock felt like coolness to molten steel. He lifted her and she wrapped her legs about him and allowed him to glide inside her. She pressed her lips to his neck, and a star-filled shock of pleasure raced through him. And he pushed deeply inside her, chasing the high, the magnificent release.

"Goddess, that's good," she said on a gasp. He caught sight of her face, and she dashed out her tongue to lick away a spot of blood. His? No, she hadn't pierced him yet. "Your cock. Us. Yeah, I think I could love you, too, Nicolo."

"What if I were evil?"

"You're not." She closed her eyes as he continued to glide in and out of her. "You could never be, even if you did play the black violin. Your soul is good. That's all that matters."

His soul? She'd forgotten he was missing one. But he didn't want to spoil her hopeful mood.

"I hope so, Brightness. Ah! I can feel you squeeze me from inside."

"You like that?"

He nodded, words unnecessary. Instead he clasped a hand over one of her breasts and pinched the nipple through the soft shirt fabric. She rocked upon him, harder, faster. She drew him out almost all the way and leaned forward. He knew she was gliding her clitoris along his shaft. Her fast breathing told him she was right there, along with him, ready to fly.

Shudders built in his body. He gripped her upper arms. Clenched his jaws. Summer cried out and quickly pressed her mouth against his neck to muffle the sound. The dash of her tongue over his vein caused him to release. The world went bright, then all colors and then all sound ceased save for his pounding heartbeats.

He was in his homeland. Alive. Vital. And in love.

Hours later they pulled in to the Parco Sempione, the large park behind the castle Sforza that had once been hunting grounds to the Sforza dukes. They stood in a shady copse listening to a street performer. Or rather, Summer stood back in the evening shade. Nicolo was currently chatting with the violinist, who had taken a break and put up a sign that he would resume in half an hour.

Nicolo had been impressed with the musician's tonality and dancing. He'd done a jig while performing, and it must have reminded Nicolo of his own performances. History told he had been very animated while playing, bending this way and that as the music captured him. Summer couldn't wait to see him perform.

"Achoo!"

She hastily glanced around but didn't see anyone with red eyes lurking about. Much as she knew she could sneeze from pollen or dust or other irritants, she was always cautious for demons.

The crunch of footsteps across the loose pebbles under the tree alerted her, and she turned. A tall blond man grabbed her about the upper arm. Only when he spoke did she know exactly who he was.

"So you two *are* in love. Happened much faster than I could have hoped for. Excellent. Once again you'll serve as useful bait to dangle from the hook, Soul Piercer."

Before she could scream, Himself swiped his palm before Summer's eyes. She blacked out.

# Chapter 21

The cloying scent of sulfur alerted Nicolo. He paused in the middle of conversation with the violinist and scanned about the park's green scenery. A family accompanied by a small dog tossed bits of bread to a flock of pigeons. Lovers kissed after a sip of wine from an amber bottle. An elderly gentleman wearing plaid slacks tilted his hat lower to shade his eyes from the sun as he reclined on the lush grass.

Summer had been standing beneath the palm tree. Where had she gone?

A silvery whisper slipped into Nicolo's ear as the violinist took up his bow and kicked down his out-to-lunch sign. He soared into a Mozart concerto. And Nicolo walked swiftly toward the palm trees. The distraction of the music did not lessen his senses. He might not be able to hear her, but he could scent her. She wore that delicious, sweet, after-sex musky smell that he'd know miles away and recognize even after decades away from her side.

And yet, sulfur pervaded the atmosphere.

Were demons in the area? He hadn't heard Summer sneeze. Had he been too involved in the discussion of Paganini's inventive harmonics with the musician to notice?

"Damn it, where is she?"

And why now had those diabolic whispers returned to him? Where was the black violin? When they had been at the Archives in Paris Himself had disappeared with it in hand. That bastard could place it anywhere in his path now, Nicolo knew that.

His father had said they would meet again.

"No."

And in a heartbeat, Nicolo knew the whispers were telling him to follow them. They would lead him to Summer.

And Himself.

Summer didn't know where she was. It felt…underground, for the musty, chalky scent. And yet the ceiling, a dome looming perhaps three stories above her head, seemed to let in daylight. Some kind of strange illumination lit the dusty air. The circular cell was vast, yet she could see the walls, fronted by equally spaced columns that looked carved out of red stone or clay. The floor was packed red dirt.

Sulfur whispered into her nostrils.

A tall, Nordic man with a blond, buzz-cut style and angular cheekbones leaned against one of the columns, arms crossed high over his chest. An ice-gray suit looked a fashion mistake stretched onto his muscular physique.

Summer knew it was an illusion. A glamour. And not one that particularly appealed to her.

"What's with the Zoolander look?" she asked of Himself.

"You do not care for it? I was trying to blend in."

"A blond? In Italy? Achoo! Damn it!" She hated that he'd so easily taken her away from the park. Must have used some devilish thrall on her. Asshole.

The man morphed into a tall, bearded looker with piercing blue eyes and a striped red-and-white shirt. An Italian gondolier?

"Oy." Summer paced. "I thought you appeared to people in the guise of their greatest temptation?"

"How's this?"

Suddenly Nicolo stood by the column, long dark hair curling over his shoulders. A rich velvet suit coat revealed a lacy-cuffed white shirt. His arms spread as he waited her summation.

Summer gulped back a gasp. "That's not fair, or ethical. He's your son, for the goddess's sake."

"Touché." Spreading back his arms, the image of Nicolo was shed, seeming to peel back and away from the black leathery flesh and muscle beneath, until finally the devil Himself stood before her in all his wicked incarnation of horns, hooves and glinting razored fangs. "Better?"

"Absolutely. I prefer you that way. Least I know what I'm dealing with. So you got a thing with kidnapping me? Really. Last time we did this you had taken an innocent little baby to do your dirty work. Didn't go very well for you, did it?"

"Now I remember why I find you so distasteful."

"Please. I was a freakin' baby. There was not a distasteful bone in my body then. I'm still a pretty cool chick, if you ask me."

Himself rolled his red eyes. "So says the vampiress who drives men to madness with a single bite."

"Not all the time!" she protested.

"Yes, all. You don't track their lives after you have taken what you want from them."

"No." She slunk back against the wall. He was a liar. Nothing he said could be trusted. And yet, he'd always told Nicolo his truths. She rubbed her upper arms and shivered. "Why am I like this?

Himself grinned. "I did it."

"What?"

"It was a little going away gift to you as a baby. I do shit like that. It's my job."

"I hate you."

"Wouldn't have it any other way."

"It's not going to work, you know. Nicolo has resisted you for decades. And look at him now. He's alive and doing well. He looks and feels better than he ever has, and he's starting a new life. He doesn't need any fabulous powers."

"Bringing him back to life wasn't my doing. When you bowed the violin that fateful morning you raised a facsimile of my son from the grave."

"A facsimile? What, you mean like a clone or doppelgänger?" Summer caught her forehead in a palm. Oh, please let her have made love with a real man and not some creepy golem. Or something worse. "Please, tell me he's not a zombie."

Himself chuckled. A tilt of his head caught the overhead illumination on his horns and they gleamed. "He is demon in a human shell. Trapped like those pitiful corporeal demons who feed off any soul's shell they can inhabit. Though Nicolo is quite soulless."

"I don't get that. I don't sneeze around him. I'm allergic—"

"Not really. It's merely a traumatic residue you carry around with you. You don't have to sneeze. If you were mentally strong you could accept that you don't need that crutch."

"It's not a crutch. I sneeze before I even know there's a demon near me. That can't be psychosomatic."

"It is. But then, you are but a miserable and hapless vampire."

"I am not hapless!" Summer thrust out her arm, splaying her fingers, as if to throw magic at him. She'd give anything to have such power as to knock the bastard off his leathery black ass.

"You wish it?" Himself queried. "I can make that happen. Give you magic untold."

"Fuck you."

"My son's girlfriend? I could manage that."

"You're disgusting! Goddess to hell, I hate you!"

Himself's satisfied moan roiled in his throat. "Your hate feels delicious."

Truly? Was the sneezing thing all in her head? As for the soul piercing…

"Take it back. I don't want to be a soul piercer."

"Ah. A bargain, perhaps? What will you offer me to lose such an ability?"

She squeezed her eyes tight. No making deals with the devil. Just. No.

"As I suspected, you are too weak to be so bold. As

for Nicolo," Himself continued, "he won't survive much longer in the human host without dire physical consequences. So your zombie theory is partially true. He needs to come fully into his legacy, you see. This second life is not as you would believe—a second chance. It is his only option. If he does not choose that option he will falter and—sooner rather than later—degrade. Unless he accepts his power."

"And turns into something like you?"

The bastard actually puffed up his chest proudly. "He would be exactly as me."

"That's gotta annoy you. Can't there be only one of you? One Dark Lord. One big, ugly, disgusting—"

A swipe of his hand through the air sent Summer flailing backward. Her shoulders hit a red stone column, and breath chuffed from her lungs. She dropped, landing on the ground on her ass, which hurt like a mother. If she hadn't seen the demon move, she would have guessed it had been a Mack truck that had instead hit her. Whew! Yet with the appropriate oath on her tongue to fling at the bastard, she had the sense not to give it voice.

Instead she prayed Nicolo would not find her. But if he did not, then he would degrade? Did that mean die? Probably. He was demon? Hell, this day just got better and better.

"If he does find me," she muttered, "it won't matter. He is determined to never play the violin."

"That was *before* he confessed his love to you," Himself said. "Now he's invested his heart like some poor sob story of a human. He has someone to protect. A reason to relent his steadfast refusal."

Ah fuck. Would Nicolo ransom his life for love? The

other option, of course, was not playing the violin and degrading. Neither was any better than the other.

Summer dropped her head onto the dirt floor and closed her eyes. Never had she wanted to sink her teeth into someone—some Dark Lord—so badly and then tear and rip and annihilate.

Following the whispers, Nicolo strode swiftly out of the park. He passed people on the street, brushing their shoulders roughly as he could not be concerned to actually watch where he was going. He was being led. And he was not going to like what he found at his final destination.

But he couldn't move fast enough to get to her. If his father had Summer he couldn't imagine what she must be going through. Pray, the bastard did not harm her. Of course, if the old man wanted him to agree to the bargain, he had best be sure she remained untouched and safe.

Because that was what this was about. He would not be able to free Summer without first succumbing to the brimstone bargain. And he would do it. She was an innocent in this horrible nightmare he'd been summoned to act upon. He would sacrifice his freedom to free her. No question about it.

Because the other option, to let the devil have her and him go on living? Unthinkable.

"Quicker," he muttered.

And in that instant the world blurred and his body moved by the massive buses and buildings, and then it soared into the sky and he felt the flick of tree leaves as he moved over the canopy of green. Faster, wind rushing through his hair. His eyes open, he spread back his arms and for one moment allowed himself to feel the joy of flight. Of weightless transport through the clear, pale sky.

*It will be yours*, assured the whispers.

And Nicolo smiled in anticipation of such a skill being his to command.

But too quickly his mirth regained presence of his fear and frustration. He would not let Summer down. She had not let him down from the moment she had found him wandering the Italian countryside. Even if becoming like his father meant he could never see her again, at the very least, he would know she was safe.

Suddenly, Nicolo's body righted in the air and he dropped. Falling what seemed parasongs, he wrapped his arms about his chest as the velocity increased and the rush of the passing world bruised his skin. Settling into darkness and then a dimly lit cavern, he came to land with a gentle touch of shoes to a red dirt ground.

Inhaling dust and dry air, he straightened, taking in the surroundings of the circular auditorium crafted from stone and dirt. His eyes fell upon Summer, lying on the floor. He rushed to her and rolled her to her back. As he smoothed a palm over her cheek, she felt warm, alive. Her hair slipped softly through his fingers. Tears choked at the back of his throat, and his heart burst with relief. Pulling her up into his arms wakened her, and she slipped her arms about his waist and hugged him tightly.

"I knew you would come for me," she said. "But I wish you hadn't."

## Chapter 22

Nicolo held Summer to him as if to let go she might be swept away and he'd never see her again. The odds of that happening were far too great. He sensed another presence in the cavernous room. But he wouldn't turn to acknowledge the man who claimed to be his father yet who had never earned such a title. Every moment he now had with Summer he must remember. Her scent. The texture of her skin against his. The slide of her hair over his cheek. The possessive grasp of her hand clinging to his shirt.

Never had anyone meant so much to him, save his son. Why had he been given this second chance, only to have it so cruelly ripped away?

"I love you," he whispered.

The silvery whispers in his head laughed a vile tone that curdled in his gut. It was what his father had been waiting for. A reason for Nicolo to bow before the devil Himself.

"Don't love me," she said.

"Too late." He kissed her then, wanting to embed one last impression of her onto his skin. To fix her to his memory.

The world lived in her kiss. The laughter and cocky attitude that made her exclusively Summer. The softness of her sighs and the wicked tease of her sensuality spilled over him, immersing him in love.

"It hurts," she whispered.

"What? Did he harm you?"

"No, here." She pressed a palm over her heart. "You make me feel so much. I know that's a good thing, but it's painful, as well. A good pain I hope to never lose."

"I don't want to ever lose hold of you," he said to her.

"Then don't play that violin."

"If I do not, you will be sacrificed."

"But, Nicolo…"

"Could you love me if I changed to that monster who lurks in the shadows?"

She nodded her head up and down, and then it moved in a sort of circle. Of course she could not love a monster. Who could?

"You won't become a monster. You are too kind. I have to believe that your goodness will overwhelm any evil."

He'd like to believe that, too, but knew it could not possibly be true. With reluctance, Nicolo pulled away from Summer and helped her to stand. She hugged him, and he put his arm around her back to keep her close.

Only now did he search the shadows of the circular

emporium for his greatest nemesis. The man who had given him life. Twice over.

The horns were the first thing he saw. He hated that Summer had been here alone with such a creature. But then he knew she was strong and probably hadn't flinched to stand before one so wicked. She hadn't sneezed since he'd arrived. He wasn't sure if that was a good or bad thing.

"So you finally have me where you want me," Nicolo said.

"Is that your surrender?" Himself stepped forward. In his hand hung the black violin and bow. The creature held it before him. "Play."

Heart dropping to his gut, Nicolo sucked in a breath when Summer squeezed him tighter about the waist and slid her hand to clasp within his. He looked down into her blue eyes. Mercy, he didn't want to lose her. She was all he had in this modern world. And if he never met another soul or made friends or walked onto the stage again then she would be enough.

"You guarantee Summer Santiago will leave here safely and never again be bothered by you?" Nicolo asked.

"I do. But you should ask she not be bothered by you again, as well. Would you wish her life be destroyed by your presence once you've stepped into your legacy?"

What sort of birthright was it to know he was demon and the son of the one thing in this realm most evil and reviled?

Summer clutched his hand tightly. "Don't say it," she said softly. "We will see each other again. We must."

Yes, he wanted that, too. He could not fathom never again holding her or feeling her soft skin against his.

"Just you," Nicolo reiterated to his father. "Stay away from Summer Santiago. And her family and friends. Including anyone she cares about."

Himself inclined his head. "Unfortunately, she cares about you. So that last request will be ignored. Deal?"

Nicolo sighed deep in his throat. His fingers ached to touch the bow. To feel the music once again. To own it. It pleaded for his submission. For his mastery. To be played and to finally sing the exquisite song it had been made for.

He'd always been a gambler. Time to make the greatest gamble yet.

Nicolo nodded. "Deal."

Stepping forward, he stretched back his arm as Summer would not let him go. The look on her face was a mixture of dread and hope. At a moment when all hope was lost. He lifted his chin and dropped her hand.

*"Ti amo."* A simple "I love you."

*"Je vous aime,"* she reiterated in French.

Nicolo turned and crossed the dirt floor. From above, eerie illumination misted about the curved ceiling like a spacescape speckled with starlight. It beamed down far enough to light his shoulders but not the floor. His strides were slow, reluctant. And then he forced courage into his bones and straightened his shoulders and walked proudly toward the destiny that had been hounding him since his birth so very long ago.

Himself opened his taloned fingers, and the violin moved from his grip, through the air, to hover before Nicolo. Exquisite and sublime, the ebony body gleamed with promise. He lifted a hand to grasp.

"Come home to me, my son," Himself said. "Take the throne beside me."

A shiver traced Nicolo's spine. What throne? Was he to be seated in some vile Hell for all his days, expounding punishments and torture upon poor souls? What powers would he receive, exactly?

He dropped his hand.

"Tell me what I will have," he said.

"Is it so important to know, when a refusal will see your lover's head torn from her body?"

Nicolo tightened his jaw. How dare he speak the cruelties they both knew would occur.

"She suffers enough as the Soul Piercer," Nicolo said. "Never touch her. Ever."

"Agreed." And Himself shared an odd look with Summer.

"She should leave now," Nicolo requested.

"No!" Summer called.

Himself shook his head. "She must be your witness. And then she will know you are not worth the risk should either of you attempt to reunite after today."

"What is it to you whom I take as my lover? Will I not be allowed such after I have assumed this vile birthright?"

"Very well. Ruin her life. It is a good start actually. You must learn that being my kin has its requirements— lacking emotion and a willingness to hurt others at all costs."

"Enough." Nicolo grabbed the violin. "I will never be like you. No matter what I become. I promise you that."

Himself hissed and stepped back. His eyes glowed red as he crossed his arms and waited.

Nicolo could feel Summer's anticipation, but he did not turn to face her. He could not. He wanted to remember only her kiss and the look of adoration in her eyes.

Instead he closed his eyes and felt the power of the violin hum through his system. It vibrated in his veins. Forged with a new power, he felt immense. His fingers curled about the bow, lightly taking their place. He put the base of the instrument against his shoulder and chin. It fit perfectly, the bone-hard chin rest conforming to the shape of him. He played the fingers of his left hand over the neck to summon muscle memory.

And then he could no longer resist the intriguing comfort and the one thing in this world that spoke for him. His voice. His heart. The soul he once had.

The first note, clear and long, opened the room with the spectacular presence. He would not play a composition, but instead follow the instrument's direction. It lured him into an A minor scale that rapidly trilled and sparkled with harmonics. His joy spoke, followed by his screaming terror. His spine arched and bent forward as his body began to dance to the music.

Summer fell to her knees. The terrible beauty in Nicolo's performance made her weep. It was exquisite. Monstrous. Sublime.

Diabolical.

The notes shivered in her heart. And she knew that with every note he bowed or plucked his very being was altering, changing, growing into that which made Himself smile so wickedly from behind him.

He played a song she did not know, yet also knew it belonged only to him and the black violin. It showcased his incomparable skill and musicianship. And it shivered a cold prickle into her neck.

And with a wicked run that spanned four octaves and ended in a dashing bounce of bow over strings, Nicolo began to change. As the music moved faster, rushing toward some wicked cliff, his body lengthened and his shoulders grew wider. His spine, bent and moving sinuously, suddenly arched backward. Nicolo cried out in pain. The bow didn't miss a note.

A rapid scale taunted his body into a side bend as hooves grew at his feet, cracking open the leather shoes he had so valued. Powerful thighs split his pants, and underneath the skin was red and then black and then a deep crimson to match the color of the blood which Summer loved to smooth over her tongue.

Nicolo shouted as a horn erupted from his temple and then the other. They grew to curves that looked so heavy they should bring him down. Yet he stood tall, still bowing, dancing wildly to the violin's command as he transformed into demon.

And when he spun about and met her gaze for a moment Summer saw the humanity in his pale gray eyes. And a teardrop. And then the irises turned red and he growled, revealing fangs within the deep maroon structure of the demon he had become.

He pulled the bow in one final dash across all four strings and flung back both arms as he shouted a final entreaty to the heavens. The shout turned to a growl and then a deep and rumbling cry of—not defeat, but rather triumph.

He reached out a taloned hand toward her. His jaw shifted, and then he pointed to her. "Out!"

Summer shook her head. She didn't want to leave. Not now when he must need her most. She would not leave him!

Himself stepped beside his son, his hooves stirring up the red dirt in clouds about their ankles. Nicolo had grown taller, and even more physically powerful. The twosome standing together presented a wicked and diabolical force that would make any man cringe and cower into the shadows.

With a flick of Himself's hand Summer found herself back in her own bedroom. Alone.

She fell to her knees and gripped the bedspread and began to cry.

# Chapter 23

The moon was full. It had been four days since Summer had stood in the red-dirt emporium and watched Nicolo transform into something she still didn't know how to define. Would he stay away from her forever? She couldn't bear that.

Her gut ached and her skin itched. She needed blood. Had tried to ignore the hunger, and now she was desperate as she took the stairs down from beside the Pont Neuf to the sidewalk beside the Seine. It was well after midnight, and the summer beach parties had packed up and gone home. Only the derelicts and a few lonely souls remained out on the streets.

Here by the river she scented desperation and evil. Whoever walked ahead of her near the underpass for the next bridge had done something terrible. Who better to gift with madness?

No. She didn't want that for any person, good or bad. Truly, had every bite she had ever taken plunged that person into madness?

"That's wrong. I can't… I'm more evil than Nicolo could ever be."

Tonight it didn't matter. In fact, she wanted to dowse herself in the darkness. Perhaps that would draw her lover back to her.

Stepping up behind a man dressed in jeans and a black hoodie, she put her arm on his shoulder just as he turned. Knife in hand, the blade stopped before it entered her gut. The man smirked and, seeing it wasn't someone he thought would cause him harm, he tipped his chin up at her. "Nice surprise."

"Not for long," she said and slapped a hand aside his face, tilting back his head.

She sank in her fangs and felt the knife blade dig in at her waist, but it didn't puncture skin as her teeth pierced his body. Vile cologne wafted into her senses, but was quickly muffled by the surprising richness of his blood.

The man's knees bent and he went down. Summer followed, drinking of him greedily and straddling his leg as she held firm to his chest to keep his neck at her mouth. Across the Seine the glint of a bonfire sparked in her peripheral vision, and the shouts echoed from late-night revelers, who were unaware of her stolen meal. Of the stolen life.

She could feel the man's heartbeats course through her, fast and then slower. His hand slapped the cobblestones. He moaned, falling into the overwhelming swoon. The Soul Piercer gave pleasure with a promise of everlasting madness.

She pushed him away. Blood spattered her chin and

shirt. He fell in a splay of limbs onto the sidewalk and into the shadow of the overhead bridge.

Had she killed him? She'd drunk with incautious abandon. She'd only wanted to satisfy her dark hunger. Had not paid attention to his life slipping away. If he was truly dead then she'd take his nightmares into her and the macabre dreams would give her a taste of the madness she had gifted him.

To check for life, she pressed her fingers over his bloody neck. That reminded her she'd not licked the bite wounds. She bent and dashed her tongue over the two punctures, and in that moment felt the pulse of life.

"Mercy," she whispered. "Rest well. I'm sorry."

And she got up and ran off. She needed to get her head on straight. She needed…

Him.

The next afternoon Summer settled onto the couch in her parents' living room. Her mother was reading a cookbook for reasons Summer could not comprehend. They often sat in silence with one another, her mother browsing through photos on the iPad or working out new routines for her acrobatic skills act she performed with the Demon Arts Troupe.

After a few minutes, with a heavy sigh, Summer tilted to the left and collapsed in an angst-filled sprawl across the couch.

"Hey, sweetie," Lyric said, setting the cookbook aside and pulling up her knees in the chair where she sat opposite her daughter. "What's the big sigh for? I haven't seen you like this before. Ever. It must be a man."

Summer smirked. "Seriously? Am I that much an open book?"

"It was a good guess." Lyric pulled back her straight blond hair and then released it in a swish over her shoulders. "I remember man troubles. I'm not that old, you know."

"I can't imagine you and dad ever having troubles."

"I knew many a man before your father."

Summer thrust up a hand. "I don't want to hear about it."

Lyric chuckled. "Oh, the stories I could tell."

Her mother had grown up in a sort of Mafioso family that had been filthy rich and greedy. Fortunately, Lyric had gotten free from her mother's control and had managed to create a good life for herself.

Summer asked, "What's with the cookbook?"

"Baby food," Lyric said.

"What? Who's pregnant? What baby?"

"Just wishful thinking. I saw it in the bookstore and couldn't resist. Kambriel and Johnny have to have a baby soon. I want to do the grandma thing."

"Seriously?"

"You don't think I'd be good at it?" Her glamorous-without-any-makeup mother rubbed her knuckles against her shoulder. "I might be a damn bit better at it than Grandma Viviane."

Lyric had never gotten along with her mother-in-law, the vampiress Viviane. A woman who had gone mad after being buried in a glass coffin beneath the streets of Paris, alive, for over two hundred years. When she'd been rescued, she'd been pregnant with Vaillant—Summer's dad— and Trystan, his twin brother. Although they both had different dads. And Trystan was a werewolf. Long story.

"You'd be great at the grandmother thing, Mom." She did have a weird domestic bone that had put Summer in curls all through her childhood and even a few hand-sown dresses. Ugh.

"So when can I start dreaming about you giving me grandchildren?"

"I have to get married first. And you know me."

Lyric sighed. "That long? I could be waiting centuries."

"I don't know what tomorrow will even bring. Right now there's Nicolo."

"The musician Johnny mentioned? He plays violin? I've always had a thing for musicians."

"Did Johnny also tell you he's Nicolo Paganini, raised from the dead?"

Now Lyric stood and crossed the room to sit beside Summer. She stroked her fingers through her daughter's hair and shuffled back to allow Summer to prop her head in her lap.

"I think I've fallen in love," Summer offered. "He doesn't have a soul, Mom. Do you know what that means?"

"I'd never make a judgment. You tell me what you think it means."

"It means I can drink his blood and it doesn't affect him at all. He is clear and sane and isn't at all mad."

"Wow."

"Right? But Himself said I would go mad if I kept drinking from the soulless."

"You spoke to— Summer?"

Summer sat up and turned to face her mom, whose beautiful green eyes had never looked more worried. "Nicolo is Himself's son. We had a run-in with the Big Guy the other day."

"Oh, Summer, what have you done?"

\* \* \*

"I've fallen in love," Summer said later as she looked down over the Seine, twinkling with street lights reflecting on the water's surface.

She'd climbed to the top of Notre Dame and sat at the base of one of the buttresses along the nave. A favorite place for her to escape and get away from reality. But when her phone jingled, she checked the text. It was from Johnny. You know Himself almost destroyed Kambriel. Nicolo will do the same to you. Walk away.

Word traveled fast in the Santiago family.

She didn't send a return text. Instead she broke the phone in two and tossed it into the river.

"I will never walk away."

She just didn't know how to find him. If she called Himself to her would Nicolo follow? An insane desperation made her whisper Himself's name.

With the devil's name on her tongue for a second time she caught her head in her hands—and then said the name out loud.

Heartbeats racing, she imagined a reunion with her soulless lover and how they would live together ever after. Years. Decades. She growing mad with every drop of blood she took from him. Just like her grandmother Viviane.

Shaking her head, Summer did not say Himself's name a third time. Instead she jumped from the roof and landed in the pebbled back courtyard behind the cathedral and walked through the formal garden. A homeless woman sat against the stone wall connecting the Île de la Cité to the Île Saint-Louis.

Running her tongue along a descending fang, Summer advanced on the sleeping woman.

\* \* \*

Summer wandered into her home and left the lights off. Normally she would feel refreshed and alive after drinking blood. And sure, she could sense that her body had received the vital nutrients it craved, but she was too down to care. She missed Nicolo. She wanted *him* at her mouth, not the neck of some stranger.

Pulling her shirt off as she wandered into the bedroom, she eyed the open bedroom window and couldn't even care that she'd left it open. The curtains blew in the breeze, lifting like gentle white faery wings. She tossed her shirt on the bed then sensed—she was not alone.

Spinning to take in the room, her eyes landed on the chair beside the window. A man sat there, palm to his forehead, observing her silently. No smile, or frown. But within his eyes worlds spoke. No, they screamed for the tragedy he'd had to endure and then wept for the nightmare that had resulted.

"Nicolo," she said on a gasp. A smile stretched her cheeks, but too quickly she calmed herself with a hand to her racing heart.

When she rushed toward him, he said, "No. Stay there. Back by the bed. Sit, please."

Summer slowly stepped back until her legs hit the bed and she sat. He merely looked at her. So she returned the curiosity. Dressed in velvet and lace, he looked well. Handsome and sexy, as usual. Not…evil. Or demonic. Or as if he'd been through hell the past few days. She could only imagine that he had been.

And she hadn't sneezed. Curious.

In an elegant glide of masculine strength, he stood and crossed the room, then stopped before her. He cupped her head with his hands and tilted it up to kiss her mouth. He kissed her deeply, seeking the core of her in that moment. And she let him inside willingly, desperately.

"You taste of near death," he said and then pulled her up to stand, and in a move she didn't even see coming, lifted her by the thighs and turned to press her against the wall. "Delicious."

As he kissed her hard, she wrapped her legs about him. His hands moved up to her bare breasts and tweaked her nipples. She moaned into his kiss. His intensity was urgent, wanting. He could take anything he wished. She would give him everything.

If only she could give him her soul.

She sucked his lower lip than gave it a playful bite. His eyes met hers in a defiant question. She smirked and dove to kiss his jaw, then bit there, without breaking the skin. He bent to kiss her breast and to roughly suckle at her nipple. Long fingers moved over her other breast, creating a symphony of moans and pleading murmurs in Summer's throat.

Tearing open his button-down shirt, she pushed it down his arms, her fingers clutching his hard biceps. He was solid and so hot. And it seemed he could not get enough of her in his mouth, for he fed greedily upon her skin, her lips, her breasts.

Summer rocked her hips, and he groaned with pleasure. Slipping down a hand, he unzipped and shimmied down his pants and then helped her off with hers. Cupping his hand between her thighs, his fingers danced over her folds. She gasped, encouraging him as he slickened her moistness over the head of his penis. The thick, hot intrusion of him within her burst as a shivering sigh. He hilted himself, thrusting rhythmically, quickly, faster and deeper.

She clung to his hair, head tilted back and sucking in her bottom lip. He burned her with his fiery desire, his incessant want. An insatiable quest to drive himself into her, to own her. She loved it. She loved him. She had to have him.

All of him.

Summer bent forward to bite his neck, fangs piercing deeply. Nicolo cried out a wanting shout as he held her to him, allowing her to feed as he continued to thrust within her. His cock rubbed her clit. His blood spilled down her throat. His fingers dug into her flesh, holding her to him, keeping her there. Wanting. Needing. Owning.

His body began to shudder, and he slammed himself deep within her, holding her head to his neck. As she took in his wickedly dark, thick blood, Nicolo tremored and came inside her. He pushed her back against the wall, meeting her forehead to forehead. Gasping, hissing, he moved a hand down to slick his fingers over her clit.

That simple move stirred her over the edge, and she shouted a cry of joy as the orgasm shimmered through her being. And then she clutched her head and laughed an unrecognizable and fearful chatter of madness.

"Yes, mine," he said against her eyelid. He kissed her there. She giggled and purred for him to give her more. More blood. More, more, more.

His body pulsed one more time, jerking his hard, muscular form against her, and then he pulled her from the wall and spun to lay her on the bed. Crawling over her gasping, sighing form, he studied her face. "You are mine?"

She nodded and huffed out eagerly, "Yes. Always. But, Nicolo, I felt—"

"You felt my darkness. The exquisite prick of your own soul falling apart. Get used to it."

"More," she pleaded. "Drive me mad, lover."


Nicolo stood before the open window, catching the rising sun on his naked body. The curtains wafted about his legs and thighs, tickling his erection. The neighbors may see him. He didn't care. He wanted to enjoy the light he had been without for what had seemed like years. Ages.

A monster's lifetime.

After playing the black violin he had descended to Beneath at his father's beckon. Himself had shown him his throne. Indeed, the vile thing existed. Metal and bone, and sheened with the dark lacquer of lost and abandoned souls. He had sat upon it and felt immense power surge up and fill his body.

And it had felt right.

And oh, so wrong.

He'd gotten back to Summer as quickly as possible, but though it may have been days for her on this realm, she might never fathom how long he had been away from her. And he would never tell her the horrors he had witnessed or that he had come to participate in. Because he could not bear to fall in her eyes. It was a hope he had clung to. So long.

Of course, he had allowed her to bite him last night. He only hoped she would not learn all the evils that had been born of his hands through his blood. And if his knowledge of the Soul Piercer had any validity he hoped the giggles had not been a precursor to her soul losing grip on reality.

For as long as he could remain here, in her presence, he felt he could fight the call to serve his wicked father. But already that skin-tightening buzz that moved across his scalp warned he had work to do. Tonight. It would begin onstage. He had a few hours yet.

A few hours of bliss that he would never take for granted and would commit to memory for all his days when he must be away from his Brightness.

She rolled over on the bed, one arm outstretched. Her pale skin was as marble, and her breasts were topped with hard, rosy buds. He'd pushed himself inside her relentlessly. Still he wanted more. He needed to fix her scent inside him, inoculate his blood with hers…

Yes, perhaps he could do just that. Take the taste of her with him. Because he had the fangs. He could do whatever he wished with them. And he'd used them to snarl, cut and defile so many times. Ah! He mustn't think of it when in Summer's presence.

Without opening her eyes, she smiled. Her fingers curled, gesturing him to come to her. And Nicolo followed, a willing sycophant. He knelt on the floor before the bed, looking over her gorgeous figure. With a finger he traced from her wrist, up to her elbow. Her smile clued him it must tickle her. He'd been rough with her earlier. He'd forgotten softness. Now, he was compelled to know her softness. For just a moment.

And then forever.

Up her arm he glided his fingertip, memorizing the silken fabric of her skin, the hard dash of her collarbone and sweet rise of her breast. And when he touched the rough, ruched nipple, he could no longer hold back the urgent desire to have her inside him.

Willing down the vile fangs that had initially frustrated him—how to speak and open his mouth?—now he was expert with them. With first a gentle kiss, he then bit into her breast.

Summer lifted her head. "Goddess, I didn't know you could— Oh…"

Her erotic murmur played music in his ears. As did her blood perform music in his veins. It danced into him hot and slick and rushing. No souls with this taste, a respite for him. Simply Summer. He could not compose a finer melody. Greedily he fed upon her, squeezing her other breast and kneading at it. He moved onto the bed, and his erection fit against her thigh. She spread her legs and directed him inside her. Pierced at breast and between the legs, she was his, pinned and taken.

"Nicolo," she cried as a brutal orgasm rocked her body beneath him.

He pushed up with one hand, blood dripping from his mouth to land on her pale breast. The air felt light. His cock was engorged. The high of her blood dizzied him. He didn't need to come. For her essence running through him gave him so much more. It bonded him to her. He felt he would always know her now. Wherever she went, her heartbeats belonged to him.

And perhaps even…her soul. Had he taken part of it into him?

"I've never been bitten," she said as she came down from the shuddering orgasm. "That was so freakin' good."

A virgin to the bite? And it had been his first bite, too. The first one performed out of love and not evil. Poetic, for the Dark Lord's son.

He'd been crowned the Dark Prince by his father. It was a title that reviled him. Yet at the same time, he'd worn it well and would continue to do so. He must. For if he did not Summer Santiago would die at his father's hand.

# Chapter 24

They'd showered together, and with but a shake of his head as he wandered into the bedroom to gather his clothes, Nicolo's hair dried.

"Now that's a trick I would love to have," Summer said. She pulled on a black silk robe, and her wet hair clung to her upper back.

He smiled briefly as he pulled up his pants. She suspected smiles were not easy for him anymore. He seemed so serious. Didn't say much. Just…took. Which had been entirely all right for her, the past hours of wild and adventurous sex.

Oh man. Being bitten. That was fifty kinds of all right. And maybe they had bonded. She hoped so. The brief moments when she'd lost a handle on herself and wasn't sure to laugh, cry or shout, had passed. She felt sane. She would remain so.

Fingers crossed.

She sat on the end of the bed and watched Nicolo button up the black shirt, wanting to pull aside his hair for him, but really she just felt exhausted and relaxed and so deliciously worn out.

"You going to stay?" she asked.

"I've a concert at the opera house in a few hours. You will come."

"I will?" Of course she would! But it had been a command. Even if she was happy to see him she didn't take well to orders. "How'd you manage a concert? You've only been gone a few days and— When did all this happen?"

"It's been arranged," he provided simply as he turned to retrieve his shoes. They looked similar to the bespoke ones he had valued. Slipping his feet into them, he then combed through his hair with his fingers and flipped the dark tresses over a shoulder. "You will come?"

"Of course. But I'm not sure I can get a ticket this late."

"That has also been arranged. Pick up your ticket at will call. I'm eager to perform."

"I bet you are." She traced his body up from his feet to the powerful thighs, and there at his hips he'd propped a hand as he stood before the window, eyes closed, taking in the daylight. Not a creature, she tried to convince herself. Still good. "So are you going to talk to me, Nicolo?"

"Isn't that what we are doing?"

"About what you've been up to. What's happened since you played the black violin? Have things… changed for you? I want to know what's going on. You're different."

"How so?"

"You're distant."

He lifted a brow that undressed her and pushed his cock inside her *like that*.

"Yeah, I know, all that sex was not distant. But you, you've changed. You seem set aside. Is it the bargain? What *are* you now? You drank my blood. Which was freakin' awesome. But—"

"Summer, please. I don't want you to know the Dark Prince. I simply want you to know Nicolo."

"I do know Nicolo. I love Nicolo. But the Dark Prince? Where did you get that name?"

"My father gave it to me. If you should ever need me, call me three times."

Yikes. Just like calling Himself. And he'd said it as if he were resigned to accept the title. Not even resigned. He owned it.

Avoiding eye contact, he murmured, "You will regret loving me."

"Never. I will always love Nicolo."

"But not the Dark Prince?" Now he met her gaze defiantly, shoulders squared. "Does he scare you?"

She shook her head. "I've not met him. Or maybe he's standing before me right now. I don't know. Yes, I suppose I have met him. He's the stoic, silent guy who won't talk to me. He is also the man who took me relentlessly until I collapsed in bliss from utter exhaustion. Do you still love me, Nicolo?"

His jaws tightened, and he clasped a hand into a fist.

"We're quite the pair now," she said. "The Dark Prince and the Soul Piercer."

His gaze glanced away from hers as he nodded. But he couldn't speak it.

She wouldn't press. Maybe he couldn't? Was he under some sort of demonic surveillance? She had no clue what his life was now like. And he apparently wasn't willing to share.

"The concert then," she said.

"Yes. Be there. You will be my focus. I won't be able to do this without you."

Her jaw dropped open, but she couldn't find a reply as he strode out of the bedroom. She didn't hear the door open and close, but knew he had left the house.

"The Dark Prince," she whispered. And a chill rippled across her shoulders.

The concert was in less than two hours. Summer browsed through her wardrobe rack of jeans and tops and the one dress he'd already seen her in. Well, there was that other dress she kept in plastic. She owned that dress because her sister-in-law, Kambriel, had insisted she buy it so she could at least *do the sexy* once in a blue moon.

With a sigh, she tugged on the red velvet cling dress that had spaghetti straps and dipped to reveal her breasts, but wasn't so low in the back. It stopped midthigh.

"I can do the sexy. And it's the color of blood."

She teased her tongue along the bottom of a fang and then pressed her palm over the breast Nicolo had bitten. The wound had healed, but she could still feel him there, luxuriating in her, taking her in, making her his. He'd indulged in her life's blood.

Two vampires could bond over sharing blood. They simply had to agree, like a sort of marriage contract. But what about a vampire and the Dark Prince? She had no clue. Did she want a clue? It was good to have a clue.

"Maybe not," she muttered as she dug about for some high heels. The black leather Louboutins were plain, but the red sole matched her dress perfectly. "Ready."

He'd told her to be there tonight. Hadn't asked her nicely or requested she attend. He'd commanded she be there to be his focus. And that had felt grand. Like he'd needed her. She wouldn't let him down.

"So does this make me the Dark Prince's girlfriend?" She wasn't sure if she should smile or cry.

The opera house was filled, yet somehow Summer had garnered her own private box with seven empty seats around her. She felt guilty for the indulgence, and then she felt special for the gift Nicolo had given her. Or had he? *It's been arranged* was what he'd told her. By whom?

Probably best if she didn't know the answer to that one.

Looking down over the audience on the main floor, who were enraptured by the up-and-coming Nicolo—as the placard had advertised—she wondered how many of them would guess he was the great Paganini. Certainly none of them had in mind to suspect a dead legend had returned to the stage. They may make comparisons, for though he played new compositions his style was definitely the same, but they should only mark him a genius, the next Big Thing.

For the first half of the concert he avoided playing his own works, and he'd even slipped in a Bitter/Sweet song that no one might recognize for the allegrettos, harmonic runs and trills he'd added. He was a master and she admired his talent.

His eyes met hers frequently. She was his focus, and each glance quickened her desires. Yes, those glances seemed to gleam red instead of his usual gray irises. It had to be the stage lights. *Please let it be the stage lights.*

But she wasn't stupid. Summer knew exactly who she was dating. And she was mostly good with that. Because he seemed like the same guy. What could have possibly happened to him in the few days he'd been gone? He hadn't turned evil yet. She prayed for that.

And thinking of his talents, she settled back against the soft velvet seat and closed her eyes to the music as memory of his fingers on her skin warmed her all over. She pressed her legs together, squeezing tightly to summon the curl of an orgasmic hum at her clitoris. Nicolo could fuck her with that sound. And she allowed it to flow through her and master her senses.

Softly, she sighed as an orgasm high up in her clitoris vibrated a sweet reaction. She'd have to do the fangirl thing and take this musician home with her. She wouldn't be completely satisfied unless she did. But she wondered now, as she again glanced about the audience and noted the women leaning forward in their seats, how many were also swooning. Dreaming of the same thing as she: winning the sexy violinist's regard.

The man on the stage was truly Nicolo. He had to be. No trace of the Dark Prince lived in those dancing fingers and swaying body. Music was his substitute soul. It was his anchor to this realm. And she had to make sure he stayed anchored and did not fall into the pit of darkness his new title would surely lure him toward.

How to break the curse of his birthright? Was it possible now that he'd transformed? Did he want it broken? He'd resisted it so valiantly in his previous life. Much as he would say he'd consigned himself to his fate now, she would never believe. He'd sacrificed to save her. She had to stay strong for the both of them.

The black violin, which he now played, would surely transform him into something else. She wished he were playing anything else, even the purple electric violin owned by Domingos.

"The Guarnerius," she whispered. His favorite violin, the one he called *il Cannone*. Nicolo had said something about Himself not liking that violin because it was innocent. And what else? "He'd called it his balance," she murmured. "A balance between good and evil?"

Could playing that revered violin return Nicolo to the man he most wanted to be?

It was currently displayed in a museum in Genoa. They'd not had the opportunity to stop and visit it during their train trip as Nicolo had wished—because the whole musician-becomes-the-Dark-Prince thing had happened. But a visit was certainly in order. Perhaps even a heist. If she could put that violin into Nicolo's hands…

She had to do it. To see if it might transform him back to a simple man. Without a soul.

The audience suddenly straightened as the next song began with a rising and falling series of scales, each time the highest note stretching higher, his fingers stretching farther, his control over the audience increasing until he broke into a furious dash.

He played "The Devil's Trill," a Tartini sonata, much faster than normal. It moved erratically, irrationally, impossibly quick. He beat his own speed, racing, luring as he walked to the edge of the stage and bent forward as he played to the crowd. Come, listen, follow me. Marvel over my skill.

The whole performance had a Pied Piper touch to it. Weird.

And they did listen and marvel. Some audience members stood and held their hands to their chests in awe. Others called out *"salut!"* and "bravo!" And as the song was over too quickly and the applause began, Summer noticed something strange within the audience. As the people looked to one another to comment about the performance, she could see their faces. Red eyes flashed here and there. Like demon eyes.

A sneeze tickled her senses, and she suppressed it with a finger to her nose as the applause increased. But she could not hold it back and she let it loose, sitting back quickly so no one could spot her. Nicolo's eyes fixed to hers. She shrugged, yet he didn't return a whimsical "eh, just a sneeze" look. The man's gaze gleamed like coal.

Quickly looking back over the main floor, she counted dozens of people with red eyes. Was it a trick of the lighting?

A deep knowing chilled her to the bone. Had Nicolo's performance somehow changed those audience members to demon? Or had it enticed demons into unsuspecting human bodies?

"No." She gripped the balcony railing to keep from falling to her knees.

Out back of the opera house, cars zoomed by, yet Nicolo could not see beyond the bevy of women who held out programs for him to sign. They ranged all ages, appearances and colors, and he loved it. And each so easy to tempt. He could feel their degree of compliance in the auras that surrounded them. Not a single implacable body in the bunch. Though these bodies had not taken on a demon.

Those had left as soon as the music had stopped. They'd been called to their greater master's bidding. His father would be pleased. And Nicolo was merely thankful for the release to this realm to play his music.

Yes, he could do this. Travel the world as Nicolo. Just the single name. Some may compare him to Paganini. As they should. But he had moved beyond that with this performance. And with the black violin in hand he could create anything and summon many to the depths of Beneath.

He closed his eyes briefly, handing a program back to someone with grabby hands, and tried to scent Summer. That sweet, musky after-sex scent he had vowed to never forget. Had he scared her away? She must know. She had seen the results of his performance. In that moment when the final note had been bowed, their eyes had met, and he had read her dread. Her knowing.

He could feel no guilt for the act he had committed on stage. It was what he did. What he had done for so long.

"*C'est magnifique*, Nicolo!" Before him a woman in body-hugging black lace and high heels fainted into her partner's arms.

Typical. It had been a long time since he'd stood amongst the adoring and devoted. Nothing had changed.

"Nicolo." The tiniest voice spoke behind him, but

he felt her move into him and skip in his blood. For he wore her blood in his veins. And a trace of her soul.

He turned and swept Summer into his arms, leaning down to kiss her before all. A roar of cheers and applause rose, and he felt her flinch but only deepened the kiss. She belonged to him. She would not deny his followers this affectionate display.

When he pulled from the kiss, her eyes flashed a warning and she said, "I saw what you did."

"It is what I do now," he said plainly then turned to the crowd, thrusting up a triumphant fist. "*Merci! Merci!* I am humbled by your adoration."

Summer drove home while Nicolo plucked the strings of his violin. That vicious, wicked black violin created by Himself. She must put the Guarnerius into his hands. But she needed a plan.

"Stop playing that," she said testily as she pulled into the garage and stopped the car.

He set the violin in the open case in the back seat then pressed a palm to the dashboard as he eyed her with that all-knowing gaze that was darker now. Had his eyes changed from gray to black? Or maybe a blackish red?

"Do I repulse you now?" he asked plainly.

She knew that his playing had transformed some souls to demon during the concert. How it had happened was some kind of diabolic magic surely only possible through the devil's hand. Or the Dark Prince's music.

"You could never repulse me," she said, and meaning it. Because really, she was the Soul Piercer. "But you do frighten me. Are those from the audience I noticed whose eyes went red truly demon now?"

He opened the door and put out one leg. "My music summoned incorporeal demons and allowed them to enter new hosts. It is what I do, Summer." He got out and closed the door, striding toward the kitchen without another word.

She did not like his new talk little, fuck a lot, attitude. Okay, so she did like having sex with him. Was the love she felt for him merely lust? No, she'd fallen in love with him, and it hurt her heart to see how he had changed. Perhaps he was aware of those changes and chose to walk away from her to hide the remorse he felt when acting that way around her?

"I won't give up on you, Nicolo," she muttered and followed him into the kitchen.

He turned and pinned her wrists to the wall. His kisses were demanding and rough, and he quickly stripped away her dress, dropping it to the floor around the high heels. He slapped her thigh, indicating she should lift it, and as she did so, he lifted her, fingers clutching her ass, and bent to lash his tongue across her breasts.

She could succumb so easily. Fall into the perfect connection their bodies formed and then drink of him and wake in a blissful dream. But it wasn't that easy now that she'd seen him at work, leading souls toward desolation.

"Wait." She wriggled her hips as he moved to push his cock within her. "Is this how it's to be now? Just slam me against the wall, take what you will and then off to Beneath or wherever it is you lurk?"

He lifted a hand to slap her, then stopped. Slipping

out of her, he stepped back and gripped his head with both hands. Bowing before her, he shook his head. "I'm so sorry, my Brightness. I would never harm you. I didn't mean to upset you."

She bent and pulled up her dress, securing the straps over her shoulders. "I know things must be difficult for you now, Nicolo."

"You will never know."

"Then tell me."

He shook his head and zipped up the fly of his pants. "If you do not want me, I will leave."

She jumped before him as he stepped toward the door and pressed him back against the wall. "I want you. I love you. And I will not regret it as you think I will. I do understand you have commitments to being the Dark Prince. I won't question that. I know it wasn't your choice. You did it to save my life." Her voice wobbled as she stated his great sacrifice. For her. He'd done this for *her*. "It's all my fault. I should have never opened the violin case that day I found it."

He gripped her by the neck and kissed her. Softly. Then firmly. And then she was falling, spreading out her arms and surrendering to his will. Wanting to belong to him.

He kissed her top lip, then her nose, then pressed his cheek aside hers and a palm to her other cheek. "I do it for you. I do everything for you. So you will never be harmed by Him."

"What do you mean? Did Himself threaten me? If you don't do what he asks?"

Nicolo nodded against her. "Don't worry. I will always protect you."

"But that's not fair. He's got you under his thumb. At his side. Why make it so difficult for you?"

"Because he knows my heart belongs to you. And that is a threat to him."

"Then maybe you shouldn't love me? If you could break away from him—"

He pressed his fingers over her mouth and shook his head. "Too late. I am this…*thing* now. I am filled with the souls of those I have damned. If only I could release them to move on. But it is my punishment for resisting my birthright for so long."

Summer swallowed. She couldn't imagine what he must have endured.

"Only promise you will give me a few moments of brightness when I can steal the time to be with you?"

"Of course, Nicolo." She hugged him and they stood there, bound by blood and a cruel curse. "I will always be here for you."

"Thank you, my sweetest Summer. Brightness of my life. You can't imagine what holding you means to me. Feeling you. Smelling you. Being inside you. I must leave soon. I am being called."

"No, not yet. Please, I need more time with you. Will we ever have a life together?"

"I want that. Yet I'm not sure how to make it happen beyond these sweet moments."

"I'll figure something out." Like stealing his precious *il Cannone* and making him play it. It had to work. She had to try. She slipped the shoulder straps off, and her dress glided to the floor. "Take me, then. Fill me. Give me your blood."

"But you have all of me, flesh and blood, and love."

"And those souls…" She started to ask, but didn't

finish. Something about his mention of souls inside him resounded with her, but she couldn't explain why. So instead she kissed him as if she would never see him again.

# Chapter 25

Leaving Summer's embrace was torture, far worse than anything Himself could inflict upon him. And yet, the torture had been perfectly orchestrated by his father, knowing well that she was the only thing that Nicolo lived for.

If he could manage the pain on his own, he should toss her aside, empty out his cold and evil heart and never think of her again. It would be best for the both of them. And he feared that as the ages passed and his slavery as the Dark Prince continued, he would lose all emotion and the ability to love Summer would slip away. But he would cling to it for as long as he was able. She was the only thing that kept him sane.

Imagine that. The Soul Piercer granting him sanity.

Sitting upon his throne of metal and bone, Nicolo watched as the souls of innocents were counted and their demons given new life. Each connection infused him with the soul in a burst of pleasure he wanted to deny but ultimately could not.

It was impossible not to allow his mind to wander to Summer's brightness. But he must correct that wandering desire. Not allow her to invade his thoughts while Beneath, participating in such despicable tasks. For he would taint her memory, and Himself would know his heart ached.

In but a few more mortal days he would rise and tour the world. The concerts had been announced. Himself eagerly awaited all the souls Nicolo would collect along his travels. Soul collecting had become both his freedom and his curse.

Summer read the concert listings online for Nicolo's performances. The name worked for him. She had to laugh a little. He was debuting in Milan tomorrow night as the toast of Paris, a new force on the rock-violinist scene. Some compared him to the soloists David Garrett or Mark Wood, who toured with Trans-Siberian Orchestra. Most compared him to Paganini. The Devil's Violinist Risen had been one of the headlines.

If they only knew the truth.

She clicked out of the internet app on her phone and sat back in the chair. No doubt, while touring the world and playing for the masses, Nicolo would be collecting souls for Himself. He probably hated it. She hoped he hated it. A small part of him might be resigned to the evil task. Perhaps another part of him might even take to it with relish.

Anything that allowed him to play the violin must

feel all right to him. The man may reason that he had been given the gift of touring and performing in exchange for something more horrible.

And who was she to continue to pine for a man she knew was no longer kind or even innocent? Loving Nicolo was akin to admitting a love for the devil Himself.

Only, she knew better. He may have been born to the position as Dark Prince, but he'd never asked for it.

"As for those souls…" She thought again of her lover's explanation how he was now filled with the souls of the damned. It niggled at her for an inexplicable reason.

Her cell phone rang. Johnny wanted her to stop by the club tonight and hang out, she and her boyfriend.

"I can't, Johnny. I'm headed for Italy."

"I see your Nicolo is headlining already? How did that happen?"

"The guy is talented."

"Sure, but that was literally an overnight thing. Is it something to do with his rising from the dead? I thought you were going to stay away from him, Summer?"

"No, Johnny. I got it under control."

"I should come over."

"Johnny, I'm on my way out. Don't worry about me. Whatever is going on with Nicolo is for me and him to handle. He's going to be fine." She shuffled out a sigh. "Johnny, I love you."

"Ah hell."

"I mean it. I don't say it often enough. Nicolo showed me how awesome love can be. Just leave it at that, okay? I'll call when I get home!"

She hung up before he could protest.

\* \* \*

Summer was not a thief. She didn't know if she could pull off a heist. But it had to be done. And in daylight. With museumgoers all around. Because the clock was ticking. Nicolo must be in Milan right about now, preparing for the concert. Summer had to steal the violin and get to Milan before it was over and he left town. Because likely, he wasn't driven to and from his concert locations. He probably just appeared when needed.

The advantages of being the Dark Prince.

She had to work with being a plain vampire. She couldn't fly or mist in or out of a place. Couldn't even shift to a wolf and lope across the lands, such as Dracula. About all the talent she had was to enthrall a human as she sipped from their neck, allowing them to forget she'd ever been there. If only that could stop the madness.

So as she stood in the gallery that featured the Guarnerius violin behind glass, she formed a crazy plan. If she could enthrall everyone in the room—currently only four people—to ignore her, she could walk up and take the violin. As for the security staff, she'd meet that risk when it was presented.

Walking up to the glass, she pressed her fingers to it. Behind that protection, another large glass box encased the violin, which sat on a steel pedestal and which was held up by a metal frame and encased in even more glass.

This was going to get noisy.

Looking about, she was thankful two people had left the room. Only two left and no guards save for the one she'd nodded to about thirty yards down the outer hallway. He'd been half-asleep. The remaining twosome walked up beside her to look at the violin. The woman commented on its luster, the varnish obviously having been touched up from when Paganini had owned it, for surely it would have been worn to the wood after such frequent use.

"It's lovely, isn't it?" Summer said and turned to make eye contact with the man. "Hold her hand," she said deeply and focused her persuasion on him. He blinked yet did what he was told. "You won't remember me. Step over there and kiss. Yes, show her how much you care about her."

The woman lured him aside, and he bent to kiss her.

And Summer smashed her fist through the glass.

Nicolo bowed before the audience, who cheered profusely and shouted "Bravo!" and begged for more. He did have more. One final song that would call in the demons to occupy those souls open and willing enough to harbor the host.

Touching the bow to his forehead, he gave a salute to the crowd and then bounced it onto the strings in the beginning to "The Devil's Trill."

Summer walked casually to the museum's front door, the violin tucked under her sweatshirt jacket. She almost made it out of the museum unremarked, when one of the patrons screamed, "She's stealing the Guarnerius!"

That outburst set three hefty guardsmen on her ass. But they'd likely had donuts for lunch for decades, so the prospect of outrunning them didn't bother her. She ran down the museum steps and turned down the wrong street. Her car was parked in the opposite direction. But with the guards close, she wasn't going to make a U-turn.

Damn it, she was new at this midday-thievery thing. Her fingers bled from the broken glass. It had been easy enough to bend the metal frame holding the violin and take it out. Now she held the neck and bow in her left hand and pumped her right fist to pick up speed. She could outrun these guys.

But probably not the patrol car that flashed its red lights up ahead on the street. Damn those walkie-talkies. Perhaps she should take this higher and leap onto a rooftop?

She took a sudden right turn and rejoiced when she saw the thick forest ahead. Some sort of city park. New plan. Stay on the ground. She could lose them in there.

Nicolo could feel the souls shiver as their human hosts welcomed in the incorporeal demons. A bitter shock initially, and then they resumed their role as concert-goers, clapping and cheering. Subtly aware that something wasn't right. And soon enough they would surrender and lose all human consciousness. Memories, lifetimes, free will. They would be called to Beneath as soon as he left the stage. And there Himself would induct them into the flames.

He had but to take the bow away from the strings, refuse to play the song, and those souls could be saved. But it was unthinkable. He'd trade them all for Summer's soul.

Realizing, as she raced through the thick park woods, that this was getting her nowhere fast, Summer paused at the edge of the forest and looked over the violin. She wouldn't have time to drive to Milan and place it in Nicolo's hands. She needed him here. Now.

There was one way to do that.

To use his title of the Dark Prince or his name? She shook her head. No question.

"Nicolo Paganini. Nicolo Paganini. Nicolo Paganini!"

Nicolo felt the summons and quickened his pace off the stage. He slammed the dressing-room door behind him, and then before he could decide whether or not to answer such an abrupt call, he was swept to the caller merely by fact of his inexperience with controlling the beckon to such a call. The afternoon was gray with overcast clouds. The air was fresh and smelled thick and green. A pond sat close by, for he heard the chatter of ducks and the splash of wings that must have taken fright by his sudden arrival.

Feeling the horns grow out from his temples, he fought to prevent the transformation and halted it just as talons curled from his fingers and about the bow he still held. The black violin was not to hand. He must have set it down in the dressing room. But who had called him here? His father?

A pale-haired woman stepped from within the dark shelter of trees, or rather, ran toward him.

"Brightness," he whispered. "What are you—"

She shoved a violin into his grasp and tugged him across the lawn and around the pond. "Quickly. They're chasing me!"

"What is this?" It felt familiar, and yet so distant. Like something he had once cherished. Too light. Too… innocent.

"The Guarnerius. Play it! Now!"

This was *il Cannone*? Yes, of course. It had been so long. Far longer than Summer could ever know. He'd asked her once if he could visit it. He'd forgotten that conversation. And she had not because it had been but a few days for her.

"But why?" he asked.

She pulled him into the shadows behind a fieldstone wall and shoved him to a stop. Huffing and looking like a tattered doll with dirt smudging her cheek and hair wild about her shoulders, she said, "It's a theory. And we did discuss it about a week ago. Remember? That we thought it might reverse the curse?"

A week ago? Try an eternity.

Nicolo lifted the violin. Indeed, this was his precious *il Cannone*. He could feel it in his veins. And it was an odd feeling. Distasteful. His body wanted to reject it, knew it was not in his best interest, and so—he flung it away from him.

Summer caught it with a dive that landed her on the ground, one hand grasping the violin body before it could shatter against the stone wall behind them. She rolled onto her back and jumped up to stand. "What the hell?"

"I don't want that abomination. That...innocence," he spat.

"It is your salvation. I know it. It has to be. You said Himself hated it. That it was the balance between good and evil. Nicolo, do this for us."

She held up the violin. He sneered and growled, taking a step back from her. Part of him wanted to reach for it, place it at his shoulder and dance the bow across the strings. But a larger part, that dark part he'd been born to, would crush it to tinder if she so much as placed it too near him again.

"I can't," he confessed. "Too late. I am this thing now."

"You don't have to be."

Oh yes, he did have to be.

"Look at me!" he cried. He tilted his head, knowing the horns were monstrous and evil. Had he shifted any further he would be wearing hooves and a tail, as well. "I am the Dark Prince!"

Her shoulders dropped, the violin falling beside her leg. Panting—she had been running—she shook her head. "I know you want this. Us. Don't give up. Please? Nicolo...I need you."

He did not want to give up on them, but if he voiced that desire, it would only give Himself more power over him. The time had come for him to walk away from that which he most adored. To keep her safe.

From behind them shouts sounded, and out of his peripheral vision Nicolo saw flashing red lights.

"The police," she said. "I had to steal the violin. We haven't got much time. If you love me you will play the violin."

"If I love you I should walk away from you and never return. Consign myself to what I have become."

"Too late." She used his words. "Because I'll never let that happen. If I have to call you to me continuously, to look at me, to kiss me, to touch me, I will speak your name all day, every day. I'll stand before Himself and show him that I am unwilling to give you up. That bastard *can* be defeated. We've done it before, my brother and I. We can do it now."

Nicolo could not find words to protest. But he should.

She thrust the violin forward. "Play."

Nicolo glanced over his shoulder. Three policemen tracked across the park lawn toward them. And his fingers curled, as if about the violin neck. When the closest officer took out his pistol and called for them to put up their hands, Nicolo did so. He turned, facing the officers, and backed up to stand alongside Summer. Bullets were no match for him.

But he couldn't reveal himself to them. The horns— hell. He stepped back into the shadows and willed his horns away. Hopefully they had not seen them.

And when the first officer shouted for Summer to set down the violin, a twinge of defense tightened Nicolo's muscles. They would grab the instrument, unknowing how to handle such a delicate thing. They could ruin it. Break it, surely.

It had been so long since he'd held *il Cannone*. He'd told his son Achille to ensure it went to the city of Genoa after his death. Ah, Achille. He could only be thankful he'd not fallen to the brimstone bargain when his son had been alive. For if Achille were to have seen him in demonic form and to know...

It had been ages. Forever. An eternity. And yet... did he still have a choice? He was *not* this creature. He did not want to be.

And when Nicolo reached for the violin and grabbed it by the neck from Summer's hands, the sound of a pistol shot clattered in the sky. Nicolo felt the hot burn pierce his shoulder. Blood scented the air.

And Summer screamed.

## Chapter 26

Nicolo flinched his shoulder then closed his eyes and envisioned the bullet that had lodged in his shoulder blade being forced out. It did so, plinking onto a stone that edged the garden pond. Black blood dribbled into his white shirt, then stopped as he healed.

"Are you okay?" Summer asked. "The violin?"

He nodded. A team of three police officers yelled for them to put up their hands.

"Get behind me," he growled as he straightened and flexed back his shoulders. He turned toward the threat. His horns were starting to emerge again, but he forced them back. He felt Summer behind him. He could smell her anxiety and taste her sweet blood on his tongue. He wanted her. And he wanted to be everything but the Dark Prince for her.

All three officers held aim on him.

Could the music from his past really affect the evil he had become? Slowly, Nicolo raised his hands, the violin neck hung in the crux of his left fingers, the bow still gripped and facing skyward in his right.

One of them shouted to drop the violin. Another quickly corrected his partner that it was a priceless instrument. Set it gently on the ground, he insisted.

Nicolo would do neither. For in that moment he felt Summer's hands clutching at his waist from behind, peering around his shoulder. He was her protector. So he would give this one opportunity a try. It may change him. It may not, for the myriad souls that lived within him could never be crushed.

He had to try it for her.

Drawing the bow across the strings, he trilled out the first few notes. A return to the time he had once held dear, an instrument that had been his constant companion. The beginning of his end. The familiar tones shivered through his system, and he answered her coy tease to play more, faster.

Two of the police officers dropped their weapons at their sides. Their mouths dropped open. The third police officer clasped a hand over his heart and whispered, "Paganini."

Swept into the music, Nicolo found his home in a simple melody that he'd composed while on a road trip to Parma from Milan. He remembered that soft summer day distinctly for he'd called the coachman to stop so he could get out and walk into the cornflower field, where he stood amidst the blue blooms and had played to the bees, the birds, to the world.

Now sunlight filtered through the trees just behind him. Nicolo danced, his body swaying to the music's control. He caught glimpses of Summer standing nearby, tears in her eyes but a smile on her face. And he knew he could do this. Have her. Live in this realm. And not kowtow to his father.

And in a crackling burst of lightning over the pond, the water momentarily parted, tidal-waving to the edges. And there at the pond's edge stood Himself. With a gesture, the devil Himself sent the policeman away. The armed men turned and walked off, as if there were nothing out of sorts and they had been on a false call.

Nicolo stopped playing and stepped before Summer to protect her. He held bow and violin in one hand at his side. He would never again give *il Cannone* away. It was his heart, his blood and soul.

His innocence.

Himself appeared in horns and hooves. Not a wise decision to walk about in this realm as his true self, but then, he probably had the entire park warded. Though Nicolo couldn't feel any wards. And he generally sensed his father's magic as a biting prickle down his spine.

"I've had enough of that vampiress," Himself said as he stopped before the twosome. "Summer Rosanne Santiago, you have meddled enough—"

"Your vow not to harm her must be honored," Nicolo reminded. "I have served you well. That guarantees her freedom and safety."

"Nicolo, what?" she said from behind him.

"Oh, don't you know?" Himself said to her. "He's sacrificed all for you. All these aeons he's been working under my thumb, has been to keep you safe. I thought to break him of that silly love."

"Aeons?" Summer stepped around to stand beside Nicolo. Her eyes searched his. He felt her breath hush across his arm. The scent of her was too perfect. "How long have you been with him?"

"Too long," Nicolo said with the heaviness of that time served. No time to explain how time worked differently in Beneath. "It's not important. What is, is that I felt the shackles release when I played this."

"You still wear the souls of the damned," Himself growled. "You will always be mine. I am your father!" Himself insisted.

"My father was Antonio Paganini, the man who raised me in the nineteenth century. He taught me how to play violin, he taught me good work ethics, he gave me drive and morals."

"He turned you into a performing monkey," Himself spat officiously.

"You say so? Coming from the Master Over All Monkeys? Be that as it may, Antonio was my father. Your evil blood may run through my body, but you will never be more than a slave master to me."

Himself raged, spreading his arms wide, and from his hands burst out flame. Nicolo stepped before Summer once again, taking the brunt of the flame, yet she could feel the heat surely.

"If you harm her. If you take her life," Nicolo insisted firmly, "you will mark me as your enemy. And I know you don't want that because you actually do want a son. Someone to be your progeny, to look up to you. I've put on my best performance for you. Now release me."

"Never!"

"Then from this moment on you cease to exist in my eyes."

Himself puffed up his chest, but his exhale looked more like defeat than he might have wanted it to. "I cannot take away the power you have now. It is your birthright."

"Doesn't mean I have to use it for evil."

Himself clenched and unclenched a taloned hand. "You've no idea how you crush me."

"As you have commanded and crushed me. I have done everything you have asked of me, without question. Vile, evil things. Things I should wish Summer never learn about. Things I can never erase from my blood. But I have done so out of obligation to our familial connection and because… I do respect your means to an end. Someone must sit the throne of Dark Lord. Without you no one would recognize the good."

"Y-you respect me?"

Nicolo nodded. He wasn't just speaking to the man's favor either. He did respect him for that reason. He was evenhanded in his punishments and tortures. And he did keep the balance as best he could.

"You will suffer upon this realm," Himself said. "You are heavy with damned souls."

"I'll take that risk."

Himself eyed Summer. She winked at him. "I think this is your cue to leave."

"Enjoy your madness, Soul Piercer. I can wait for my son to return when you have become ash. That is, if he survives the onslaught of souls. If he remains in this realm they'll want free. That won't be pretty."

The devil swept his hand before him and extended it toward the pond. A pathway of flame formed, bridging the water and licking at the sky. Himself strode to the center and disappeared in a burst of brilliant fireworks.

"Dramatics," Summer muttered. Beside her, Nicolo

collapsed. "Shit." Blood drooled from his eyes. And his body convulsed.

"The souls are trying to get free," he said. "I can do nothing to stop it. They will burst through my pores…"

"No, that'll kill you. We have to get them out of you. How to—"

She'd simply accepted it when he'd told her he had souls in him, and for reasons she had never been able to put a finger on. He was without a soul. She harmed souls. She had felt him touch her soul when he'd bitten her. If only there was a way to touch those souls within him…

"Oh my goddess, yes!"

She was the Soul Piercer. If she could pierce the souls within Nicolo then perhaps that would grant them freedom.

Without thinking twice, Summer willed down her fangs and plunged them into Nicolo's neck. Blood spurted into her mouth. So hot and it tasted vile, black. The souls he had damned shivered. She could take them out of him. Pierce them all and set them free, and save him from dying. And with hope, the souls could move on to wherever it was they had been destined.

He gripped her shirt, shoving at her in a struggle to loosen her from his neck, but Summer held tight. His blood slipped over her fingers and clothes. "Let me do this," she managed. "It's our only hope."

He let his head fall back. And she heard the souls, each and every one of them in succession, scream as they were opened and set free. Aeons? He had been serving Himself for so long? Mercy, but he had been through hell. The prince of Hell. Of Beneath.

But no longer. She would give him the brightness required to exist upon this realm.

"It's working," he whispered. And then his head lolled to the side and his eyes closed.

Fearful he could die if she took too much blood from him, Summer took respite in knowing he was a changed being, someone as powerful as Himself. And what made him even stronger was his desire for good. So she took more blood until she could not bear to drink another drop. Dropping her head onto his chest, she spread a hand over his heart and felt the life beating within him. Strong, powerful. And then she knew no more.

The best case would see Summer's soul tainted by those she had tapped within him. Sure, they had escaped, but in the process had left remnants, dark smears upon her soul. Now it was Nicolo's turn to make things right.

With a visceral knowing, he lifted his lover's body under the shoulders. Her head fell back, exposing her neck, which was smeared with his black blood. He sank in his fangs to drink deeply of her soul. He could take Summer's soul into him until they bonded and shared one common soul. It would be the first soul he would wear with pride since the day she had resurrected him from the grave.

## Chapter 27

A week following the daring daylight robbery from the Genoa museum, Summer taped up a cardboard box and handed it over to a delivery service. Inside, she carefully packed in the Guarnerius violin. Technically, it did belong to Nicolo, but he was a different man now. He would find a new violin, one that sang to his new soul, an instrument he could use to speak to the world. Besides, with the press and media reporting on the stolen violin, the return of it should cause a media frenzy and ultimately increase the museum's profits.

Nicolo had decided to continue the concert tour that had been "arranged" by forces Summer still didn't want to question. But he wasn't working for his father, nor did he wield the black violin. That instrument was probably sitting on a shelf in Himself's lair somewhere. Summer got a kick out of imagining the Dark Lord pouting in a cozy little room before the fireplace. Behind him on shelves sat the failed instruments of temptation he had used throughout the ages. Ha!

Her new reality? She was dating, and living with, the Dark Prince. Yes, the King of Beneath's son. And while he had all the power and magic that Himself possessed, Nicolo was a free man and could do as he wished with the birthright that he had accepted as a means to keep her safe. He would wield that power for the good. Or Summer hoped he would. His intentions were pure and beneficent. Only time would tell if a man could honestly remain good with his history of having served in Beneath for aeons.

And she, well, she had taken a few donors since the night when she'd taken all the blood she could from Nicolo and released the damned souls from his body. She'd watched after the donors had gotten up and staggered home. And she'd checked back on them the next day, and the next.

So far? They seemed to be faring well and normal. Was she no longer the Soul Piercer? Nicolo guessed she was not. When he had bitten her they had bonded in blood and soul so he knew things about her now that even she did not know.

But she didn't need to take human donors often. In her lover's arms, she found sustenance, pleasure and happiness. And together, she the Soul Piercer, and he the Dark Prince, they would make it work. They had to. With a baby on the way, they both wanted to ensure their child grew up knowing right from wrong, good from evil, and to never be threatened with the promise of a power that could change lives.

\* \* \* \* \*

*Lynne Graham has sold 35 million books!*

## To settle a debt, she'll have to become his mistress...

Nikolai Drakos is determined to have his revenge against the man who destroyed his sister. So stealing his enemy's intended fiancé seems like the perfect solution! Until Nikolai discovers that woman is Ella Davies...

*Read on for a tantalising excerpt from Lynne Graham's 100th book,*

### BOUGHT FOR THE GREEK'S REVENGE

'Mistress,' Nikolai slotted in cool as ice.

Shock had welded Ella's tongue to the roof of her mouth because he was sexually propositioning her and nothing could have prepared her for that. She wasn't drop-dead gorgeous... *he* was! Male heads didn't swivel when Ella walked down the street because she had neither the length of leg nor the curves usually deemed necessary to attract such attention. Why on earth could he be making *her* such an offer?

'But we don't even know each other,' she framed dazedly. 'You're a stranger...'

'If you live with me I won't be a stranger for long,' Nikolai pointed ut with monumental calm. And the very sound of that inhuman alm and cool forced her to flip round and settle distraught eyes n his lean darkly handsome face.

'You can't be serious about this!'

'I assure you that I am deadly serious. Move in and I'll forget ur family's debts.'

'But it's a *crazy* idea!' she gasped.

'It's not crazy to me,' Nikolai asserted. 'When I want anything, I o after it hard and fast.'

Her lashes dipped. Did he want her like that? Enough to track er down, buy up her father's debts, and try and buy rights to her nd her body along with those debts? The very idea of that made er dizzy and plunged her brain into even greater turmoil. 'It's nmoral... it's blackmail.'

'It's definitely *not* blackmail. I'm giving you the benefit of a choice ou didn't have before I came through that door,' Nikolai Drakos elded with a glittering cool. 'That choice is yours to make.'

'Like hell it is!' Ella fired back. 'It's a complete cheat of a supposed ffer!'

Nikolai sent her a gleaming sideways glance. 'No the real cheat as you kissing me the way you did last year and then saying no nd acting as if I had grossly insulted you,' he murmured with lethal uietness.

'You *did* insult me!' Ella flung back, her cheeks hot as fire while he wondered if her refusal that night had started off his whole chain eaction. What else could possibly be driving him?

Nikolai straightened lazily as he opened the door. 'If you take ffence that easily, maybe it's just as well that the answer is no.'

Visit **www.millsandboon.co.uk/lynnegraham**
to order yours!

# MILLS & BOON®